## RICH IS ALWAYS BETTER...
## NO MATTER WHAT THE...

**FRANK CLARKE**—...son of 70. His chameleon charm hides a somewhat dastardly rogue who wants his golden years lined with silver...his mother's. Plus her jewels, her stocks, her ready cash.

**FLAVIA CLARKE**—A Westmount widow from the very upper crust. At 97 she still doles out orders like Queen Victoria in a vicious mood and wields her fortune like a sword to keep her relatives in line.

**VIVIEN HOWARD née CLARKE**—The disinherited daughter. She's devoted to health foods and yoga, and she's being swindled by her nearest and dearest.

**COUSIN ESTELLE**—*A/K/A* **STELLA DELLA CHIESA**—Once the darling diva of Europe's opera houses. Now she shares her stage with the ravages of time...but she's about to play her most important role.

**ROCH LARIVIÈRE**—A fence who makes a good neighbor. He specializes in objets d'art and wants to diversify into selling exotic sexual experiences to the chic geriatric crowd.

"A light, tight-paced romp, a good read for a fun-filled Sunday afternoon"
*Halifax Mail Star*

"An intensely enjoyable reading experience"
*Hamilton Spectator*

"Hilarious"
*Quill and Quire*

# DEATH is Relative

## EDWARD PHILLIPS

AVON
PUBLISHERS OF BARD, CAMELOT, DISCUS AND FLARE BOOKS

This book was originally published in Canada under the
title *Where There's a Will...*

AVON BOOKS
A division of
The Hearst Corporation
1790 Broadway
New York, New York 10019

Copyright © 1984 by Edward Phillips
Published by arrangement with McClelland and Stewart
Limited
Library of Congress Catalog Card Number: 84-091244
ISBN: 0-380-69867-6

First Avon Printing, April 1985

For: E.J.S.
L.H.W.
K.S.W.

*Between brother and brother, two witnesses and a notary.*
Spanish proverb

# Chapter 1

Whatever motivations and drives may animate the brains of the nameless millions, the guiding beacon in the life of Francis Desmond Clarke was money. To be sure, he never thought of money as mere rectangles of banknote paper with an engraving of Her Majesty on one side and a noble prospect of somewhere in Canada on the other. This was merely cash or bucks which came today, went tomorrow. To him money was cyclical, self-renewing like the moon, waxing, waning perhaps, but always there. For Francis Clarke money partook of a dual nature. It was concrete; he needed it in his bank account to support the extremely comfortable life style he had come to accept as his due. But money also partook of the abstract; palpable, prodigious, it filled his consciousness to overflowing and left little room for the gentler human feelings.

Now that Frank Clarke had turned seventy and had looked down that empty corridor to see nothing between himself and the end, he had begun to daydream a project, a monument that would carry his own name across the grave into the great beyond. But this project would take money, much more money than Frank would ever inherit through legal channels.

That thought was running through his mind as, on a certain afternoon in October, he sat in the back seat of a long black limousine which pulled into a parking lot at Montreal's Mirabel Airport, narrowly missing a Toyota sedan as it eased itself to a stop. The portly chauffeur climbed out of the driver's seat to open the rear door for Mr. Clarke, an impeccably tailored, silver-haired man who might be described as elderly but not yet old. After flicking imaginary specks of dust from his navy-blue lapels, Frank Clarke passed a hand over his sleek, barbered hair. He had no intention of undertaking Mirabel Airport alone while the driver of the limousine smoked cigarettes and listened to the car radio. Frank Clarke was paying an indecent sum of money to hire this bloody limo, rented for the occasion because he no longer cared to drive his car on freeways outside the city limits. And if the driver was being paid for a service then he was going to serve.

"*Vous devriez m'accompagner*," he said to the driver in lightly accented French. "*Peut-être qu'il y aura des baggages.*"

"*Okay, d'abord.*"

Frank Clarke gave the chauffeur a withering look.

The chauffeur touched his cap. "*Oui, monsieur.*"

The two men crossed a roadway and entered the airport concourse, which resembled a hangar more than a lobby. It has been observed that a camel is a horse designed by a committee. Mirabel is an airport designed by a government, which means it would have made an excellent Olympic stadium.

In truth Frank Clarke was filled with apprehension as he fingered the telegram tucked into his jacket pocket. ARRIVING B.A. FLIGHT 397 OCTOBER 2 STOP WOULD ADORE BEING MET STOP WILL CARRY A RED ROSE STOP WITH MAD ANTICIPATION ESTELLE.

"Estelle? Estelle! Estelle Church!" Flavia Clarke, Frank's ninety-three-year-old mother, had exclaimed, her face angular against a froth of lace-trimmed pillows. "Haven't seen or heard from her in years. Not since she retired from the stage."

"Isn't she the one who became an opera singer?" Frank had asked.

"Indeed. Changed her name from Estelle Church to Stella della Chiesa. They say she was good. Some even called her the successor to Melba. But her life off stage was no better than it should have been. A tart with a voice is still a tart!"

After making inquiries of several harried officials, Frank located the British Airways lounge. Following the usual delays for immigration and customs, the passengers began to empty through swinging doors: distracted mothers clutching cranky children, rumpled businessmen heading for the nearest martini, gangling youths gilded with grime. Frank scanned them all eagerly, looking for a woman, no longer young, carrying a single red rose. By now most of the passengers had dispersed, swallowed by the vastness of the bleak concourse. The exit door stood motionless.

Suddenly the door opened a crack, just enough to permit a hand to slide through. No ordinary hand, the long nails glistened with Chinese-red lacquer, competing in hue with the enormous square-cut ruby circled in diamonds on the fourth finger. Slowly the door opened to reveal the owner of the hand. Almost concealed behind a giant bunch of long-stemmed red roses stood a woman whose appearance even Frank, himself well beyond the age for surprises, found extraordinary. A long-sleeved jacket covered in black sequins flared at the hips over a black satin skirt which came barely to the knee. High-heeled T-strap shoes drew attention to a pair of black lace legs which could still turn a jaded head. But it was the face that rivetted attention. Framed in shoulder-length hair, which might be described as the colour of a raven's wing, the chalk-white skin threw into striking relief a scarlet mouth and teal-blue eyelids. For a moment she stood, her hand on the open door.

"*Mon dieu, séigneur,*" whispered the chauffeur.

"Cousin Estelle?" ventured Frank, taking a step forward.

"Francis, dear cousin Francis." And the apparition launched herself at her first cousin once removed, enveloping him in a cloud of roses and strong, sweet perfume.

Sorting himself out from his newly discovered relative he inquired after her luggage.

"I have suitcases, two of them. My trunks are coming by boat."

11

"Trunks? I see. Are you planning to stay long, Cousin Estelle?"

"As long as dear Flavia will have me. How is she? Tell me everything."

By now the driver was leading the porter wheeling the luggage towards the car.

The fact that his cousin Estelle had managed to snag one of the nearly nonexistent porters, an endangered species in this airport, did not escape Frank's notice. He could tell she was a formidable woman. Anyone who would cross the Atlantic ocean wearing that kind of high sleaze had to be.

"How did you manage to get those flowers through customs?" asked Frank. "They're usually strict about plants and fruit."

Estelle laughed; her laugh, like her voice, deep and husky. "But, my dear, don't you see? They're artificial." And she stepped into the limousine with the air of one accustomed to stepping into limousines. "Now come and sit beside me and we'll have a nice chat on the way in from the airport."

Frank drummed his fingers impatiently on the gleaming surface of the car as he waited while the driver shut the door beside Estelle and crossed to hold the rear door for Frank himself. He could not decide whether or not the sudden arrival of a distant cousin would work to his advantage; Frank always assessed a situation on the basis of how he might benefit. On the one hand, the arrival of Estelle Church might act as a kind of smoke screen, drawing attention away from Frank while he methodically carried out his plan. On the other hand, anyone visiting his invalid mother became, by extension, his guest as well. Although he did not live with his mother, he oversaw the running of her household, and a visiting relative could well turn out to be a time-consuming nuisance. There was no place in Frank's schedule for the spontaneous and unexpected.

"*Monsieur?*" The voice of the driver at his elbow pulled Frank back into focus. The rear door stood open. Frank climbed into the limousine and settled himself on that small segment of the back seat which had not been preempted by Estelle and her fake flowers.

# Chapter 2

Nurse Florence Harrison sat at the marble-topped table in the cavernous kitchen of the large old house, drinking instant coffee made with hot water from the tap. A coffee pot sat on the stove near a canister of ground coffee, but the pot needed rinsing and Nurse Harrison couldn't be bothered. A large, amorphous woman without planes or highlights, she sat sipping the bitter, lukewarm liquid, and wishing Nurse Gibson would be just a few minutes late for the night shift. Then Nurse Harrison would have the pleasure of informing Nurse Gibson that she had arrived late. One of the few treats in Nurse Harrison's life, aside from sweets, lay in being punctilious about other peoples' shortcomings. This censoriousness brought a glimpse of colour into the monochrome of her otherwise drab life. Beyond lazy, she would gladly have paid someone to breathe for her. Hospital work proved far too demanding; now she only took private cases where she put in her eight-hour shift and more or less allowed the patients to fend for themselves.

The rasping sound of a buzzer fixed over the kitchen door jolted her from reverie into the importunate present. "Let her wait," thought Nurse Harrison, finishing her lukewarm coffee. The buzzer replied with three short rings which compelled attendance.

With extreme reluctance Nurse Harrison heaved herself to her feet, fat in white tennis shoes, and walked with heavy tread to the foot of the staircase leading to the second floor. She looked with loathing at its broad, carpeted expanse. A single-seat passenger elevator ran up the wall beside the stairs, but it had been absolutely forbidden to the nurses. They were not being paid to ride. Angrily grasping the banister, fighting the stiff pull of gravity, she made her way up to the landing, then turned left up the rest of the stairs. At the top she turned right into the bedroom of Mrs. Flavia Clarke, whose ninety-three-year-old hand rested on the button which activated the buzzer below stairs.

"You're late. I just peed myself. You can change the bed while I'm having my bath. And hurry; I'm expecting my cousin any minute." Flavia Clarke spoke with the easy authority of one used to giving orders. Her voice, only slightly weakened by age, seemed at variance with her shrunken body.

Nurse Harrison felt raw rebellion boil up inside her; but if she quit this case then the agency, Care, Cooks, & Chars, Inc., by now aware she was lazy and truculent, would either dismiss her or send her back to hospital duty. As it was, she only worked as cover nurse, taking the morning, afternoon, or night shifts whenever the regular nurse had time off.

Going into the bathroom she filled the tub with warm water and threw in a handful of Elizabeth Arden bath salts. Decades of Christmas presents had equipped Flavia Clarke with enough Elizabeth Arden beauty products to last her comfortably into the next century.

After helping the old lady out of bed and into the bathroom, after coaxing the flannel nightdress over her head and helping her to crawl crablike into the tub, Nurse Harrison went down the hall to a linen closet the size of a small bedroom and smelling of camphor. Teasing out a quilted cotton mattress pad, contour sheet, folded top sheet, she returned to the master bedroom and began to make up the bed.

15

The creak of a footstep sounded on the stair.

"Give me a hand," said Nurse Harrison without looking around. "She's wet herself again."

"Perhaps if you had been doing your job it wouldn't have happened," replied a man's voice.

Nurse Harrison spun around to confront Frank Clarke. "Oh, excuse me, sir. I thought you were the cook."

"As you can plainly see I am not the cook. Nor is it the cook's job to help you change the bed."

"Francis, is that you?" called his mother from the tub. "Don't come in. I'm not decent."

"Mother," he raised his voice, "you have always been decent. Indecently decent," he added *sotto voce*. "Cousin Estelle has arrived. We'll wait downstairs until you are ready to see her."

Nurse Harrison shut the bedroom door. If she disliked the mother she feared the son; moreover he did the hiring and the firing in the household. She tugged the old lady out of the tub, dried her, draped her in a fresh nightdress. She combed and coiled Mrs. Clarke's still heavy white hair, pinning it on top of her head with tortoise-shell pins which resembled small croquet hoops. The final touch was a knitted bedjacket of lilac wool tied with a pink satin ribbon. Mrs. Clarke had drawers filled with bedjackets knitted by her satellite spinsters, all fearful lest dear Flavia neglect to send the customary cheque on their birthdays.

Downstairs in the front room, Estelle had sunk with careful abandon into a large wing-chair placed at right angles to an immense walnut chimney piece from which two bilious lions kept an eye on the room. Frank pushed aside the heavy brocade *portières* across which male peacocks marched in full panoply.

"Oh, my dear," said Estelle in a voice which sounded ravaged by cigarettes, although by now it was clear she did not smoke, "that is no way to make an entrance through *portières*. You reach out like this and push them aside, almost as if you were swimming the breaststroke. Once when I was singing

16

*Traviata* in Turin I made my entrance through *portières*. *'Flora, amici, la notte qui resta . . . .'* It was really quite an ugly production. The director was one of those who wanted the cast to jump onto tables to sing. We had a dreadful row. I said to him, 'Alfredo is a gentleman; he certainly wouldn't leap onto Violetta's dinner table to propose a toast.' *Libiamo*; *libiamo*. But some directors cannot look at a flat surface without having someone leaping onto it to sing." Hers was a voice filled with overtones of travel. Years of singing in foreign languages had superimposed layers of patina on vowels, obliterating origins, at least to the unpractised ear.

"Would you like a drink, Cousin Estelle?" inquired Frank. "Some sherry perhaps?"

"You wouldn't happen to have a drop of gin?"

"Yes, unless the night nurse has polished it off. I'll go check."

A few minutes later Frank pushed his way through the *portières* carrying a silver tray on which rested a bell-shaped ship's decanter, a chromium-plated ice bucket, and two cut-crystal tumblers which he placed on the circular mahogany table in the centre of the room.

"Would you like a martini? I found some white vermouth. Gin and French, as they call it in blighted Britain."

"No, thank you. Just gin — no ice. One of the pleasures of retirement is being able to take a drop. I could never drink when I was performing. Once I accidentally got a bit tight before a performance of *Pelléas and Mélisande*. It didn't affect my voice, but when I leaned forward in the tower scene to let my hair cascade down to Pelléas, I nearly fell off the bloody balcony." She took a deep swallow. "So this is your mother's house. Just what I would have expected. Solid, substantial. Flavia appears to have done well for herself.''

Francis himself thought the room hideous, a distillation of eclectic excess; old without being good. Except of course for the figurines; they were all new. The old balloon seller, the Copenhagen mermaid, a mare and her foal, all had been replaced since his sister Vivien smashed every portable object in the room during a row with their mother. Only Grandmother Van Patten's Staffordshire dogs had not been replaced, but then they had been irreplaceable.

"I suppose," he replied, "if you happen to like that sort of thing."

Nurse Harrison then battled her way through the *portières*, sucking in her lower lip and smiling what she imagined to be an ingratiating smile. "Your mother will see you now, sir."

"Would you like to ride the elevator upstairs, Cousin Estelle?" asked Frank, holding aside the brocade curtain to let his cousin pass.

"I'd adore it. I must confess I find stairs a bit taxing, with my emphysema. Not that it's serious, mind you," she added quickly, almost as if to confess illness were bad form. "Only sometimes I find myself a little short of breath."

Frank folded down the small square seat and Estelle took her place. "I haven't ridden one of these things since I sang Queen of the Night in Hamburg. I rode a tiny elevator down from the flies for my first-act aria. I was in black lamé, with an enormous sunburst headdress. I looked quite splendid. The role is a piece of cake if you have the notes, two arias and a short ensemble – and the regular fee."

Frank pressed a switch and the tiny elevator hummed to life carrying the shiny black Estelle up and around the landing. With regular, measured tread he followed Estelle up the broad staircase, turning the landing just in time to see his first cousin once removed place one jewelled hand on the door jamb, the other over her heart: the operatic objective correlative of deep emotion.

"Flavia, Flavia, is it really you?"

"Who else do you suppose it is? I suppose I should say, 'Welcome, Estelle.' How long do you intend to stay?"

"As long as you will have me." Breaking her attitude, Estelle lunged at the bed, seized the older woman's blue-veined hand,

and pressed it to her scarlet mouth, leaving a crimson smear across the back of Flavia Clarke's parchment hand.

"I hate to be touched," said Mrs. Clarke, wiping the back of her hand on the sheet. She turned her piercing blue eyes onto her son. "Francis, give Estelle the front room on the top floor."

"I thought she might use Father's bedroom," replied Frank. "She'll be down the hall, so she won't disturb you, and she will have fewer stairs to climb."

"The top floor is for company," snapped his mother. "Always was, always will be. Don't make yourself too comfortable, Estelle. I'll be moving to a nursing home shortly, just as soon as a room becomes available. Then the house will be shut, emptied, sold. You'll have to shift for yourself."

"But, Flavia dearest, how can you bear to leave this lovely old house?"

"It's way too big for one old woman. And I'm bored with myself."

Unlike most of her generation Flavia Clarke harboured no illusion about dying in her own house. Frank knew she longed for the bustle and excitement of a nursing home, where death was a daily drama and endless feuds awaited only her sure touch and abrasive personality.

"Now it's time for my supper. Then I watch one hour of television before bed. I'll see you tomorrow. Goodnight." Flavia Clarke smoothed over the folded top sheet and fluffed the bow of her bedjacket. The interview had ended.

As Frank and Estelle filed out of Mrs. Clarke's bedroom, Frank pulled the door until it stood barely ajar. Placing his right forefinger vertically across his lips he motioned Estelle to follow him down a long corridor and into a large bedroom whose forbidding mahogany furniture and deep-toned Oriental rug gave it a look of heavy opulence. Beneath that massive headboard, now fretted with tiny cracks from the drying effects of central heating, Desmond Clarke, Frank's father, had slept.

He had also died in this very bed, although Frank did not think it necessary to tell Estelle.

Frank flipped back the quilted bedspread to expose a sheet folded taut over blankets. "The bed is made up. I suggest you use this room, Cousin Estelle. It will save you climbing another flight of stairs. The door beside the tall chest of drawers leads to the bathroom."

"But, Francis, didn't your mother say I was to sleep on the top floor?"

"Mother never leaves her room; she won't know the difference. Besides, I am not about to carry your suitcases up two flights of stairs."

Without waiting for a reply Frank walked out of his father's bedroom and led the way back downstairs. He was delighted, almost relieved, at the way his mother had so obviously not made Estelle welcome. To have had his mother postpone her move into a nursing home because of the distraction of a visiting relative would not have pleased Frank, anxious as he was to shed the responsibility of the big house. Nor did Estelle seem likely to move into instant intimacy with Mrs. Clarke. Frank understood the elderly have their shortcuts to friendship: infirmities, pictures of grandchildren, a sense of hasn't the world gone downhill. Suddenly total strangers turn into old acquaintances. Furthermore Frank strongly suspected Estelle wanted something; he set little store on family affection as anything but a lever with which to get one's own way. He certainly did not want Estelle to get wind of the real extent of his mother's financial worth. The less anyone knew about his mother's affairs the better.

Downstairs in the front hall Frank ushered Estelle through the *portières*. "Make yourself comfortable, Cousin Estelle, while I take your bags up to your room."

Once back in the front room Estelle almost collapsed into the wing-chair. No theatrical attitudes informed her posture. She looked old and crumpled, a damask dinner napkin after a hearty meal. Had Frank been a compassionate man he might have felt sorry for the older woman as he reentered the room. Shorn of her stage presence her seedy glamour seemed strangely grotesque.

"How about another gin, Cousin Estelle? You look a bit done in. Travel is very tiring, after all."

"You're right. I am a bit tuckered." She reached greedily for the tumbler. "When I think of the number of times I had to simulate fatigue on stage. It takes enormous energy to pretend you are exhausted. All those marvellous death scenes: *Traviata, Lakmé, Lucia.* But perhaps my greatest death scene was as Manon. Dying of exhaustion, or whatever it is courtesans die of, I spoke the final lines as I collapsed into the arms of my lover, Des Grieux." Estelle crossed her hands on her chest like superannuated butterflies. " *'Il le faut! Il le faut! Et c'est là l'histoire de Manon Lescaut.'* " Estelle let her arms fall slowly into her lap.

Had Frank ever really thought about opera he would probably have agreed with Dr. Johnson that opera was "an exotic and irrational entertainment." And Frank had little use for the irrational, centred as he was in a world which revolved around material objects.

"Did you ever sing Wagner?" he inquired, not really much interested but mindful of the obligation that Cousin Estelle was his guest.

"Good heavens, no! I was a singer, not an umpire. And all of his heroines are so stupid!"

A commotion at the door to the dining room caused both Frank and Estelle to turn their heads. The cook, a stout sunny Italian who answered to the name of Gelsomina, punched her way through the *portières* to announce that *cena* was *pronto*.

# Chapter 3

Vivien Howard, *née* Clarke, sat cross-legged on the living room floor in her ground-level condominium apartment, meditating on beauty. Arthritis no longer permitted her to assume the lotus position, but every evening at six she cranked her way down to the floor, spread the folds of her voluminous wrap-around skirt, emptied her mind of whatever thoughts it might have held, and tried to concentrate on the other. Today's skirt was of unbleached muslin. But even though she sat immobile, so still in fact that the giant silver hoops suspended from her ear lobes hung motionless, Vivien Howard could not sustain the pure essence of the other. The now kept crowding in around the edges of the vacuum where beauty reigned supreme.

On the giant roll-top desk, picked up for a song at the Salvation Army, lay a letter. On Government of Canada stationery, almost reeking of officialdom, this letter informed Vivien Howard that the National Gallery of Canada wished to hold a retrospective exhibition of the paintings of her late husband, Randolph Howard. Already bullish in the art market, the work of Randolph Howard was beginning to gain international recognition. At a time when energetic, self-indulgent, abstract expressionism and vast, empty, geometric canvases were all the vogue, Randolph Howard stuck to what he knew best, meticulous paintings of figures in interiors, executed in egg tempera. Critics had dismissed his work, both the medium and the message, as being hopelessly out of date. But fashions in painting change almost as rapidly as the height of hemlines. The swing back to figurative painting had caused critics and dealers alike to rediscover the small, elegant panels of Randolph Howard with their soft luminosity which had been likened to that of Vermeer.

To have a retrospective at the National Gallery would put the final stamp of approval on the Howard *oeuvre*, meaning the few paintings Vivien still had in her possession would in effect help cushion her decline into old age. Having married an artist and having been almost always at odds with her family, she had grown used to a hand-to-mouth existence. In fact she had rather relished the challenge of making do. But then her step had been elastic, her back straight, both her vision and hearing sharp. Reluctantly she had been forced to admit to herself that old age requires money. She was undergoing dental treatment; she would soon need new glasses; taxes had gone up yet again; her antique refrigerator could expire at any minute.

It was not in Vivien's nature to rail against the inequities of fortune, but it did strike her as unfair that, considering the vast amount of money controlled by her mother, she should be forced to pare cheese and save string. Granted, her brother Frank (Vivien detested the name Francis) helped her out from time to time. The occasional cheque, sometimes even an envelope containing cash, would be pushed through her letter slide to land with a soft thud on the tiled floor. But the erratic nature of these donations precluded her counting on them; and there was no consistency in the amount. For all his pretentious and sporadic bursts of charity even Frank himself sometimes hardly knew where his next case of champagne or tax money was coming from. Still, he had remained on good terms with their mother, something Vivien had not been since the day she smashed the figurines, and was struck from her mother's will as a result.

What really bothered Vivien, as she sat cross-legged on the floor, trying unsuccessfully to keep present concerns from disturbing her meditation, was the knowledge that at least six of Randolph Howard's finest paintings and several of his drawings presently hung in her mother's house. But they had been reduced to the status of mere interior decorating accessories and now hung in unused bedrooms, because every room needs a picture or two to make it welcoming.

During their early married years Randolph and Vivien had been poor; consequently it was a drawing or painting Randolph had given his in-laws each Christmas. It had infuriated Vivien to realize that an elaborately framed reproduction of Monarch of the Glen would have been more warmly received than one of Randolph's meticulously executed panels.

The mantra tickled her palate but failed to touch her mind. Rolling herself forward onto her hands and knees Vivien climbed slowly and painfully to her feet. A fan-shaped pine-framed window hung over the working fireplace, for which she had paid extra. The window panes had been replaced with mirrors whose reflection returned the image of a once beautiful, still handsome woman of seventy-two with silver hair resting in a soft bun on the collar of her black turtleneck shirt. Even behind glasses, the eyes she had from her mother shone a brilliant blue.

The reflection showed her immobilized by thought. If only she could get her hands on the paintings in her mother's house. Vivien knew they weren't catalogued. Nor were they insured except as general household items. Furthermore as most of them had been relegated to the third floor they probably wouldn't even be missed.

She had approached her brother Frank about helping her to recover the paintings, but he had put on the holier-than-thou manner that made Vivien want to slap him. He couldn't possibly steal from his own mother. Just imagine how upset she would be if she found out. Vivien replied that as far as she was concerned the paintings were only on loan; Frank could return them to his sister with a clear conscience. He had turned vague and muttered that he would see what he could do.

Vivien crossed the room abruptly and flung up the sash-window. The sudden current of air blew into her face shoots from the hanging spider plant. She inhaled deeply; fresh air helped clear her brain, or so she liked to think. The vapour of carbon monoxide peppered with dust flowed deep into her lungs, but so great is the power of positive thinking she immediately felt the mists receding from her mind.

Vivien realized the best way to recover the paintings would be to slip into the house and remove them herself. But the house was never empty. Now that her mother was bedridden she had nurses round the clock. A cook came daily to prepare the hot meal, as did a cleaning woman to tidy rooms no one used. If only the house could be emptied, even for a couple of hours.

The grandfather clock in Vivien's dining room began to wheeze and crank, winding up its ancient gears to strike the resonating chime indicating half-past six. Time to eat her veal chop and the rest of yesterday's turnip, followed by bean sprouts sprinkled with wheat germ. Vivien Howard crossed into the kitchen, her feet in soft black espadrilles soundless on wooden floors shiny with varethane.

# Chapter 4

Frank held the *portières* aside so Estelle could pass freely, then held her chair as she sat at the sombre oak table. Gelsomina had cooked as if for twelve hungry field hands who had laboured in the vinyards. A tureen of fettuccine Alfredo preceded slices of veal piccata heaped on Grandmother Van Patten's huge platter. Frank never ate much, but he was surprised to see the gusto with which Estelle tucked into her food. He was about to ask whether a meal had been served on the plane but decided the question would be tactless.

"Flavia and I used to keep in touch; a few lines on a Christmas card," began Estelle between bites. "I remember her telling me you married, then divorced. And your sister Vivien married an artist, a painter. I can still remember being surprised at the news; our family has never welcomed artists into its ranks. I had to run away to Europe in order to have a career. What was he like, her husband I mean? I feel a kinship with him, even though we never met. Did he fit in?"

"Not really. But then no one fits in with Mother. She'd tell Gabriel he was playing off key or Jesus Christ that he needed a haircut."

"Oh, Francis." And they both laughed the laugh of conspirators, deriding the very person whose food they were eating.

Frank refilled both wine glasses. "I never got to know Randolph Howard really well. He was a bit of a loner, worked hard, sometimes spending months on a single painting. Mother had some of his work, but it seems to have disappeared. One of my most vivid memories of Randolph was the night Vivien brought him here to the house, to meet the family.

"It was Christmas Day, shortly after the war. I have never considered Christmas a good time to initiate anything, least of all an engagement. But with our family, no time is ever a good time. I had come to the house early, ostensibly to help Mother, to give her a hand in setting up the bar; but principally because Vivien had telephoned asking me to be there when she arrived: an ally, so to speak."

Like most people telling a story in which they figure prominently Frank was not above manipulating the facts in order to put himself in the most favourable light.

Frank had indeed arrived early at the family house on that Christmas Day. His mother needed no help; in fact she would have resented the merest suggestion that she did not have the situation well in hand. What prompted Frank to be punctual was less solicitude for an anxious sister than the realization that introducing a prospective brother-in-law into the family circle meant a realignment of power. In the internecine struggle which passed for family life *chez* Clarke, Frank could not tell whether a husband would reinforce or weaken Vivien's position. The status quo found Frank in a position of strength, particularly vis-à-vis his mother, a position he did not intend to relinquish.

Frank had always paid court to his mother. Once home from his office Mr. Clarke could not be blasted out of the house with dynamite; and it fell to Frank to escort his mother, who took any social function with deadly seriousness. She certainly did not wish to trail along her drab, disapproving daughter. But now that his sister was about to upgrade her status to that of married woman, Frank felt apprehensive. Change did not necessarily mean improvement. There might, after all, be a

27

grandchild whose future would be assured by a slice of the will.

He barely had time to hang up his Prince Albert and spread his presents under the tree when the front door gave its piercing jangle. Flavia Clarke, in a long, taupe velvet gown and the emeralds she wore once a year because Christmas was a time for green, had been pacing the living room in a fury of impatience. At the sound of the bell she kicked her train out of the way and flung herself at the door.

As always, tension made her more than usually voluble. "Merry Christmas. And a Merry Christmas to you, Mr. Howard; or may I call you Randolph, an old lady's privilege? Hang up your coat, here in the coatroom. Do shut the door, Vivien; we aren't heating the entire city. You're still wearing the mouton I see, such a durable fur. Or is it wool? Neither fish nor flesh nor good red herring, if you ask me. Come into the drawing room. The cook is furious because I wouldn't give her the day off, and the maid is dripping with cold. I had to send her home and hire a girl for the evening. I had Gladys – she's the girl I hired – set up a bar in the drawing room. I'm afraid with a cross cook and an ad hoc maid the pantry is *hors de combat*."

Vivien and Randolph muttered Merry Christmas and how do you do, then entered the living room uneasily, as if they suspected snipers hid behind the furniture. In deference to Christmas Vivien wore a floor-length skirt. Hanging around her neck on a leather thong was a ceramic ornament which looked like a chocolate chip cookie. Randolph had put on his best Harris tweed jacket with suede patches stitched to the elbows and had knotted an ascot around his neck. Out of deference to his mother's tastes, Frank had worn a blue three-piece suit.

The two men, who had previously met, shook hands and mumbled Merry Christmas. Flavia Clarke crossed the wide hall and opened the door of her husband's study without knocking. "Desmond, do be a dear and put away your stamp collection. Vivien and her young man are here and we're going to have cocktails. We don't want to delay dinner too long. Overcooked turkey gets so dreadfully stringy." She returned to the living room.

Randolph searched the tea trolly which had been set up as a bar. "Do you have any Scotch, Mrs. Clarke?"

"Scotch? Isn't there rye on the bar?"

"Yes, but I prefer Scotch, if you have it."

Frank winked at Vivien and went into the kitchen. The cook sat morosely at the kitchen table. She had come and gone over the years, hired, fired, and sometimes quitting. A tall, angular woman, she smelled a bit musty, like an old potato.

"Merry Christmas, Mrs. Cooper."

"Merry Christmas, Mr. Francis." Mrs. Cooper sighed a long sigh which drained every last drop of merriment from the greeting.

"Everything under control?" asked Frank, a shade too brightly.

"I guess. But bastin' that turkey is terrible hard on my back."

"But it will taste so good," said Frank with the hearty cheeriness of a camp counsellor. "And you make such delicious turkey soup. How's Peetee-Pete?" A blue and grey budgerigar climbed around the bars of his cage chattering crossly.

"He don't like Christmas, Mr. Francis. Can you hear what he says? 'Peetee-Pete don't like Christmas.' " Mrs. Cooper believed her budgie a Demosthenes and understood every word he said.

Frank dug out a bottle of Scotch from a pantry cupboard, smiled a greeting at the hired girl cowering at the far end of the kitchen table, and fled, anxious to escape Mrs. Cooper, fortunately made taciturn by Christmas cheer.

"Here we are," he said, waving the bottle at Randolph. "I'll pour; you say when."

"Francis, dear, I'll have a Pink Lady," announced his mother. "That's egg white in the silver jug. Not too much grenadine. Well, my goodness, let's all drink to peace at last, and a Merry Christmas. I had intended to have hot *hors d'oeuvres*, but Mrs.

29

Cooper is in such a state I decided salted nuts would be easier. Besides, there will be heaps of dinner."

As she paused for a sip of her cocktail Frank and Randolph clinked glasses with Vivien and drank. Frank was surprised to see Vivien drinking Scotch, which he knew she disliked, but he could tell she was terribly on edge.

"Mother, go and stand beside the tree so I can take your picture," suggested Frank who had brought his camera. He knew the best way to make the evening work was to keep his mother stage front and centre.

"Randolph, how do you like our tree? I must confess the idea for a white and silver tree came from Francis. It is pretty, but it does make me think of a display window for better dresses. I like a traditional tree myself. I'm really very old fashioned, but one must move with the young. The young keep us young."

With photographs duly taken, it was now time to open presents. Predictably Frank's presents were extravagant, expensively wrapped, frivolous.

At this point, Mr. Clarke, remote and hieratic in a velvet smoking jacket, entered the living room. Vivien, Randolph, and Frank dutifully stood as the senior Clarke exchanged a kiss with his daughter, handshakes with the men. Deep down Frank disliked his father, but on public occasions the son always treated the older man with courtesy and deference. The performance gratified his mother and convinced the world that young Clarke wasn't a bad sort really. All he needed was something to do.

For his father Frank had purchased a stamp, antique, apparently quite valuable. Mr. Clarke cleared his throat, which meant he was pleased.

Now it became Vivien's turn to present her Christmas offerings, books, wrapped in dark green tissue paper and tied with limp red ribbon. They were received as books are usually received by people who do not care for reading.

"By the way, Vivien dear," began Mrs. Clarke, "thank you

30

for the lovely poinsettia. There simply wasn't room for it in here, what with the azalia from the Masons and the cyclamen from the Leslies. Did I tell you I saw Morna Leslie just the other day? Still the social butterfly, but she looks as old as God. She didn't take kindly to her change of life." Mrs. Clarke dropped her voice on "change of life" as evidence of a fine sensibility. She also dropped her voice on Jew; cancer; the curse, meaning menstruation; toilet; and pregnant. "But then Morna Leslie never did have much bone. I was having lunch with Phyllis. We went to that little French place. I don't remember the name, but it had red-checked tablecloths. Phyllis had the sole."

Frank had always deplored his mother's tendency to talk in footnotes. "Another drink, Randolph?" he asked, rising.

"Yes, thank you, Frank." Gratitude rang in Randolph's voice as he rose to hand his tumbler to Frank.

Suddenly, with a flash of blue and grey, the budgerigar swooped into the room and attempted to light on the Christmas tree. Not finding the dense needles to its liking it fluttered for a moment before coming to rest on the edge of a parchment lampshade.

"Jesus Christ, Vivien!" Randolph went ashen. "You didn't tell me there was a bird in the house."

"What's wrong? Don't you like them?"

"Can't stand them. Call me when it's gone." He ducked into the large coatroom beside the vestibule and pulled the door shut.

The bird gave a couple of chirps and dropped a stool onto the lampshade. Mrs. Clarke sprang to her feet. "He'll ruin my shade. Treva, Treva, come in here at once. Peetee-Pete is loose again. He's dirtied onto the parchment shade and it will bleach a stain. Quickly, bring a damp cloth. And get him back into his cage. He's upsetting Mr. Howard. And do hurry."

The budgie fluttered across the room to land on a gilt picture frame. Mrs. Cooper cranked her way into the room carrying a damp tea towel.

"Look at that. He's ruined my shade!"

Frank spoke. "Nobody will ever notice, Mother. The shade is mottled anyway. Turn the stain to the wall. Think of it as that much more antiqued."

Mrs. Clarke crackled with indignation. "Treva, take Peetee-Pete back to his cage at once, and see he doesn't get loose again. It's bad enough to have sand and seed husks crunching underfoot in the pantry without his laying waste to the entire house."

"Yes, Miz Clarke." She shuffled across the room holding out an enticing forefinger. "Come on, Peetee-Pete, good birdie." But the budgerigar, drunk with freedom, winged his way across the room to perch on the black Wedgewood *jardinière* which held the azalia.

"He's scairt," announced Mrs. Cooper, reproach in her tone. "You'll have to leave."

Vivien knocked on the door of the coatroom. "Randolph, are you all right?"

"For the moment. Where is it now?"

"Just about everywhere. I didn't know you were afraid of birds."

"You do now. All the decent ones have gone south for the winter."

"Anything you want? We have to go upstairs now so Mrs. Cooper can coax him back to his cage."

"Pass me my cigarettes, will you?"

As Vivien fetched the cigarettes from a side table she heard a rattle, a clank, and the half of the doorknob holding the shank fell onto the floor of the front hall.

"Dammit, Vivien, I'm locked in here."

"There's no point in freeing you until Peetee-Pete is back in his cage. We're going upstairs now."

Ten minutes passed before the budgie could be coaxed onto Mrs. Cooper's outstretched finger to be grabbed from behind by her other hand. It screamed and bit her sharply all the way back to its cage.

It took Frank another five minutes to coax the doorknob into a position where the shank, worn round by years of use, would turn back the latch. As a cross Randolph stepped free Vivien handed him a fresh drink and a lighted cigarette.

"I think I'll tell Gladys to bring on the soup," announced Mrs. Clarke sailing into the pantry from where her voice carried clearly through the swinging door. "No, Gladys, I said use the cut-glass dish for the cranberry sauce. You forgot to put ice in the drinking water. Mr. Clarke will carve the turkey on the sideboard. And don't forget to warm the gravy boat."

She pushed through the swinging door, flinging her taupe train out of harm's way. A small woman of immense energy, she made the ions dance even before she entered the room. "Now then, everyone; drink up."

A few moments later, the maid, numb with inadequacy, appeared meekly in the doorway to announce madame was served.

The Scotch broth, dense with bits of barley and cool from having sat too long, was cleared away, largely uneaten, by the terrified maid. Randolph had racked up more demerit points by requesting permission to smoke and, without waiting for formal consent, had lighted his cigarette and dropped the used match into the silver nut dish which sat in front of his place. As the maid backed through the swinging door under the weight of an enormous turkey, Vivien spoke.

"Gladys, please bring Mr. Howard an ashtray."

Mrs. Clarke shot Vivien a look. Protocol demanded that Vivien ask her mother to ask the maid to bring an ashtray.

"Bring Mr. Howard an ashtray," repeated Flavia Clarke, squaring her padded shoulders and reaffirming her position. "And you have put out the wrong carving knife. This is the knife Mr. Clarke uses for roast beef."

The girl wilted through the swinging door to correct the mistake. Mr. Clarke took up position at the sideboard where the overcooked turkey meat had already begun to flake from the bones.

"I always buy a large bird," announced Mrs. Clarke to no one in particular. "We eat it hot, then cold, then Mrs. Cooper makes turkey tetrazzini, and finally it ends up as soup. Thank you, Gladys. Don't forget to bring in the gravy. Mrs. Cooper makes delicious gravy, Randolph. Simmers the giblets all day on the back of the stove."

Meanwhile back at the perch the budgerigar had just made the discovery that the door to its cage, although shut, had not been properly latched. As the maid pushed her way back through the door the bird made its second bid for freedom, swooping past the end of her nose into the dining room. With a shriek she dropped Grandmother Van Patten's gravy boat. It shattered, sending a wave of giblet gravy across the pantry floor. *Whoosh* went the bird three times counterclockwise around the dining room before alighting on top of the corner cabinet.

"God almighty!" Randolph jumped to his feet so quickly his chair tipped over backwards. Taking refuge once more in the coatroom, he emerged, a minute later, dressed to go outside. Ducking into the vestibule and shutting the door behind him, he called Vivien, who came to stand on the other side of the door.

"Randolph?"

"Vivien, thank your parents and make my excuses. I'll see you back at the flat." He left the house.

Ignoring the mess, Mrs. Clarke marched into the kitchen and fired Mrs. Cooper on the spot. Mrs. Cooper replied that Miz Clarke could save her breath to cool her porridge because she was quittin'.

"Well don't quit until you have finished the dishes," replied her erstwhile employer, who then took to her room with a "splitting" headache.

The evening quickly unravelled. Mr. Clarke retreated to his study to gloat over his new stamp; and, leaving the budgerigar in undisputed possession of the dining room, Frank drove Vivien home.

It turned out to be Frank himself, over lunch one day, who

broke the news to his mother that Vivien and Randolph intended to get married. When she began to expostulate he looked at his watch, signalled for the cheque, and suggested they had better hurry if they wanted to be on time for the movie.

Frank was Randolph's best man at the small, unpublicized wedding.

After he had made certain Estelle was finished Frank rang the small silver bell. Gelsomina carried in a large bowl of salad. Estelle helped herself generously. Out of politeness, Frank took a few leaves. He did not much care for salad, believing it was rather like eating one's way across a lawn.

"It doesn't sound to me as though Randolph made a favourable first impression," observed Estelle. "First impressions are so important, especially to an actress. When I made my entrance as Norma I had to dominate the audience before I sang my first recitative. Did Randolph manage on subsequent meetings to ingratiate himself?"

"Not really. He wouldn't allow Mother to push him around. He was never rude, just quietly obstinate. And I hardly need tell you Mother likes to have her own way."

"Odd about the bird. I shouldn't have thought the help would have been allowed pets. But then again this is North America."

Across the table Frank could see his cousin Estelle's eyelids beginning to droop, the result of gin, food, and jet lag. He rose, signalling the meal had ended, and pulled Estelle's chair away as she stood. On small matters of social protocol Frank remained punctilious, part of his protective colouring.

He pointed Estelle at the stairs, then left the house, anxious to avoid the night nurse who would soon be coming on for her shift. Nurse Gibson had a platoon of accident-prone relatives about whom she loved to complain. She also mistook good manners for interest, so whenever she was on duty Frank skulked about his mother's house like a stowaway.

# Chapter 5

The following morning Frank Clarke poured himself a cup of tea and sat down at the kitchen table in his upper duplex apartment. Opening the morning newspaper, he flipped through the pages to the obituary column. Scanning it eagerly he stopped short at an entry: Evans, Thomas, in Montreal on Friday, September 30. Thomas Evans, silly old fart. They had gone through high school together over fifty years ago and had kept in touch through occasional meetings on the street. And now high school hero Thomas Evans was dead, bald and toothless, to be buried with the pacemaker he had carried in his chest for the last eight years.

Frank took another sip of tea, filthy drink; but during his last general checkup his doctor had suggested he give up coffee. "Only a suggestion, mind you, Frank." Patterson Smithers had looked grave. "The old ticker is in pretty good shape, I must admit; but I'd like to keep it that way. The less caffeine the better, as far as I'm concerned. Now drop your trousers and lean over the table."

"Yes, Dr. Smithers," replied Frank, who never called the doctor by his first name. Although many years the doctor's senior, Frank had no wish to be on a first-name basis with a man who referred to the heart as "the old ticker," and who furthermore had stuck his middle finger all the way up Frank's rectum.

Still, Frank listened to his doctor for the straightforward

reason that he wanted to outlive everyone else he knew. Living is the best revenge.

Frank had not always collected obituaries, any more than he had looked carefully into the future and seen his own demise as the inevitable outcome. For most of his adult life he had lived through a continuous present, tomorrow no more real than is Christmas Day to people enjoying a picnic on the twenty-fourth of May. His past he shed annually, the way a snake sloughs off its skin.

Some men have a talent amounting nearly to genius for protracting adolescence. In the case of Frank Clarke he experienced for the first time on his sixty-fifth birthday the kinds of misgivings which normally assail adult men of forty. Frank belonged to that almost extinct species of men who, without resorting to welfare and unemployment insurance, manage to live a lifetime without ever having worked. By exploiting his looks and charm, by being financially dishonest and sexually unscrupulous, Frank had slithered and sidled his way through more than sixty years without coming up short.

At this point in his life Frank had no real financial worries. Once his mother died he would be well off. But it had begun to filter through to Frank, some time around his sixty-fifth birthday, that people he had known all his life were beginning to die off. Moreover the obituaries he collected often listed accomplishments, honours, children, all of whom would preserve name and memory after death. The idea, vague at first, had begun to trouble Frank that once he had been called to Abraham's bosom all trace of him would vanish, except for the casual memory of a handful of people. The idea had begun to grow, to cover its skeleton with muscles, sinews, flesh, and in doing so forced its way further and further towards the forefront of his consciousness. With his demise would come oblivion. As the deaths of his contemporaries began to sift into the obituary column Frank started to cultivate an uneasy sense of his own mortality. And what had he to show for his three-score years and ten?

To understand a problem is already an approach to its solution. Once Frank realized he craved a memorial, the question narrowed itself down to what. Having no particular skills to trade off he soon came to realize he would have to leave something, an endowment, a collection. Having always enjoyed the graphic arts, most particularly drawing, the idea came to Frank that he build up a small but select collection of those master drawings which had not already been absorbed into major museums. Bequeathed in his name to an important gallery, The Frank Clarke Collection would bridge the now and the hereafter, granting him the kind of concrete immortality that religion promised but, Frank felt quite certain, never delivered. Were he to amass enough first-class drawings he might be able to hold out for a gallery in his own name: The Frank Clarke Gallery housing The Frank Clarke Collection. The beautifully bound and richly illustrated catalogue would become the cynosure of every curator between Montreal and Dallas. It was a goal well worth scheming for.

The kind of superlative drawings Frank wished to collect, however, had become scarce and expensive beyond his present means. All that stood between Frank and immortality was money. And his mother had money, all the money he needed to realize his dream of a collection. He needed to get his hands on his mother's assets; furthermore while she was still alive, before her death and consequent inheritance taxes poured funds he coveted into government coffers.

Where there's a will there's a way, as his mother was fond of saying. Frank had been trying to persuade her to cut him in for a larger portion of her estate, so far unsuccessfully. For a time he had even considered the idea of having her declared incompetent and committed. But hearings on family issues could turn very messy, and his mother became lucid to the point of brilliance when it came time to discuss her assets. Reluctantly, he had abandoned the idea. However circumstances had provided Frank with another way to gain access to his mother's assets, moreover through legal channels.

Frank spread the newspaper flat on the kitchen table after

he had made sure the only familiar name in today's obits was that of Thomas Evans. From a drawer in the kitchen table he took a pair of barber scissors. Clipping the obituary neatly from the paper he put it into a biscuit box which sat on top of the refrigerator. Across the lid of the box a platoon of Grenadier guards paraded for eternity in front of the British Houses of Parliament.

Then Frank went into the bathroom. After removing his glasses he showered and shaved, leaning over the handbasin to bring his face closer to the mirror. Although creased by wrinkles, the skin across which he drew the razor was still pink and fresh beneath once fair, now silvery white hair. But the nearsighted eyes retained their brilliant, arresting blue. It was a face that still carried intimations of boyhood, as if it had passed from adolescence to old age without the intervening stage of manhood. Those who knew Frank Clarke well called him a sweet old man. Others who knew him better said he was a smooth operator.

Frank rinsed his razor under hot water. Running through his mind like a litany went the opening paragraphs of the power of attorney granted to him six months ago by his mother. This power of attorney gave Frank total and absolute control over her property. He had committed the preamble to memory.

"On this fifth day of May, nineteen hundred and eighty-three, BEFORE: MTRE. MARTIN T. MAXWELL, the undersigned Notary for the Province of Quebec, practising in the City of Montreal, APPEARED: DAME FLAVIA McCUTCHEON, retired, of the City of Westmount, Province of Quebec, therein residing at 25 Mayfair Crescent, unremarried widow of the late Desmond Bruce Clarke (hereinafter called the 'Constituent'), who does by these presents, nominate, constitute and appoint her son, FRANCIS DESMOND CLARKE (herein the 'Attorney'), of the City of Westmount, Province of Quebec, therein residing at civic number 317 Berwick Road, to be her true and lawful Attorney and for her and in her name, place and stead, to do any and all of the following things, namely:

39

1. To manage and administer both actively and passively, all property, movable and immovable, belonging to the Constituent, whether now belonging to the Constituent or devolving from estates or successions in which the Constituent is or may be interested, or accruing to him in any other manner, without exception and in consequence . . . ."

And so it continued, for fifteen beautiful pages. The consummation devoutly to be wished had finally come to pass, spearheaded by the notary himself, Martin Maxwell. Granted, Frank had done a little spadework first, taking the family notary out for an expensive lunch à la carte with three wines. Over a piece of excellent Stilton, Frank had broached the subject of his mother's possible move into a nursing home. He hated the idea of taking his mother out of her own house; he knew his late father would have wished his widow to die under her own roof. But, here Frank paused to refill Martin Maxwell's glass, the situation had grown intolerable. Finding adequate staff had become next to impossible. He had been dealing with an agency, but the people they had on call were a gaggle of slatterns. His sister Vivien had been estranged from their mother for some years now and never went near the house. He himself was not getting any younger; he hated to think of what would happen to his mother if anything happened to him. Who would look after her then?

The notary swallowed a burp and agreed that a nursing home seemed to him the best solution.

"I'm glad you see it my way," Frank had said, "but the home I have in mind is some miles outside the city limits. It's going to be a dreadful nuisance chasing out there every time I need her signature on a cheque or a sales contract."

"What you should have is a power of attorney."

"Power of attorney?"

"Exactly. Allows you to act for your mother; makes you her total and absolute representative."

"What a good idea!" exclaimed Frank, as though the entire purpose of the lunch had not been to lead precisely to this point. "But you know Mother. I seriously doubt she'll be prepared to relinquish that much control, certainly not if I ask her."

"Let me speak to her," suggested Martin Maxwell. "I'm sure I'll be able to bring her around."

"I do believe you're right," agreed Frank. "More champagne?"

"Don't mind if I do," replied Martin Maxwell, his normally red face now almost purple from the aftermath of an enormous lunch. In fact it had occurred to Frank that Martin Maxwell didn't really look too awfully well.

"Why don't you come and see Mother tomorrow morning?" suggested Frank as he signalled for the cheque.

As Frank had predicted, Mrs. Clarke followed the suggestion of her notary because she was paying for his advice. She belonged to the generation who dispensed advice freely on all subjects but only followed such suggestions as were paid for by cheque. She was fond of quoting her dear late husband, who always said you got nothing for nothing in this world. "And Desmond certainly did very well for himself," she would add, almost defensively. Secretly she would have preferred her husband to practise a profession rather than be involved in trade.

Desmond Bruce Clarke had taken the solitary talent with which he had been endowed and pushed it to its uttermost limits. A sombre, graceless man, he had an instinct amounting to genius for making money. At a time when most people in the East thought of Alberta as an obstacle separating Toronto from Victoria, he saw it as the province of the future. He bought real estate in downtown Calgary when it was still a small provincial city. He understood the North American economy moved on energy: electricity, oil, natural gas. He also invested in banks. Knowing the uncertainties of the stock market he purchased a large amount of gold when it still sold for thirty-five dollars an ounce. He prospered greatly.

At some point between deals he took time out to court and

41

marry Flavia McCutcheon, a pretty, high-spirited girl of whom it was said she was strong minded. She bore her husband a daughter, and two years later, a son. Desmond Clarke looked at the children, swaddled in christening clothes, as though they had been left on the doorstep in a basket. Only momentarily puzzled by these new lives, for which he had been responsible, he forgot them and returned to his financial concerns, leaving the children entirely to his wife.

Flavia Clarke undertook motherhood fully determined to create the children in her own image. That she failed totally came not from her lack of energy and drive but from the strong and distinct natures of the children themselves. By eight years of age Vivien had become if not a thorn in her mother's flesh at least a piece of Velcro worn next to the skin. From the moment she started to walk Vivien had wanted to become an actress, lining up her dolls in rows and performing bits from Shakespeare. A tawdry touring company, to which the children had been dragged for "exposure," had put Frank to sleep but enthralled Vivien, kindling longings she was to carry for the rest of her life.

For Flavia Clarke the stage was only a rung or two above prostitution in the hierarchy of feminine occupations. And Vivien had the misfortune to be a girl during the pre-history before consciousness raising. The juggernaut of society ordained that she would marry, early and well. She did neither, but nonetheless found her path onto the stage blocked on every side.

Frank, on the other hand, defeated his mother by appearing to be exactly what she wanted him to be. An emotional chameleon, he changed colours at will, whatever fit the mood of the moment. He was Mother's little man, her favourite son, her best beau. He had charm, a magic ingredient made up of equal parts manners, grooming, a built-in social barometer, and a capacity for conversing with those many years older than himself.

Mr. Clarke Senior remained only dimly aware of his family.

His remoteness lent him mystery, and the children tended to behave when he was present. Added to which he was known to have a bad heart; his uncertain health only furthered his distance. But almost more than death itself he dreaded the spectre of his fortune being dissolved, broken up, passing out of the family. He saw his money as his memorial, and drafted his will with an attempt to grasp at permanence beyond the grave.

His entire estate was left to his two children as executors in trust, the revenue going to his wife for as long as she lived. Not only would Flavia be cared for, but the capital could not be touched until her death. It also meant paying inheritance taxes only once. Realizing however that at some future date it might be prudent to sell the real estate and reinvest the money, Mr. Clarke made a provision that all surviving members of the family must agree to sign the deed of sale. He must have understood how unlikely it would be that his wife and children would sit down and agree on anything, much less the sale of property thousands of miles away.

The trust fund set up by her husband left Flavia Clarke a wealthy woman. However, the older generation of her own family was by now beginning to die off. A late and only child, Flavia Clarke became heir to windfall after windfall: diamonds and railway stock from her maternal grandmother, Flavia Araminta Van Patten, after whom she had been named. Her grandfather, Andrew McCutcheon, left her a hotel and a slice of seashore on Cape Cod. From her own mother came emeralds; from her father two apartment buildings and a stack of government bonds as thick as the Montreal telephone book. In her own right Flavia Clarke became a rich woman, and she proceeded to cultivate the eccentricities and petty tyrannies of those for whom wealth is a weapon.

After a bitter fight, she disinherited her daughter during what was an emotionally turbulent period for Flavia Clarke. Not only did she cut her daughter off without a cent, she found herself on very chilly terms with her son Francis, who had seen fit to marry a woman of whom she did not approve. Claudia O'Leary was a divorced woman. She had independent means, and she quite obviously touched up her hair. Besides these not inconsiderable drawbacks she had been outspoken on the subject of her mother-in-law to those who felt it their solemn duty to repeat the uncharitable words that Flavia Clarke's body temperature was higher than her IQ. "That woman," seldom if ever referred as "Claudia," became *persona non grata* in the Clarke household.

Happily for Flavia Clarke, perhaps even for Frank himself, his marriage broke up shortly and coincidentally after Vivien had been disinherited. Flavia Clarke was never to know the real reason for the divorce, nor did she much care. Claudia O'Leary Clarke might have forgiven Frank for having an affair, but not with her best friend's husband.

A free agent once again, Frank lost no time in reconciling himself with his mother, who kept her son in tow with a monthly allowance backed up with presents, a car, a fur coat, a gold identification bracelet, sometimes just plain cash. In exchange he was required to dance attendance. And in spite of holding down no regular job or practising architecture, for which he had been trained, Frank worked very hard. Catering to the whims of a wilful old woman required a degree of self-discipline which equaled at least that demanded of those who work regular business hours. And when finally a combination of age, infirmity, and urging by her notary, persuaded her to grant her son Francis a complete power of attorney over his mother's assets, Frank saw his years of service to his mother begin to pay off. He now had total control of her money.

Frank liked to think he had thirty years to live, and he had plans for those thirty years. Quite simply his plan was to use his power of attorney to liquidate his mother's holdings in stocks and bonds and translate them into cash, the encroachment to be explained by the expenses of his mother's illness. This subverted cash would be used to purchase drawings with which to build up The Frank Clarke Collection. Now if he

44

could only persuade or intimidate or even bribe his sister Vivien into agreeing to sell the Calgary holdings and reinvest in equity, to be subsequently liquidated, he would be well on his way to appropriating the entire estate for himself.

Flavia Clarke, however, had begun to harbour her own vision of permanence. She knew there were to be no grandchildren. And like her dear late husband with his monument of money, she started to have intimations of immortality. She too wanted a monument to bear her name into the indefinite future; furthermore, the letters of her name were to be chiselled right into the stone. And when provincial legislation was passed enforcing French-only signs outside buildings Flavia Clarke amended her will so that her name would appear on the wall of the main lobby in English: The Flavia Clarke Memorial Wing. She would have preferred her name to be visible from the street, but "Le Pavillion Commémoratif Flavia Clarke" simply would not do.

The question remained what sort of building was to be so honoured. Not a hospital certainly; Flavia Clarke regarded illness as a form of self-indulgence and did not believe it should be encouraged. She mistrusted intellect, most particularly in women, thereby ruling out any university. People in nursing homes had memory lapses and might forget their benefactress. She decided to endow a wing for a senior citizens' home, one which only those with immense private fortunes could afford. Maple Grove Manor seemed just the place, where blue-rinsed ladies with garnet brooches at the throat took tea with silver-haired gentlemen whose Saville Row suits hung loosely on their thin frames. The Flavia Clarke Memorial Wing would rise, a reminder to future generations of geriatrics of her selfless generosity. And there was precious little that her son or anyone else would be able to do about it.

That was until Frank was granted power of attorney. Once the document had been drafted and signed five months ago Frank began at once to put his master plan into operation. He went to his mother's bank and opened a daily interest savings account under his own name. Then he called his stockbroker to sell his mother's holdings of Consolidated Canneries, after which he sent the stock certificate, along with a certified copy of his power of attorney to the stockbroker's office by registered mail. A cheque duly arrived payable to Flavia M. Clarke c/o Frank D. Clarke, which Frank took to the bank. He made out a deposit slip on which he entered the number of his own daily interest savings account. On the back of the cheque he wrote "For deposit only" and the account number. He waited in line, smiling and urging several customers to go ahead, because at his age he was in no hurry, until one of the newer tellers became free. Frank pushed the deposit slip and the cheque under the window. The teller checked the slip and the amount of the cheque. As no cash was to be withdrawn she did not question the fact that the cheque was made out to Mrs. Clarke, and punched the deposit into Frank's account. He walked from the bank three thousand dollars richer.

A few days later he repeated the procedure, using a different stockbroker and a different branch of the bank. He never sold for more than two or three thousand dollars, amounts which would be punched into the computer without question. Cheques for larger amounts had to be authorized, and the chief teller or the manager might well question the designation of the cheque.

After depositing the initial sale he continued on up to his mother's house where he proceeded to put phase two of his operation into effect. Frank was anxious that his mother move to the Willowdale nursing home. Once she was safely installed he could unload the big house and the attendant responsibility. Best of all, he would no longer be obliged to deal with staff. Knowing that if he made an outright suggestion that she move into a nursing home she would dig in her heels and give him an outright refusal, Frank took an oblique approach. A few days ago, he began as he pulled up a chair to the side of Mrs. Clarke's bed, he had driven out to visit Grace Cartwright, an old friend of his from years back. Grace was now well into her eighties and had given up her flat to move into Willowdale Manor, reputedly the finest nursing home east of the Rockies. Grace hadn't wanted to move, not one bit. She hated the idea of leaving her own home. But, my dear, you should see her now; happy as a clam. She's made a host of new friends; she loves not having to worry about meals; she plays bingo three times a week and is taking a course in off-loom weaving. Furthermore she furnished her bed-sitting room with her own things, including her big colour TV console which has its own cable hookup, so when she feels like being by herself she simply shuts the door and has meals on a tray. She is quite delighted with the place.

Grace Cartwright did not exist, of course; Frank had made her up. Unfettered by fact he was able on subsequent visits to his mother to embroider at length on this Avalon, this Oz, this Shangri-là of nursing homes. For the first month Flavia Clarke listened without comment. By the second month she was making guarded inquiries: "I suppose it's dreadfully expensive. Do they have a handrail beside the toilet?" After eight weeks of hearing about the fortunate Grace Cartwright, Mrs. Clarke chafed impatiently and told her son Francis to put down her name on the waiting list for a room. Frank did not think it necessary to admit that his mother's name had been on the waiting list since May 5, the day the power of attorney had been signed. He dutifully agreed to comply with her request.

Now, leaning over the basin, Frank rinsed his face with warm water, splashed with cold, brushed the teeth which were still attached to his gums, then dressed. Without pausing for breakfast, he drove up the hill to his mother's house. Using his key he opened the front door just as Nurse Gibson, the night nurse, came down the stairs. Tall, gaunt, angular, in earlier times she would have been burned at the stake as a witch. She appeared to be quite sober, not always the case early in the morning; but she took good care of her patient and was the only nurse about whom Flavia Clarke did not regularly complain.

"Good morning, Mr. Clarke. I just got your mother up. She is ready to see you now. I'll go and fix her breakfast."

Frank nodded, and climbed the stairs to his mother's bedroom.

"Morning, dear," he said, "and how are we today?" He bent over beneath the faded silk canopy of the massive four-poster to kiss his mother on the forehead.

"As well as can be expected, with a house full of layabouts underfoot. And now Estelle. Is she up yet?"

"I doubt it. She was exhausted after her flight. And she told me over dinner that one of the pleasures of retirement was never getting up before noon."

"And wasting a perfectly good morning. What do you suppose she really wants, after all these years without a word? Only a bit of scribble on a Christmas card. I scarcely know her."

"Ostensibly she wanted to come for a visit. At least that's the impression she gave me. She was very tired, and I was reluctant to grill her."

"What did you two talk about?"

"She did most of the talking, reminiscing mostly: her Susanna in Saltzburg, her Rosina in Rome, her Norina in Naples; and how tenors are separate but not equal, with a resonating chamber where their brains should be." Frank did not think it necessary to tell his mother the true nature of the dinner-table talk. The mere mention of Randolph Howard's name caused Mrs. Clarke to bristle with antagonism, and Frank did not wish to tamper with his mother's mood.

"Sounds to me as if she has turned into one of those bores who live in the past." Flavia Clarke plucked fretfully at the sheet. "Francis, I do wish you would move me into Willowdale."

"Mother, how many times do I have to tell you your name is on the waiting list, right at the top according to the director. The second the Grim Reaper empties a room you will be moved." Frank drew a chair up to his mother's bedside.

"Have you heard the news about Constance Chadwick?" began Mrs. Clarke as he seated himself. "Fell down again, and this time she broke her hip. They may have to put in a pin. She's years younger than I am. I suspect she had been drinking."

"Probably. I understand she has a bit of a problem in that direction."

"She must be a dreadful worry to her poor son Geoffrey. Fetch me another pillow, will you, dear?"

Frank tucked the pillow, whose case had been trimmed with tatting, behind his mother's thin shoulders. "I ran into Evelyn McMaster outside the bank the other day," he began. "There, is that better? She has cut up her sable neckpiece and used it to trim her trenchcoat. She said she grew tired of the reproachful little glass eyes. I must say she looked bizarre. She told me Phoebe Portland has left the Unitarians and become a Catholic convert."

"Phoebe always was an independent thinker. I'm sure that's why she never married."

"Mother, I think we should have a little talk . . . about the will." He carefully avoided saying "your will" in order to give the subject distance.

"Did you hear what happened to poor Muriel Baldwin? She went to her button box and swallowed a handful of blouse buttons. Thought they were aspirins. Poor thing. She must be quite senile."

"Mother, about the bequest to the old people's home—"

"Senior citizens' *residence*," interrupted his mother.

"Sorry. What I mean to say is do you really want to leave the entire half of your estate to build a wing? That will leave only half for me. You know perfectly well I will have enough. But poor Vivien. She's not at all well—and I worry about her future."

"Your sister hasn't spoken to me in years. And when I die she'll get half your father's estate. Poor Desmond. And just imagine how proud you'll be to see The Flavia Clarke Memorial Wing when it's completed. You might even want to move in there yourself. You're not getting any younger."

"Think of Father. He would just hate to see all that money go out of the family."

"His money, yes. But remember we're talking about my money." The old lady smoothed the sheet with blue-veined hands. "Alice Pratt telephoned me to say that Gertrude Pritchard is on cortisone and has blown up just like a balloon. Poor thing. Such a pretty woman she was too, although she never did have good bone. I can still remember the year she came out. She wore lace."

"Even a quarter of your estate would be enough to build two wings."

Mrs. Clarke pressed the buzzer. "I'm going to have my breakfast now. And it's time for my medication. Come back tomorrow."

Frank crossed the room apparently to look out the window but really so his mother could not see him take three deep breaths to calm himself. The idea of his mother's will leaving half her estate to Maple Grove Manor always put him into a rage. His mother had the tenacity of a terrier, a tenacity unfettered by intelligence. Unlike a dog, however, she could not be disciplined. Never mind. If his plan to liquidate the assets continued to go smoothly there wouldn't be enough money left when his mother died to build a goddamn sunporch onto Maple Grove, let alone a wing.

Frank walked towards the door. "I'll come by tomorrow," he said as he left the room.

Mrs. Clarke could not relinquish the last word. "Tell the nurse to hurry with my tray."

Frank mouthed a rude word as he started down the stairs.

By the time he regained the ground floor Nurse Gibson was on her way upstairs with his mother's breakfast. Frank picked up the telephone in the room which had once been his father's study, all leather and dark wood and glass-fronted bookcases. He dialled a number.

"Imperial Securities," said a switchboard voice.

"Mr. Burns, please."

"One moment, please." After a brief pause a voice came onto the line. "Burns here."

"Mr. Burns, it's Frank Clarke."

"Good morning, Mr. Clarke. What can I do for you?" The voice sounded as though it might smell of Old Spice aftershave.

"I'd like to sell two thousand shares of International Potash – for Mother."

"Do you intend to reinvest? I could recommend – "

"No, thank you. Just sell."

"They may want a certified copy of your power of attorney. Some transfer agents will accept a photocopy, but others drag their feet. It may prevent needless delays."

"Very good. I'll bring you one along with the stock certificate."

"I presume the shares are registered in your mother's name."

"Yes, they are."

"Shall I make the cheque out to her?"

Frank paused for a moment, as if thinking. "No, why don't you just make it out to me. Same difference, really."

"Very good, Mr. Clarke."

Frank replaced the receiver; his palms made a whispering sound as he rubbed his hands together with satisfaction. Everything was going smoothly. Next month he would fly to New York for an auction at Christie's when a pair of splendid Matisse drawings would go onto the block. By then he would have the necessary funds. Frank leaned heavily on the legal principle that in any transaction the good faith of the parties is taken for granted. And if he lost a little in the transactions? All he had to do to cheer himself up was to think of what the government would take in inheritance taxes even before half his mother's estate went towards that goddamn memorial wing. Frank looked at his watch, a Rolex given to him by his mother after he had kept her company on a cruise up the Saguenay River. Half-past nine read the hands, neatly encapsulating one quarter of the dial; too soon to go to the bank.

On a sudden impulse Frank went down the flight of steep,

narrow stairs leading from the pantry to the cellar. Almost all the other houses in the neighbourhood had basements; but the old Clarke house, one of the few remaining wooden structures in the community, had a cellar, dank, musty, and filled with things that go bump in the night. Most people familiar with the house were reluctant to go down into the cellar unless armed, but Frank loved it. As a child growing up in the house, the cellar had been his refuge, filled with hidey holes so precious to a child comfortable with his own company. The large, dim space was filled with relics of a way of life now long past. A gas ring still sat beside the washtubs where the laundress, whose large ironing table sat covered with cardboard cartons, could make tea for herself and the gardener without bothering the cook. Now the dirty laundry went out; and the garden, once a showplace, was being untidily reclaimed by nature gone to seed, and overrun by those very plants and shrubs which, pruned and manicured, had formerly been the envy of the entire community.

A workbench of lumber seasoned to the toughness of fibreglass sat beneath racks of tools: screwdrivers and chisels, whose wooden handles spoke of life before plastic. Nuts, bolts, screws, nails, washers, sat in neat rows of discarded jars whose age had raised their status from that of trash to that of collectibles. Beside the furnace, a massive silver structure which once burned coal but had since been converted to oil, crouched a toilet, modestly isolated in its own cubicle. The cistern, perched high on the wall, could be coaxed, via a length of chain ending in a wooden handle, to release a flood of water across a high, flat porcelain surface on which stools rested like exhibits in an avant-garde gallery.

Frank crossed to a large storage cupboard and opened a door held shut by a butterfly nut. It creaked open to reveal shelves beneath which sat a small, square safe, itself a collectible. With sure fingers Frank spun the dial as tumblers clicked into place. Opening the heavy door he drew out a large square box of tooled green calf. Inside, on a bed of white satin now yellowed with age, lay the emeralds which had belonged to his grandmother. Suspended from a chain of square-cut diamonds hung five large pear-shaped emeralds, burning with their own inner light. In the centre of the circle formed by the necklace lay the earrings, two more pear-shaped green gems hanging from a single diamond stud. Mrs. Clarke kept them in the house, less, Frank well understood, out of sentiment because they had belonged to her mother than because they were the most valuable thing she owned. Every so often she would ask Frank to fetch them just so she could sit and hold them in their box, her eyes bright with ownership.

God! Weren't they splendid. And one day they would be his, along with everything else. Frank closed the box and placed it in the safe, for the time being. Sold judiciously, translated into cash, they would swell his coffers and help to underwrite The Collection. The second his mother moved into Willowdale Frank intended to remove the jewels to his own safety deposit box. In fact, since his mother had wanted to avoid the expense of insuring them, they were not scheduled. Nor were they mentioned specifically in the will. Frank did not intend to declare the emeralds for succession duties. They would simply disappear. He would take them to his fence, Roch Larivière, a friend of Frank's since childhood. As children the two men had grown up across the street from one another, which gave them the opportunity to share their first dirty jokes, their first cigarettes, their first fumbling attempts at sex. Roch now ran a clandestine business as a receiver of stolen goods, and thus far had not run afoul of the law. Good neighbours make good fences.

At some point he must get himself down to Roch's apartment in Old Montreal to deliver his mother's opal and diamond brooch for which Roch claimed to have a buyer. He might even try to get down later this afternoon. Frank pushed the small but heavy door shut and spun the dial. Then he closed the wooden door, obscuring shelves filled with glass jelly jars and boxes of solid paraffin wax.

If Flavia Clarke had allowed the occasional concern to penetrate her adamantine assurance, one of these concerns was that because of her money she might be thought an idle woman. Making jams and jellies was one of the ways through which she established her right to be considered a housewife who toiled.

Sometimes, on a whim, Flavia Clarke wrapped the birthday or Christmas cheque, with which she kept her coterie of friends obedient, around a jar of preserves. On one occasion the grape jelly, which had failed to set properly, leaked all over the cheque, making the writing illegible. The recipient then telephoned her to say her grape jelly had ruined the cheque. The suggestion that her jelly could be less than perfect so incensed Mrs. Clarke that not only did she not replace the spoiled cheque, she struck the recipient from the charmed list.

Frank left his mother's house at fifteen minutes past ten. Walking briskly down the long path leading from the front door he stepped onto the sidewalk, almost colliding with a small girl walking a cocker spaniel puppy on a lead. Still young enough to consider all humans as siblings, the puppy wagged its stump of a tail and jumped all over Frank, wiping its paws thoroughly on his trousers. In the process the chain tangled itself around Frank's legs, now covered with muddy paw prints. Stepping backwards to avoid the dog's importunate affection, he tugged sharply on the chain. Suddenly taut, it pulled the child off balance to land sharply on her knees. The concrete sidewalk peeled off several layers of skin.

"If you would learn to control your puppy . . . . " began Frank, his voice devoid of sympathy, as he lifted the howling child to her feet. At that precise moment the child's mother walked up to them.

In a flash Frank was kneeling beside the sobbing child, dabbing at skinned knees with a spotless white handkerchief and murmuring "There, there, dear" in honeyed tones. Somehow his legs had become tangled in the lead, he explained to the anxious mother; he was so terribly sorry. The mother apologized in turn to Frank, making a grimace of adult conspiracy and assuring him "That Puppy!" was slated for obedience school the second it was old enough. She led the now sniffling child away to be disinfected and bandaged while the girl digested what was perhaps her first lesson in the duplicity of the male sex.

Across the street, at their bay window, the Petrie sisters, Ines and Edna, stood like Siamese twins nodding approval. One of the sisters, no one could remember which, had been married years ago; but conjugal life had left no trace. They had materialized in the window just in time to see Frank kneel to rescue the fallen child. Such a sweet man he was – and so devoted to his mother.

Frank drove from Westmount into the neighbouring community of Notre Dame de Grace. Our Lady of Grace; it did sound better in French. He parked his car near a small branch of a large bank and went inside. Approaching the information counter with diffidence he smiled shyly at a young woman with enormous glasses and masses of kinky hair to whom he confided that he had a cheque. He would like to open an account; was it – he seemed to falter – a daily interest savings account? All this banking business seemed so complicated. He couldn't make head nor tail. When he was a boy, banks – but she wouldn't be interested in that. He was sure she was a very busy woman.

Beneath the dacron sweater, only slightly balled under the arms, a faintly maternal urge began to stir. Now all kind efficiency, the young woman took charge, opening a daily interest savings account with the cheque for ten thousand dollars, the proceeds from a recent sale of Trans-Canada Pipeline stock, to be rolled over every thirty days. Frank did not use the term "rolled over," although that is what he meant. Instead he said "extended."

As the young woman applied herself to the paperwork Frank stood, shoulders slightly stooped, smiling good-naturedly into the middle distance; a paradigm of gentle incompetence. "Isn't there something I could do to help?" he inquired, knowing perfectly well the young woman thought he should not be wandering about loose.

By the time he left the bank, Frank had cajoled his way into a term deposit issued in his own name. He also left the young woman with whom he had dealt pleased to have been of help to this nice old man who thanked her warmly and smiled the sweetest smile.

As he slid behind the wheel of his car he made a mental note to pick up some pastries for his mother. Frank went out of his way to humour his mother's whims. By keeping the forefront of her consciousness occupied with minutiae, small gifts and quarrels with the nurses and bits of gossip about those friends who had not succumbed to the Grim Reaper, he kept her mind away from epic issues. He avoided topics like whatever happened to the Royal Doulton dinner service, which had already been sold by Frank for a nice piece of change, or whether she should bother having Grandmother Van Patten's diamonds reset. The diamonds in question had already been reset, by their new owner.

# Chapter 6

Back in the upper duplex of the building he owned (he would have preferred the lower but the doctor insisted that stairs were good for the heart), Frank fed the goldfish. Bette, Greta, and Marlene rested torpidly on the coloured pebbles covering the bottom of the bowl. As he sprinkled flakes of dry food, which broke the surface tension of the water, they darted up to dine. Once a day he fed the fish; Sunday mornings he changed the water and washed out the bowl.

It had become Frank's practice to take a nap after lunch precisely from two to three. His adherence to a routine did not spring from that inflexibility which is often a symptom of the later years but from the conviction that a routine is efficient. This particular day was no exception; Frank lay down for his accustomed hour.

Afterwards, instead of putting the kettle on his own stove, Frank drove up the hill to his mother's house for tea and a chat with Cousin Estelle who by now ought to have surfaced from her bedroom. Unless she were adventurous enough to explore the kitchen herself she probably would get no tea. Gelsomina, the cook, did not arrive until five, and the nurses refused to make anything at all unless it was for the patient. They made exceptions for Frank, however, as their jobs depended on his good will.

How sick he had become of managing staff: three nurses a

day for morning, afternoon, and night shifts, with Nurse Harrison as replacement; a cook; a cleaning woman – all feuding and forming alliances. Ordinarily Frank would have preferred a resident housekeeper to oversee the entire operation. The last housekeeper had come highly recommended, reliable, honest, and a gourmet cook to boot, meaning she put bay leaf in stew and baked a cake without using a mix. From the first Flavia Clarke had resented Mrs. Innes, a statuesque woman from Barbados, with café-au-lait skin. "There's a touch of the tar brush there!" Mrs. Clarke had announced the second her new housekeeper was out of earshot. In skin, as in most things, Mrs. Clarke thought in terms of black and white. But a touch of the tar brush hinted at cross breeding, miscegenation, rapes; it brought to mind images of caramel-coloured children in shopping bags abandoned in washrooms of welfare agencies. Consequently, when one day Mrs. Clarke summoned the housekeeper to her room in order to complain about lumps in the tapioca pudding, the outcome of the interview was a foregone conclusion.

At first Frank had been furious. Having a resident housekeeper took much of the load off his shoulders. Until a suitable replacement could be found he had to deal with help on a day-to-day basis from the agency.

The second he shut the front door behind him, the *portières* slowly parted to reveal Estelle wearing a long chocolate-coloured robe of the sort which used to be called a housecoat. Far more than a dressing gown, not quite a ball gown, its skirt fell in elaborate folds to the floor in front, fanning into a train behind. A long scarf of the same supple fabric covered her head, the ends crossing under her chin and falling down her back to the floor. Giant sunglasses concealed her eyes, although not even a bold sunbeam ever dared affront the gloom of the Clarke front room.

"Dearest Francis, at last you are here," she began in her husky contralto. "The very first line Lucia sings as she comes on stage has been running through my mind all afternoon.

58

*'Ancor non giunse?'* " Has he not yet arrived? And here at last you are."

"Indeed, Cousin Estelle. Have you had tea?"

"No."

"Did you get some lunch?"

"After a fashion. I came downstairs around noon, and that nurse was in the kitchen, the one with the fat feet. 'Who are you?' she demanded. Naturally I ignored her and went to open the refrigerator. 'You'll have to come back later,' she said. 'I have to make Mrs. Clarke's lunch.'

" 'My good woman,' I replied. 'I am not accustomed to taking orders from the help. Now while I prepare myself a light breakfast you can make up my room.' She muttered something – I am certain it was rude – and flounced from the kitchen. And my room is still not made up."

By now, Estelle had sunk into the Italian provincial couch whose faded blue satin cover badly needed redoing. The padded back was held in place by row upon row of fabric covered buttons, an upholsterer's nightmare. She sat sideways, her left hand resting in her lap, her right braced against the back of the couch. It was a singer's pose, her body upright, ready to support sound on an invisible but powerful column of air.

"Cousin Estelle," began Frank. "Unfortunately you are now in Canada, a country where democracy has quite undermined the concept of service. There are no masters any more, only union leaders. Our working-class lives its life in panic terror lest it be called upon to perform one tiny task that lies outside the job description. The nurses who come to the house are here to care for Mother. That is all they are prepared to do. We will not dwell upon the fact that most nurses on private cases are lazy sluts, unable or unwilling to undertake hospital work. Mother needs constant care, and I am not about to push and pull her on and off the toilet. I will speak to the cleaning woman who comes in three days a week about doing up your bedroom and bath. Now I will see about getting us some tea."

By the time Frank returned to the front room Estelle had

moved to stand in front of the fireplace, one elbow resting on the mantelpiece, in three-quarter profile to the room. By turning her body she caused the train of her robe to sweep into a graceful curve.

The heavy pile carpet muffled Frank's steps so he was able to stand observing his cousin without her being aware of his scrutiny. Her presence made him uneasy, if only because he did not really know why she had come to Canada. The actress she had once been informed every movement and gesture; whatever she was thinking never translated itself into speech without first taking into account the audience, the setting, the lighting, and the effect to be achieved. Whether or not she could in some way interfere with his master plan he could not as yet tell. He sensed in her a will of steel. His own mother was a strong-willed woman, but her determination expressed itself through imposing her wishes on a small circle of people. Estelle, on the other hand, had risen to the top of a demanding and competitive profession. No matter what assistance she may have had along the way, it remained her own drive and determination which had caused her to scale the Everest of success. He suspected she could be a powerful ally as well as a daunting opponent.

He knew Estelle was somewhat younger than his mother. But even by the most lenient standards she was an old lady. At present she appeared in good health; not even the emphysema of which she complained appeared to hinder her. But she had reached an age when the body can suddenly break down, and were she to fall suddenly ill Frank realized he would be responsible for seeing she was cared for. On the point of moving his mother into a nursing home where she would cease to be his direct responsibility he grew apprehensive at the thought of being landed with another elderly female invalid. Expense aside, he bloody well did not want to be bothered. At the moment the only thing he could do was to shepherd Estelle safely through her visit and make certain she boarded a plane for the flight back to London in the not too distant future.

"Tea will be along in a minute," he said by way of announcing himself.

Frank sat in a lumpy upholstered armchair draped with lace antimacassars. "Cousin Estelle, why did you come to Canada?"

He had hoped to catch her off guard. But she was ready.

"To visit my dear cousin Flavia. Why else? And to meet her charming children."

"I see," said Frank, thinking that this sudden surge of family feeling was coming on somewhat late in life. "Have you any idea how long you intend to stay?"

"Until my welcome has worn out," replied Estelle archly.

"I am only asking," continued Frank, "because any day now Mother will be moving into the Willowdale nursing home. That does not mean you cannot stay on here. But you will be alone, except for the cleaning woman who will continue to come in."

Nurse Harrison's large backside upholstered in white polyester pushed its way through the *portières* as she backed into the room carrying a tray. Pointedly not looking at either Frank or Estelle she put the tray heavily down onto the circular table and beat her way back through the curtains. Estelle seized upon the interruption.

"By the way, I telephoned Vivien earlier this afternoon and she asked me by for a bite of supper. She said I was to tell you to come along if you could."

"I won't be able to make it. I have an engagement. There's a half-bottle of gin in the pantry. I strongly urge you to take it with you. Vivien serves dreadful things to drink, like Campari, and Kir, and red and white vermouth mixed together."

"Thank you, I will," said Estelle crossing to the tray. Frank watched her pour, quietly amused. She handled the teapot as though God were sitting front row centre.

"Pouring tea always reminds me of the time I sang Despina

in *Cosi Fan Tutti*. I was the maid and my first entrance was carrying a tray with two cups and a pot of hot chocolate. I thought it a silly part, all that business about disguising myself as a doctor, and then as a notary drawing up a bogus marriage contract. But that was long ago, early in my career. It was as a dramatic coloratura that I built my international reputation."

Estelle handed Frank a cup. "Francis, I had a visit with your mother after she had eaten her lunch. From what I was able to ascertain – I was reluctant to ask outright – she no longer speaks to your sister Vivien. As I am to dine with Vivien tonight I wonder if you would mind telling me why. I would hate to appear tactless, more so since I will be meeting your sister for the first time. Of course if you would prefer not to talk about it . . . ."

"Not at all. In a word, Mother and Vivien had a row, the day of Randolph Howard's funeral, as a matter of fact. Vivien got drunk, angry, and pasted Mother. They haven't spoken since."

"You mean Vivien struck your mother – physically?"

"Knocked her flat."

"Dear me."

"We came back here for lunch after the service," began Frank. "The funeral had caused us all to bury the hatchet, but in a shallow and well-marked grave. The cook managed to delay lunch; and instead of the proffered glass of sherry, Vivien got into the gin. She was already tired and upset, and from what I was able to figure out Mother managed to say all the wrong things. Vivien got angry, and you know how these scenes can escalate."

Before the Cadillac limousine had even discharged its passengers at the front door of the Clarke house, the air was thick with tension. Frank's wife Claudia had refused to return to the big house for lunch. In her smoke-cured voice she announced her intention to take Vivien to lunch very soon, when they would both get pissed to the gills, then added in a stage whisper that she had no intention of sharing soggy soufflé with Mother McCreep. She jumped into her Sunbeam Talbot and tore out of the cemetery. Flavia Clarke overheard and took offence. As a result of this unfortunate marriage Frank had fallen from grace and now lay in the burning lake of his mother's disapproval. With one snip Frank had cut, to his mother's displeasure, both the apron strings, and now met her as equal, not dependent.

After Claudia's abrupt departure, the members of the Clarke family shook hands with the representatives of Randolph's family before returning to the big house for lunch. Frank, Vivien, and their mother stepped from the limousine, filed up the front walk, and entered the house with a sense of heightened formality, almost as if they were being filmed for a documentary.

Dressed in black, the two women sat talking. Frank could still remember how his mother kept a good black dress just for funerals; Vivien had mixed and matched. Vivien did not have much to say, nor was she given the chance to say very much. Funerals filled their mother with energy; they were times of high drama, the Proctor and Gamble hour made flesh. She had been galvanized by the death of her own husband; the days simply were not long enough to reply to sympathy notes, scribble thanks for flowers, dispose of his possessions. Vivien took her father's gold cuff-links which she had made into earrings. Frank took the stamp collection, which he promptly sold. Nobody it seemed wanted the complete novels of Surtees bound in calf or a bisque bust of Byron. Flavia Clarke asked Vivien whether Randolph wanted three pairs of pyjamas, nice warm flannelette, brand new, still in cellophane. Vivien told her mother Randolph never wore pyjamas. To the best of Frank's knowledge that was as close as the two women ever came to discussing sex.

"Oh, Francis," exclaimed Estelle, covering her mouth with both hands. "You do make me laugh."

Frank thought that anyone who had looked at as many ceilings as Cousin Estelle had little right to be coy. But he understood she was trying to ingratiate herself.

"Lunch was delayed," he continued. "Mrs. Cooper had attempted a soufflé and failed."

"But I thought she had been fired after Christmas dinner."

"She was. But Mother needed her too badly, not as a cook but as a foil. Anyhow Mother suggested we all have a glass of sherry . . . ."

The arrival of Frank pushing the tea-trolley bar caused a temporary diversion. Frank poured sherry for his mother, vermouth for himself. Vivien crossed to examine the drinks trolley while Frank placed the cut-crystal stem glass on the table beside his mother. Ordinarily a moderate drinker, Vivien felt recent events called for something with authority. Demonstrating more courage than conviction she made herself a dry martini and took a long, bitter swallow.

"I think it would be an excellent idea for you to give up your flat and move back here," began her mother, who now lived alone in the big house and was bored to tears with her own company. "Just think; you could have your father's bedroom, bathroom, dressing room. It's practically a flat."

"Thanks anyway, Mother, but I think I'll stay put for the moment." Vivien took a second swallow.

"There is absolutely nothing to be gained by living alone. You'll brood. And if you should go back to work, although I can't imagine why you would even consider it, just think how agreeable it would be to have a hot meal waiting when you got home."

"I'd like to take a few weeks to sort myself out before I make any moves." A third swallow drained Vivien's glass and she moved towards the trolley.

"Suit yourself. You always have – and it is polite to ask."

"May I have another drink?" Vivien deliberately left out "please." It had always galled her to be treated like a poor relation in the house where she had grown up.

"Yes, of course. Still it would be pleasant if you moved back in." Once their mother had taken hold of an idea she worried it the way a terrier puppy worries an old glove. "Think of all the things we could do together: concerts, theatre, bridge; you really must learn how to play."

Vivien sat sipping her drink without reply.

During this exchange Frank also sat silent. Were Vivien to move back into the house as her mother's companion she could easily work her way into a position of influence. But, considering the basic antagonism between the two women, the possibility seemed unlikely. Still, the chance remained. Until his marriage Frank had been the principal influence on his mother, manipulating her so obliquely she remained unaware of the ruse. Always in the back of Frank's mind lay the ambition to be cut into his mother's will for a larger share of her estate.

Frank put down his teacup and checked himself. Until he better understood what Estelle was really about Frank did not want to expose himself to her any more than was absolutely necessary. Self-interest, like body lice, must be dealt with in private, denied in public.

"How did Vivien take to the idea of becoming your mother's companion?" inquired Estelle.

"Not very well. When Mother suggested they take a cruise together, Vivien burst into tears. I guess she found the prospect of trailing around various watering holes as one half of a pair of Westmount widows pretty depressing. But Mother did not give up. I don't really have to tell you she won't take yes for an answer."

His mother's invariable formula for dealing with tears was to remind the distraught person that the world teemed with those far more unfortunate.

"Now, now, Vivien. We must all learn to live with our losses. Tears don't really solve a thing. Just think of all those people in Great Britain who lost their homes during the war. And it isn't too early to start thinking about your future."

"My future!"

"Yes, your future. Sooner or later you will have to consider the possibility of marrying again. A sober, serious marriage. You have had your marriage for—romance." "Romance" was Mrs. Clarke's code word for sexual intercourse. That she even brought the subject up showed how seriously she meant her words to be taken. Flavia Clarke herself had embarked upon marriage convinced that sex was a duty, a belief her late husband had done little to dispel. As a result sex had always been one of the forbidden topics in the Clarke household. And to admit the sexuality of one's own children was as unthinkable as admitting to company that the smell of boiled cabbage lingered in the front hall.

"You have passed the age of childbearing," she continued, "but there are widowers."

"Mother, are you serious? We have just come from burying Randolph, and you are trying to marry me off to some old fart with three children and a pot belly."

"I don't mean at once, Vivien, and there is no need to be coarse. To begin with, a prompt remarriage would not be seemly. All I ask you to do is consider the possibility."

"But you must realize that before I marry again I have to have at least a couple of years of sleeping around. You know: cab drivers, delivery boys, the man who comes to read the meter. And I shall drink heavily and have a black, coloured, negro lover, definitely blue collar, who will beat and humiliate me. I shall sit in drafts and eat desserts and ignore Christmas cards and become generally debauched. Then I shall meet a good, kind, established doctor or lawyer or Indian chief whose strong, pure, undefiled love will redeem me. Finally I shall run a foster home for retarded children. I have it all worked out."

Frank could see Vivien growing really angry. It was at this point he remembered an urgent appointment and rose to leave. This rift would serve his purposes nicely.

"But what about my soufflé?" demanded his mother.

"I'm not hungry really, Mother. And I know you and Vivien have a great deal to talk about." Before either woman could object Frank had slipped out the front door.

"And then what happened?" In her eagerness to hear the conclusion, Estelle forgot her attitudes and leaned forward as any curious old lady might.

"The argument escalated rapidly. I had to piece the story together from remarks Mother and Mrs. Cooper let drop. Vivien refused to talk about the episode; but Mrs. Cooper, you may be sure, was lurking in the dining room where she wasn't listening but couldn't help hearing. Mother made a crack about Vivien and Randolph living together before they were married. Some parents are like junkies when it comes to criticism; they just can't do without their fix of disapproval. It must have been quite a scene; it certainly impressed Mrs. Cooper. Vivien cleared the room of small objects: the old balloon seller, the old knife grinder, the Copenhagen mermaid, even a pair of King Charles spaniels which had belonged to Grandmother Van Patten and were supposed to be very valuable. I don't think she actually threw the figurines directly at Mother, but rather around her."

Flavia Clarke sat immobile on the love seat as figurines hurled by her daughter exploded musically into shards. One of the King Charles spaniels smashed the glass covering the engraving of Salisbury Cathedral after Constable. It was only after Vivien had cleared all surfaces of small breakables that she turned to larger game, reaching for the large cut-glass bowl filled with fruit no one was permitted to eat. Mrs. Clarke leaped into action. With the agility of an athlete she sprang across the room, spun her daughter around, and slapped her hard across the left cheek. "That will do, Vivien, thank you very much."

Vivien had never been struck in her life, nor had Frank.

Punishments had always taken the form of banishments, treats denied, pleasures postponed. The blow was guaranteed not to sweeten her disposition.

And just as she had never been struck before, Vivien had never hit anyone, at least not seriously. But the blow she landed on her mother's jaw was serious, so much so in fact it knocked the older woman to the floor. Vivien stood in the centre of the room, a Winged Victory, albeit with arms and head. The room lay in shambles; her opponent lay prone. There remained little for Vivien to do but leave the house for what turned out to be the last time.

Although unhurt, Flavia Clarke took to her bed for a week and was "not at home" to the outside world. Within the house she was "in" only to the maid, who brought meals on a tray; and to her notary, Martin Maxwell, who, under instruction from Mrs. Clarke, removed Vivien from the will.

"That's quite a story," said Estelle, "particularly to one like myself who has had little or no experience of family life. But tell me, Francis, once you realized Vivien was drinking rather more than was good for her, didn't you try to intervene? I'm sure you must have realized trouble was brewing."

Frank looked pointedly at his watch. "Goodness me. I didn't realize how late it is. I'll have to dash, Cousin Estelle. I hope you enjoy your evening with Vivien."

Frank ducked out of the house without even going upstairs to see his mother. Had he stuck his head in the door to say hello she would have insisted he keep her company until her supper tray arrived. Frank was fully prepared to give his mother anything she wanted, except his time. She had already devoured more than her share of that.

# Chapter 7

Frank turned his car down the hill in the direction of the St. Lawrence River. He had not been lying when he told his cousin he had a prior engagement, having telephoned Roch Larivière earlier in the day to suggest he bring by the opal which now lay in a small satin envelope locked into the glove compartment of his car. Besides, he had no wish to spend the evening in his cousin's company; he found it both trying and tiring to edit his real motives as he filled her in on family background. Already he had lost his footing once and let slip how he had hoped for a larger share in the will. So much had been left out as he told her about the funeral: how his marriage had been foundering on conjugal shoals. Frank had only hinted at how strongly his mother disapproved of both her children's marriages. Nor had he even come close to the emotional morass in which he and his mother manoeuvred for supremacy.

And like a surgeon with a probe Estelle had touched the weak point in his story. Why had he let Vivien hang herself? Why had he not used his charm and tact to defuse an explosive situation? Why had he sidled out? The answer was beyond simple. He had wanted to see his sister discredited, to see her share of the will diminished and added to his own.

Frank had no intention of depriving his sister of material comforts. Once he gained control of his mother's money he would make sure Vivien enjoyed a much higher standard of living than she presently did. Nothing she needed or wanted would be denied. It was just that he couldn't bear the thought of her sitting on a large block of capital, like a brood hen, while it slowly hatched into coupons and dividends. No art collection ever got itself built that way.

He pulled onto Dorchester Boulevard. Now he must prepare himself to deal with that nelly old queen, Roch Larivière. Frank had grown heartily tired of the camp behaviour he had tolerated in his youth. However, he had a knack for adapting his behaviour to suit the situation in which he found himself.

Frank drove his car down Beaver Hall Hill. After threading his way through narrow streets in the older quarter of the city he spotted a parking space. Neatly backing his car into place he shut off the engine. Then, unlocking the glove compartment he removed the satin envelope containing the opal, and put it in his pocket.

He walked two short blocks to a grey limestone building, formerly a warehouse, which abutted the sidewalk. Inside he rode the antique elevator with its flexible latticed gate to the upper floor where he pushed a buzzer.

"Fanny, dearest!"

"Roxanne, my sweet!"

"Don't just stand there like the Avon lady, come inside."

Frank Clarke walked into the top-storey apartment of Roch Larivière. Roch owned the building, renting the lower floors at exorbitant rates to young professionals who had grown up during the sixties. They were prepared to be gouged for a monthly rent which allowed them to live in the most newly chic part of town and to brag about exposed fieldstone walls to those who could boast only brick.

At first glance Roch Larivière appeared to be one of life's losers. In spite of his French name he did not speak a word of that language, having been raised by an English-Canadian mother and a British nanny who, moreover, had instilled in him an intense dislike of French Canada. He had spent most of his adult life as a homosexual at a time when the government felt it had every right to invade the bedrooms of the nation. And at a time when fashion imposed an anorexic emaciation, he was immensely fat; bald, smooth, and buttery, like a debauched Oriental deity.

But he had learned to use his resources, not least of which were drive and intelligence. Disinherited by his ultra-conservative father for having been caught in a compromising situation with the chauffeur, who was dismissed on the spot without references, Roch began with no experience whatsoever to shift for himself. At first he had himself kept by a series of older men, calling himself Rick Rivers for his French lovers, Roch Larivière for the English. Aside from catering to their sexual tastes he offered them absolute discretion, a legacy from his childhood. Then his youth and beauty ran out, but in the meantime he had cultivated a taste for beautiful things: furniture, china, paintings, jewellery, silver. He had also learned a good deal about them. Over the years he had feathered the love nest with enough valuable objects to set up shop; and that is precisely what he did, operating out of his house to cut down on overhead.

He had a shrewd sense of acquisition, never asking too many questions about the antecedents of an object, just as long as it had beauty and pedigree. His good faith as third-party owner of a movable object was not therefore compromised. Occasionally there were borderline cases, one or two even bringing police inspectors to the door. But Roch had discovered that those investigators who could not be bought off with straight cash could be persuaded to accept the favours of beautiful young women, or men, whose names, numbers, and photographs he kept on file and to whom he paid a retainer. Roch would have thrown up his plump hands in horror at the merest suggestion that he was a receiver of stolen goods. It was just that he believed beautiful objects should be under the care of those who truly loved them. And if he accepted a fee for bringing collector and prize together? Well, after all, a lady has to live.

His apartment looked as though he had just come home from a garage sale at Buckingham Palace. Objects in prodigal profusion were stacked on chairs; they spilled from tables and stuck out of drawers. Roch knew the exact location and worth of everything in the house. Moreover he had a good idea of whom to put in contact with what.

"Come to the kitchen," said Roch as he closed the door behind Frank. "It's the one place where we can sit – and a little white rum never hurt anyone." He moved his bulk with agility as he threaded his way to the rear of the apartment. Frank followed, careful not to tread on the train of Roch's robe, a garment cut like a monk's cassock stitched from mauve satin.

Seated on twisted wire chairs at a table which had come from an ice cream parlour, they sipped rum and soda.

"Cheers, Precious Treasure," said Roch lifting his goblet; he never drank from a tumbler. "What have you been up to?" His voice sang with innuendo, giving the most pedestrian statements overtones of sin.

"A little bit of this, some of that."

"Well – I've been up to a good deal of that." Roch rolled his eyes. "Only last night, as a matter of fact, I had the most beautiful Adonises you ever saw."

"I believe the correct name is Adonis."

"There were two of them. It was pure heaven. One in front and one behind."

"Did they communicate by walkie-talkie?"

"Dearest Fanny is a mean bitch."

"If the mule fits, Roxanne, wear it."

"Look, I'm not about to turn into one of those old tarts who turns to God and good works. Seriously, though, I've been thinking of expanding the dating service. So far I've only operated on a private basis for my best customers – and to buy off those Nosy Parker police. But, face it, Fanny; times are tough. Nowadays people are less concerned with beautiful objects than in scraping up enough cash to pay their real estate taxes. And during depressed economic periods people fall back more heavily on their fantasies. And many of these fantasies are, let us say, amorous. Offer them an opportunity to turn these fantasies into flesh, implement their imaginations, and then turn their lusts into lucre."

"Sounds good. From beautiful objects to beautiful bodies. And with the unemployment rate so high there is a vast pool of youthful energy out there waiting to be tapped."

"Precisely my point. But this will be no ordinary dating service. Discretion will be assured, in fact guaranteed. Most of the clients will be vulnerable to blackmail. My 'employees' will be well taken care of, just as long as they avoid private enterprises; for which the consequences could be quite painful. It will be a carriage trade service. No offensive advertising. You've read the ads in those cheesy magazines: 'Nine inches of pure pleasure waiting to plug your pussy.' Tacky, tacky. To begin with, we will go metric. Two hundred millimetres sounds far more impressive than eight inches. We will market sensitive sexuality, fairy-tale foreplay, fantastic fellatio, caressing cunnilingus, soulful sodomizing, thrilling threesomes. But I need a name, a logo; something that will set my agency apart from the others, the vulgar ones. I had thought of 'Flesh and Fantasy'."

Frank thought for a minute. "Too much of a mouthful. Too many words. It would degenerate into F and F, which sounds dirty."

"What do you think of 'Rent-a-Rendezvous'?"

"Again too much of a mouthful. And 'Rent-a-Date' sounds a bit street."

" 'Eclectic Escorts'?"

"No, no, Roxanne. Half your clientele won't know what the word 'eclectic' means."

"Oh dear, I suppose you're right. What would you say to 'Assignations Anonymous'?"

"Too therapeutic. It sounds like the kind of organization one would join in order to give up sex, not indulge in it. You want a name which suggests you're offering more than sightseeing, dinner perhaps, and a casual fuck. You want to hint at the unmentionable." Frank snapped his fingers. "I have it! 'Escorts Unlimited.' "

Roch clapped his plump hands together. "That's it! Perfect! Simply perfect, my Fanny. But now we have a little business to transact. I believe you have the opal?"

Frank took the small envelope from his pocket and slipped the brooch out. Roughly the size of a fifty-cent piece, the smooth surface of the opal glittered and danced with tiny specks of prism colour reflected and magnified by the surrounding diamonds.

Roch placed his hands together so only the tips of his fingers touched. "Splendid, simply splendid. But there's going to be a tiny problem"

"What's that?"

"My client is interested only in the opal. I explained there were diamonds, but I didn't realize they were so large."

"What do you suggest?"

"My advice – if you really want to unload – is to take the opal out of the setting and sell the diamonds separately. They're worth far more than the opal, but it's the opal I have a buyer for. I can have my jeweller do the job. And I may even be able to sell the diamonds, if you wish."

Frank thought for a moment. The brooch wasn't doing anyone any good sitting in a strongbox. And if he took it to a jeweller to sell as estate jewellery there would be delays, maybe even questions. Here he was certain of a sale. Roch took forty per cent as commission. A large slice, granted, but one paid for convenience and anonymity.

"Fair enough," said Frank. Sell the diamonds. Get whatever you can."

"And now, my Fanny, I have something to show you." Roch heaved himself to his feet and glided into the bedroom. He returned with a small portfolio which he laid carefully on the kitchen table. Inside, wrapped in protective plastic, lay a drawing. In pristine, economical strokes of pen the artist had described a woman, seated, draped in a tunic, and holding a hand mirror. Behind her stood another woman, similarly draped, arranging the hair of the woman who sat. Across the bottom a signature uncoiled itself, as familiar as the logo of a multinational corporation: Picasso.

Frank's eyes widened in astonishment. "Where on earth . . . ."

"Tut, tut, my sweet. Let us just say it has come into my possession. And you are the first person to whom it has been shown."

Frank stared in rapture at the signature. Lying on the table was a drawing which could be the cornerstone of his collection.

The two men began to dicker. Roch had an immensely valuable drawing, but Frank knew the provenance was extremely dubious. It would have to remain under wraps for quite a while. Roch, in turn, understood Frank very much wanted the drawing. But Frank had once spoken of a silver tea service, Georgian, hall-marked, a service which belonged to his mother but which he had been kindly storing in his own apartment. And was there not a sapphire bracelet still in the safety deposit box? Roch compressed his bulk into a monument of concentration; although he did not close his eyes his pupils appeared to shrink. The opal, the diamonds, the silver service, and the bracelet in the strongbox – all in exchange for the Picasso.

When bargaining Frank appeared to go slack, as though only his skin were holding his skeleton in place. He paused as if weighing off one value against the other. How about the opal, the diamonds, and the sapphire bracelet – but not the silver service.

Roch appeared to smile; his jowls rearranged themselves while the face from the nose up did not move. "You drive a hard bargain, my Fanny. And to think we went to school together." His pseudo smile faded into an incipient pout.

"Roxanne, *mon coeur*. If you scotch-taped that drawing onto the wall of the men's room in Central Station, Interpol would nab you before you got halfway across the ticket lobby. The opal, the diamonds, the silver service, but not the bracelet."

Roch shrugged his massive shoulders in mock defeat. "Very well. What can I do?"

"Done?"

"Done!" The last brisk and businesslike.

The two men shook hands, Roch's nearly covered by a broad cuff of mauve satin. Roch opened the door of the freezer compartment which took the top quarter of his refrigerator. He removed a plastic container, which had once held a gallon of chocolate-ripple ice cream, and put the opal on top of the other jewellery inside. The container was almost full. As he did so Frank fastened the string ties of the portfolio prior to taking it away. Roch shut the freezer door and turned to place his large hand flat on the portfolio lying on the table.

"Just one tiny moment, Precious Treasure. As I have just been shamelessly taken advantage of, I feel I must at least see the silver service. Shall we say tomorrow at the same time?" He slid the closed portfolio onto the top of the refrigerator. "Tomorrow evening you will depart with that under your arm."

Frank rose to leave. "Don't bother; I can find my way out."

Contrary to popular belief there is honour among thieves, but only up to a point.

*   *   *

After leaving Roch's apartment Frank drove straight home, his mind filled with the Picasso drawing. As he let himself into his duplex he heard his telephone begin to ring, and went to answer it.

"Hello?"

"Mr. Clarke, it's Graham Macafee from Willowdale Manor. I've been trying to reach you." His voice came over the line like corn syrup, smooth and sticky. "I'm sorry to say we lost one of our residents early this morning."

Frank quashed the impulse to ask, "Where? Did you look

under the bed? Perhaps in the bottom bureau drawer?" Instead he replied, "Is that right? Does that mean you have a room vacant?"

"Indeed it does. And your mother's name is at the head of the waiting list."

"When will the room be ready for occupation?"

"If we get the cleaning staff to work first thing in the morning, the room should be ready, shall we say, after one P.M.?"

"Very good. I'll get Mother organized to move tomorrow afternoon."

"Please call as you're on your way, Mr. Clarke. We like to greet our new residents and make them feel right at home. We're all part of one big family here at Willowdale."

"I'm sure you are," replied Frank. "Tomorrow afternoon, then. Thank you for calling, Mr. Macafee. Goodbye."

As Frank hung up the telephone his reaction was to execute a pirouette of sheer delight, but he reconsidered. A wrenched back or pulled ligaments would be most inopportune. Tomorrow was to be departure day, D-Day. Flavia McCutcheon Clarke would exit from the big house for the very last time. The big house, with its antediluvian roof and pre-Cambrian plumbing, would fall to the wrecker's ball. Once and for all he would cease to deal with nurses, cooks, cleaning women, that bunch of sluts who live off the infirmities of the well-to-do.

Frank changed out of his suit into his Yves St. Laurent dressing gown and Gucci slippers. The body over which he slipped the robe showed its seventy years through small but well-defined love handles and a modest pot. The skin still had tone and texture, his legs had not turned into cottage cheese, and his small, flat pectorals had proved surprisingly resistant to the pull of gravity. As a boy Frank had been the ninety-seven-pound weakling at whom the late Charles Atlas aimed his ads. Just a few weeks of "dynamic tension," isometric exercises by any other name, and you too could punch the bully on the beach who kicked sand into your eyes. Frank ignored the dynamic tension and hit the bully with a rake. His body had always been free from hair and that on his head had turned to silver naturally. Frank found himself vastly amused at the spectacle of men, no longer young, hair metallic auburn with Grecian formula, skin tanned with bronzer, trendily unbuttoning shirts to reveal gold medallions emblazoned with zodiac signs nestling in chest hair the colour of polar bear fur.

He poured himself a glass of port and stood studying a drawing propped up on the mantelpiece, his most recent acquisition; a British drawing for which he had negotiated successfully. A young woman stood leaning her arm on the back of a chair. She wore a shawl, two irregular black triangles over the billowing sleeves of her nineteenth-century gown. Hairpin strokes of the pen, loose, free, formed a background for the head, the wash defining the lower cheek and neck a triangular shape echoing the two sections of her shawl. Pen and brush had been freshly used but with the underlying control which signals the true professional. Not a truly major drawing, perhaps, but one any collector would be proud to own.

Tomorrow its place would be taken by the Picasso. Frank closed his eyes and remembered the two figures, one standing, one seated. A feeling of perfect contentment filled him to overflowing. His beautiful drawings, so much more immediate and intimate than paintings, were well worth a little discreet larceny. In fact his intrinsic dishonesty almost became virtue when one considered the alternative. A retirement residence for the recycled rich.

Frank stood sipping his port. The future stretched ahead, clear, straight, unbending as an autoroute. And yet, and yet; there remained the problem of Estelle. Frank wondered if perhaps he ought to have accepted Vivien's supper invitation where he would have been able to monitor the conversation. Who could tell what sort of mischief those two harridans might get into, left to their own devices, their tongues loosened by vermouth and gin. Damn Estelle anyway! Of all times to materialize out of a past which she seemed more than ready to relive vicariously through any captive audience.

For a moment Frank regretted his inability to be overtly rude, especially to a member of the family. To have told Estelle the simple truth, that she was totally unwelcome and nothing would please him more than her immediate departure, lay beyond his scope. Having been a social creature all his life Frank found himself so steeped in the niceties of etiquette he found it far easier to use courtesy as a weapon than to be truthfully blunt. Yet once his mother had moved into Willow-dale and the nurses along with the cook had been dismissed, Frank wondered how long Estelle would choose to stay on in a large, empty house, high on the hill overlooking the city, far from shops, with only her mirrored reflection for company.

Frank shrugged his shoulders. Tomorrow's task was to move his mother. The following day he would get to work on dis-lodging Estelle. Once more he looked at the drawing. More companionable than people, food, drink, television, or even sex, the drawing filled the room with its small but vivid pres-ence. Furthermore all his daydreams of power, manipulation, and self-transcendence found their outlet in his plans for The Collection, plans he intended to pursue with all his will. And the energy of Frank's will was enormous. He remained after all his mother's son.

# Chapter 8

As Vivien Howard attempted to spread the serape over the most badly clawed spots of her sectional couch she was seized by a moderately bad case of hostess anxiety. The serape looked decidedly makeshift, even though the Mexican vendor in the Oaxaca market had assured her it was *"muy typico."* From behind the shut bedroom door the Siamese cats, Yin and Yang, howled their incarceration.

It was not the notion that Vivien had never met her dinner guest which alarmed her, nor even that the stranger was a relative, although somewhat distant. Rather it was the knowledge that the unknown person with whom she was about to break her own, freshly baked, whole grain bread, had been an operatic soprano. Vivien had always enjoyed opera but on the primary level of musical theatre. In Vivien's mind sopranos fell into one of two categories: English women with sensible Oxfords and crocheted tams who sang *Messiah* in Leeds, or tempestuous Mediterranean divas who clobbered reporters, feuded with other sopranos, and stormed out of performances. Estelle Church sounded innocuous enough, but Stella della Chiesa struck terror to her heart. Estelle, the blackest of family sheep, who in defiance of her parents had eloped with her voice teacher Neville Church, and had gone onto the stage. Furthermore her career had blazed across Europe, albeit some years ago. And now this faded legend had accepted to partake of Vivien's modest, although highly nutritious and balanced meal.

The bell rang. Vivien took a deep breath and opened the door.

In a froth of dove-grey chiffon, arms outstretched, scarlet mouth and cerulean lids aquiver, Estelle stood poised as if for flight. "Vivien, Vivien Clarke – at long last. Dear Cousin Vivien!" Seizing her putative hostess by the hands, Estelle aimed a kiss at each cheek, kisses that did not actually touch the recipient but manifested themselves as moist little explosions under each ear. It was a technique perfected over the years on devoted admirers visiting her dressing room after performances.

"How you are, Cousin Estelle?" replied Vivien, temporarily overwhelmed by the idea that one could be at once tempestuous and Canadian. "Please come in and sit down."

"Charming, perfectly charming. Did you do it yourself? You must have. It's so – so personal." Estelle spoke to buy time as, with unerring eye, she surveyed the room. Deciding against the couch covered with that hideous whatnot; the rocker, an old lady's chair; the butterfly chair, from which she would never be able to extricate herself; Estelle swept over to the Morris chair, ducking the spider plant, and seated herself as though expecting a downbeat.

"Will you have something to drink, Cousin Estelle? Kir? Campari and orange juice? Vermouth and mineral water?"

From her reticule Estelle drew a mayonnaise jar holding a clear, colourless fluid. "I'll just have a drop of this, if you don't mind, dear. No ice, please."

By now Vivien had come to realize that her guest didn't bite; she curled herself somewhat stiffly onto the couch with a glass holding two colours of vermouth. "How long do you plan to stay in Canada, Cousin Estelle?"

"I don't really know. Your mother – I understand the two of you do not speak – is moving into a nursing home any day now and the house is to be sold." Estelle laughed, a stage laugh totally without mirth. "I can't say she's overjoyed to see me. I saw her for about five minutes yesterday when I arrived, and this afternoon I was summoned for an interview. She pelted me with all sorts of personal and disagreeable questions. Why did I dye my hair? Wasn't I too old to dress the way I did? Had I put anything aside for my old age? Most extraordinary. Back in England I should have thought her rude, but perhaps things are different in Canada. I can't remember; I was only fifteen when I left."

"No, Cousin Estelle, Mother is rude, and a bully and – but why get into that now?" replied Vivien, wisely skirting the yawning cesspool of family life. "What have you been doing? Since you left the stage, I mean?"

"I taught for a number of years. What retired singer does not?"

"Is your husband still alive?"

"No, he died a long time ago – penniless, as is the case with most musicians. We had separated by then, but I paid his bills at the end. Domesticity does not go comfortably with a career as a performer. If you are a performing artist, a great – and I was great – your art becomes your life. Few people realize the discipline, the dedication, and the sacrifice involved. It is almost like a religious vocation. Mind you, I had plenty of admirers, male admirers. They fell in love with my voice and my beauty, and then they tried to own me. I never met a man who was prepared to accept that he was secondary to my career. So I ended up with a casket of jewels, living alone."

Vivien could think of nothing to say.

"But please don't think I am feeling sorry for myself," continued the older woman. "I had a glorious career. I would have liked to have had children – what woman does not? But motherhood is a common experience. To bring the entire audience of La Scala to its feet with an E-flat at the end of the Mad Scene from *Lucia*, to take countless curtain calls with flowers raining down onto the stage; that is not a common experience."

"I don't suppose it is. Tell me, Cousin Estelle – "

"Please call me 'Estelle.' 'Cousin Estelle' sounds so terribly formal."

"Certainly – Estelle." The two women laughed, their laughter warming the room.

"I wish I knew more about opera," said Vivien. "Did you ever sing Puccini? I ask only because I guess he is my favourite operatic composer."

"I was not a Puccini soprano, which is to say I sang bel canto, not verismo roles. Bellini, Donizetti, Rossini, Verdi, Mozart, were my composers. I did sing one Puccini role, though, that of Lauretta in *Gianni Schicchi*. I was young when I sang the part; it was one of my first appearances on stage. It's quite delightful, really. Puccini's one comedy, in one act. The libretto is taken from an episode in Dante's *Inferno*. Buoso Donati has just died, and his scheming relatives are dashed to find he has left his fortune to a religious order. The young man Rinuccio, a tenor naturally, suggests they send for Gianni Schicchi who arrives along with his daughter Lauretta, a soprano. She loves Rinuccio, but cannot marry him as his family looks down on Gianni Schicchi as '*gente nova.*' Learning that nobody yet knows of Buoso Donati's death, Gianni Schicchi comes up with a plan. He will impersonate the dead man, dictate a new will which will benefit the family, after which Donati's death can be made public. He pulls on a nightshirt, climbs into the canopied bed, and the notary arrives. After leaving each relative a bequest, Gianni Schicchi leaves the bulk of Donati's estate to himself. The family is helpless because they fear the consequences of tampering with a will: the amputation of a hand and banishment from Florence. Naturally they are furious, but what can they do? Gianni Schicchi chases them out of what is now his own house, then steps forward to speak directly to the audience and explain that what he did he did for the sake of the young lovers. A happy ending: the young people get the money. Would you mind if I had another drop of gin, dear?"

"I wonder if it wouldn't be a happier ending if the old people got the money," said Vivien rising to her feet to refill Estelle's empty glass.

She padded soundlessly on rope soles into her small kitchen where she poured neat gin into her cousin's wine glass. Then she checked the oven, turned down a burner, and returned to the living room.

Estelle did not hear her cousin return. She sat collapsed in her chair, her hand with the giant ruby covering her eyes.

"Are you all right, Estelle?" said Vivien, setting the wine glass down on a table beside Estelle.

"Yes, quite all right, thank you, dear."

"You're quite sure?" Vivien hovered but did not crowd, her presence quietly reassuring.

"To tell you the truth, Vivien, I am a tiny bit drunk. Don't worry. I shan't fall down or be ill. It's just that I'm so very tired. The trip and everything. I must confess I had a small drink while I was waiting for the taxi."

"Would you like some food?"

"Not just yet." Suddenly, unaccountably, Estelle began to weep. Tears streamed down her white, creased cheeks as she fumbled in her bag for a handkerchief. With an effort of will she stemmed the flow, dabbed at her eyes, and took a swallow of gin.

"How tiresome of me. We've only just met and here I am making a spectacle of myself."

"Estelle, there is something wrong, isn't there?"

For just a moment the older woman hesitated, visibly struggling against the temptation to confess; but the combination of tears, gin, and a sympathetic ear proved too seductive.

"Yes, I suppose there is. In a word, Vivien, I'm broke. Absolutely penniless. All I have left in the world are my jewels, a few clothes, a trunkful of costumes, and some scrapbooks. Oh, I suppose my jewels are worth something. But were I to try to sell them what I would get is only a fraction of their worth. And they have a value far beyond pounds or dollars. They are mementoes of men I once knew, and loved. All that remains. The landlord raised the rent on my bedsitter in Earl's Court, and I decided to take a gamble. You see this ring?" The hand at the throat displayed the gem. "There was a matching bracelet. I sold it to pay for my plane ticket, one way. What had I hoped? I suppose I had hoped that Flavia would take me in. We are both old ladies now, tattered remnants of a family that has always been small. I knew there was money. I thought she might overlook past differences, neglects. Flavia, along with you and Francis, are my last surviving relatives. But I gambled and lost. Even were she not moving out of that large empty house she obviously doesn't want me around. I am an importunate nuisance, nothing more. Francis has been polite, but distant. Poor Vivien, I must be boring you to tears."

"No, Estelle, you are not. Please go on."

"I don't have to point out to you that London is not a city for the poor. Some months ago an acquaintance gave me a ticket to the Royal Opera in Covent Garden. I wore this dress under an old trenchcoat and rode the Underground looking like a charwoman. As I made my way to my seat someone recognized me and whispered, 'Stella della Chiesa; it's Stella della Chiesa.' Word spread through the theatre like a gale. The entire audience rose to its feet and applauded me. It was lovely, quite thrilling really. The opera was *La Sonnambula*, one of my roles. The soprano slurred her embellishments and acted as though she were directing traffic under water! An admirer bought me champagne at intermission. It ended all too soon. I rode the tube back to Earl's Court and went to bed in a cold room. Nobody ever offered me a lift home. They had granted me that one self-congratulatory moment of adulation, and that was that. I almost wished I hadn't gone."

Estelle paused for a sip of gin and to study the effect of her story on the audience. Even though Vivien stood lowest in the pecking order of the Clarke family, Estelle realized a weak ally is better than none. So far Flavia had shown herself openly hostile; Frank stood aloof, almost aggressively neutral. Without Vivien, Estelle knew she could drown.

But Vivien listened avidly. Shaking her head slowly from side to side, she radiated sympathy. "It must be hard to have been famous. I guess there is something to be said for obscurity, after all."

Satisfied with the reaction, Estelle continued. "I want you to know I did my homework. I learned about your Medicare program. I knew that if Flavia took me in she would not be obliged to pay my medical bills. When I think of all the wonderfully romantic deaths I died onstage; a far cry from the tedious reality of growing old and breaking down. If only I could say with a flourish, 'My heart is weak,' or, 'I am ravaged with cancer,' something with a bit of flair. I have emphysema, but that is neither glamorous nor fatal. I am quite simply wearing out. And perhaps for the first time in my life I don't know what I am going to do."

"Don't give it another thought, Estelle. You can move in here with me."

"Oh, Vivien, my dear Vivien. I shall start to weep again. I don't expect you to take me in."

"I'm quite serious, Estelle. I have two beds in my room, and plenty of storage area in the basement."

"How truly kind you are. But it wouldn't work out. To begin with you have cats."

As Yin and Yang had long ago given up complaining and gone to sleep Vivien showed surprise. "Did you open the bedroom door?"

"No, but my sinuses are beginning to close. I'm terribly allergic to cat hair."

"I'll board them with a friend."

"Vivien, my dear, kind, generous Vivien; it wouldn't work, even without the cats. Two older women, accustomed to living alone? Set in their ways? At least one with an ego the size of the Royal Albert Hall? It wouldn't do. But something will turn up; it always has. Believe me; you will be my ace in the hole. I think that is the term. I may be down, but I'm not out."

Estelle smiled, then drew the ruby ring from her finger. " *'Riponi quest' anello,'* " she said, handing the ring to Vivien. "Put by this ring – as Desdemona says to Emelia. I refer of course to the opera."

"I can't take your ring, Estelle. It's way too valuable."

"A gift has no value unless the giver values it herself. The ring, and the bracelet that I sold, were given to me by an Italian count. But in Italy every third man claims to have a title. Here, try it on. If I did not wish you to have the ring I would not have offered it."

Estelle placed the ring in Vivien's palm. She had been genuinely touched by her cousin's offer of shelter, but it cannot be denied that a large jewel helps to cement an alliance.

Vivien slid the ring onto the fourth finger of her left hand, where it concealed the plain gold wedding band she still wore.

"It's beautiful, Estelle. It's also my birthstone."

"All the more reason for you to have it. And now I think I am very interested in having some dinner."

# Chapter 9

The following morning Frank scalded the Sèvres teapot, spooned in the tea, and set it to steep for a full five minutes. The paper had been delivered promptly, and as was his custom he turned immediately to Births and Deaths. As his eye picked off names, like a sniper shooting bottles off a wall, it became evident that not a single funeral notice concerned anyone he had ever known. He reread the page, more slowly this time, paring Christian names down to their more common nicknames: Richard into Dick, Margaret into Peggy. But not even the familiar and friendly form could evoke a former acquaintance. The Grim Reaper had been goldbricking.

As an afterthought, Frank glanced at the lead obituary accompanied by a photograph, so obvious he had not paid attention. The photograph seemed vaguely familiar. As he read the name Frank felt a jolt of recognition: Martin T. Maxwell. All the obituary would admit was that Martin Maxwell had died suddenly, at his home. The following paragraph listed his numerous philanthropies; outside his legal practice he had been a pillar of the community.

The sudden wave of feeling which swept over Frank sprang less from the awareness that someone he had known for twenty-five years was dead than from a terrible anxiety about how the news would affect his mother. For twenty-five years Martin

Maxwell had been her notary, presiding over the frequent and dramatic changes in her will and charging her plenty for the service. She had stoutly refused to deal with any other notary in the firm: Martin Maxwell or no one. And now that Frank was pressing his mother to alter her will in his favour he feared she might possibly refuse to deal with a notary other than Martin Maxwell himself.

Frank himself had been on the point of buying Martin Maxwell another enormous lunch with an eye to enlisting his aid in persuading Mrs. Clarke that the bequest to Maple Grove was excessive. Frank well knew he was bucking popular sentiment. With thousands of families wondering daily where to unload their old people, a senior citizens' residence carried the same popular appeal that an orphanage did during the thirties. Now babies were in short supply and geriatrics a glut on the market. But shorn of the solemn, avuncular presence of Martin Maxwell, Frank realized that in terms of the will he had returned to square one.

Still, the situation had to be faced; and Frank decided he had better be the one to break the news to his mother. Thoughtfully he clipped the obituary and put it into the biscuit box. He showered, letting the hot water cascade over his body, while he pondered the way to best present the news. Perhaps he had better play up the prospective move to Willowdale; and while his mother was fussing and fuming about what to take, which robe to wear for the ride out – was it to be by ambulance or limousine? – he would slide a "by the way" into the conversation and casually mention the notary's death.

After drying himself Frank shaved, then dressed, this morning in dark grey. He had pared the art of dressing down to its barest essentials. His suits came in only two colours, dark grey and navy blue. All his shirts were blue, his shoes black, his silk ties of conservative stripes.

As he was about to leave the apartment, he was detained by the telephone. The voice on the line belonged to his sister.

Without the usual inquiries after his health and whether he had slept well, she launched without ceremony into the reason for her call.

"Frank, we have got to do something about Cousin Estelle."

"Do we, now? And what? Before you answer let me point out that Cousin Estelle is quite capable of looking out for herself. Anyone who has had an operatic career lasting over thirty years is tough, tougher than either of us, I venture to say."

"Now, Frank, don't be like that. Estelle is an old lady. Did you know she is absolutely flat broke? She had to sell jewellery to buy her plane ticket."

"I see. Well, now." Vivien's revelation explained Estelle's presence in Canada, and Frank did not welcome the news. "Now what precisely would you suggest?"

"I told her she could come and live with me. But she is allergic to cats, and my condo is small. I thought perhaps she could stay on at the big house."

"Did you, now? You know, of course, that Mother is moving out to Willowdale, possibly even today; and the house is going to be sold."

"When did all this come up? I thought Father had arranged his affairs so Mother would never have to move out of her home."

"She's bored with her own company. The move was her idea, believe me. And you know what she's like once an idea takes hold. Besides, I'm tired of the responsibility. It's an old house, and something is always going wrong."

"I understand. But we could still set Estelle up in a small flat, and furnish it with things from the house. And I can have Randolph's paintings back at last. I'd be glad to help you, Frank, in any way."

"Slow down a bit, Viv. Supposing we do set Estelle up in a small apartment, as you suggest, who is going to pay the rent? Who is going to pay for her food, and those drag-queen outfits she wears? Who is going to look after her when she falls and breaks a hip on the ice because she doesn't know the first thing about our lovely Canadian winters? Did you know she has emphysema? That means when you or I catch a cold she gets pneumonia. Who is going to nurse her?"

"I'd be glad to look after her, if I could have a bit of financial help. Surely Mother's estate is adequate to support one old lady whose wants are few."

"I have always noticed how easy it is to be generous with someone else's money." Preoccupied as he was with getting his mother moved, and dealing with the death of Martin Maxwell, Frank could not cope with this now and bought time by offering his sister a minor conciliation. "Let me think about it, Vivien. The house will not be sold at once, and even when it does sell it will have to be cleared out. All this takes time. Estelle can stay on until the last minute. By that time we will have worked out some sort of solution. Now I must dash."

He rang off, furious. Talk about goddamned nerve! Sending a telegram: "WOULD ADORE BEING MET." Here I am. Take me in. Look after me in my old age. And furthermore listen while I tell of how I sang Lakmé for the crowned heads of Europe, Semiramide for a sheik who covered me in diamonds, Marguerite in Madrid where my admirer was Spain's leading matador. Moreover, Estelle had made common cause with Vivien. Perhaps it was this alliance that gave Frank the most irritation as he slammed out of his apartment. His one consolation lay in the fact that he still controlled the purse strings.

He drove to his mother's and, using his key, he let himself in the front door as quietly as possible. Down the long corridor that led from the spacious front hall into the kitchen Frank could see Nurse Harrison seated at the kitchen table, asleep, one fat cheek resting on her fist. He went quickly up the stairs.

Flavia Clarke's bedroom door stood ajar. Frank looked stealthily inside. His mother lay asleep. He wondered for a moment whether he should wake her. Then he looked again. Something about the angle of her body struck him as odd; she appeared to have slid off the pillows and her eyes were open. He stepped through the door and crossed to the side of the bed. As he looked down at his mother he realized with swift, absolute certainty that she was dead. The glazed eyes, the partially open mouth, the pallid skin, all telegraphed death, not sleep.

What followed within Frank was not a rush of filial feeling, a gush of sorrow at the death of the sole surviving parent. Grief takes time to realize, to unfold, to expand; it remains an emotion demanding leisure, and Frank felt himself chased by the clock. What caused his chest to tighten and his heart to pound was the realization that her death could not have come at a more inconvenient time. The death of the constituent renders a power of attorney instantly invalid. With his mother dead, Frank had in his possession a totally useless document; its official pages and scarlet seal were reduced to the status of souvenir.

Dead? With her assets only beginning to be liquidated? With all those securities still unsold and one half of the Calgary property now legally belonging to Vivien? With Maple Grove Manor about to inherit a mini-fortune, not to mention the obscene amount in death duties now due the government? By permitting her heart to stop beating Flavia Clarke had consigned her son Francis to oblivion. He looked down the avenue of his life and saw not The Frank Clarke Gallery but nothing: a void. He had counted on his mother living at least two more years. Wasn't it just like her to die, at the precise moment everything was falling so neatly into place. Her ultimate demonstration of selfishness.

Wait! So far no one but he knew that Flavia Clarke was deceased, and with or without pain no longer mattered. As long as she was not officially dead she was still alive. Furthermore, as long as she remained undead the power of attorney continued to be valid. His only concern at the moment was that somehow he had to perpetrate the illusion that his mother still lived. Frank stood at his mother's bedside, temporarily immobilized by shock at her death and feeling anger bordering on rage at how this death had wrecked his carefully laid plans.

Rapidly quelling these inconvenient emotions he felt a ruthless determination asserting itself not to permit this setback to interfere with his master scheme. He must somehow contrive to conceal her death. On the possible consequences, moral and legal, of attempting to suppress this irreversible fact, he did not allow his mind to dwell. His whole future lay at stake; he must act now, without delay.

Closing the bedroom door he went unsteadily downstairs and into the kitchen. Nurse Harrison still dozed, but her head was beginning to slide. Gravity slowly but inexorably pulled at the pudgy fist until it slid away and her head jerked forward, snapping her awake. Catching sight of Frank in the door she gave a little gasp of dismay.

"Oh! Excuse me, sir. I must have dozed off. I'll go right up and check in on Mrs. Clarke."

"I just looked in, Nurse Harrison, and she's fast asleep." Frank smiled his most charming smile. Hiding behind the smile, he forced his voice to sound normal. "You poor woman, you must be tired. Why don't you run along and I'll hold the fort until the morning nurse gets here."

"That's very kind of you, sir. But if the agency got wind I'd left before the end of my shift . . . ."

"Don't worry. I won't tell if you won't."

"But if your mother should wake before Gibson gets here . . . the moment she opens her eyes she wants to be taken to the toilet."

"I thought Gibson was on the night shift."

"She was, but she has a bit of a problem with the bottle, as you may know." Nurse Harrison's voice took on the unctuous tone of one who loves malicious gossip. "She asked for the day shift so she could be kept busy. Sitting up all night with nothing to do; well, it puts temptation in her path. And the agency didn't like her drinking on the job. I'm covering for the night nurse who's sick."

"How did the agency find out about Nurse Gibson? I never mentioned anything."

"Oh, sir, I really thought I had to say something. I felt it was my responsibility, towards the patient, I mean."

"I see. In any event she will be here shortly. You go home and get some rest. Two shifts in one day is a lot of work. You look tired. I know Mother is a demanding patient. Now you just run along."

Frank made a gesture similar to that of a headwaiter showing diners to a table. If only she would get off her backside and move it.

"Very well, but perhaps I had better pop up and look in on Mrs. Clarke, just to make sure."

"That really won't be necessary, Nurse Harrison. I assure you everything will be all right."

Still expostulating over how she really shouldn't, Nurse Harrison scrambled into her topcoat and collected her purse with a speed and dexterity she seldom showed around her patients.

As he heard the front door close behind her Frank expelled air from his lungs in a wheeze of relief. One nurse had been dealt with, but she had already been prepared to leave. The incoming nurse, all geared up to go on duty, would require more careful handling.

Frank sat at the kitchen table only too aware that the buzzer from his mother's room was never again to ring. He wished Nurse Gibson would arrive. The sooner she was here, the more quickly she could be dismissed. But there was more to it than that. After Nurse Gibson had been dispatched, what then? How was he to create the illusion that his mother still lived when her corpse lay in full view of anyone who opened her bedroom door? Obviously the body had to be taken from the master bedroom. But where? Concealing a body in the deep freeze had become a cliché, in life as well as literature. Besides, Mrs. Clarke had steadfastly refused to own a deep freeze, just as she had resisted owning a dishwasher, a blender, an electric kettle, or any other appliance that might have made life easier for staff.

For just a moment Frank toyed with the idea of carrying his mother's body down to the basement bathroom, laying it flat in the bathtub, and covering it with a layer of clear paraffin wax, just the way she used to seal her jams and jellies. But he shuddered at the thought. If there were only some legitimate way to get the corpse out of the house.

The sound of the front doorbell snapped him alert. Frank went to the door and let in Nurse Gibson, crisp and angular in her white uniform and looking as if she had arrived by broom, not bus. He went straight to the point. "Nurse Gibson, would you be kind enough to step into the kitchen. I'd like to have a word with you."

Obediently, the incoming nurse followed Frank into the kitchen where he motioned her into a chair. She cast longing eyes at the coffee pot, but decided to comply.

"Nurse Gibson: as you no doubt know, Mother has wanted for some time now to move into the Willowdale nursing home. Yesterday I had word from the director that a room has become available. Also, to my pleasant surprise, a cousin from England has arrived in town. She happens to be a nurse and she will help me move Mother to Willowdale. No offence meant, of course; but I know Mother would prefer to be with members of her own family when she makes the change."

For his own protection Frank stuck to the truth, or what would have been the truth were his mother still alive. By simply turning his mental clock back a few hours he found himself on surer ground than he would have been had he totally invented a scenario.

Nurse Gibson's bony nose gave a suspicious sniff. "What about Mrs. Clarke's medication?"

"The instructions are all there in the daily journal you have been good enough to keep. Naturally the journal will go with us to Willowdale."

"You're going to need help," stated Nurse Gibson. The prospect of moving Mrs. Clarke out to Willowdale promised diversion.

"Between my cousin, myself, and the ambulance attendants, we'll manage nicely. I should have telephoned the agency to warn you not to come, but things happened rather suddenly and it slipped my mind. I shall see of course that you are paid for today's shift." Frank took folded bills from his pocket, neatly clamped by a silver money clip. Peeling off two twenties and a ten, he handed them to the nurse. "Why don't you take the day off and go shopping. Thank you for being so good to Mother."

Nurse Gibson made a few clucking noises of feigned reluctance, but soon enough the money was safely shut into her handbag. "And now I'll just go and say goodbye to the patient."

Frank's voice remained steady, even cutting; but his left hand gripped the back of his chair. "I would prefer you not to go upstairs. Mother is resting up for the ride in the ambulance and I would rather she were not disturbed." His smile softened the steel in his voice. "Now you just run along and have a day off. And don't forget to put in for a full day's shift." Frank rose and held out his hand. "Goodbye, Nurse Gibson. It's been a pleasure having you on the case."

Baffled but powerless the woman stood. A day's shopping could not begin to compare with the excitement of a visit to Willowdale, settling the patient into her quarters followed by lunch in the cafeteria, lingering over cups of coffee with cronies from former cases. But she made her way down the hall, unable to resist her employer's determination. At the foot of the staircase she paused. "I really hate to leave a case without saying goodbye to the patient."

"I'll explain to Mother why you did not go up. I know she'll understand."

He opened the front door. Cool October air flowed in and around Nurse Gibson, cutting her once and forever from the Clarke house. The door shut firmly behind her. Frank turned the deadlock and attached the safety chain.

So far the operation had been a piece of cake. But the sense of release quickly sputtered and died as Frank let his eyes follow the staircase up to the landing and his imagination continue up to the second floor. What was he going to do about Estelle? From minor inconvenience and possible financial liability she had suddenly taken on monstrous proportions. Her very presence had become a major obstacle. His first thought was to get her out of the house while he dealt in some way with his mother's body. But how? Suggest Vivien take her sightseeing? He could scarcely imagine Vivien and Estelle ambling arm in arm down trendy Crescent Street or trailing through the neo-gothic splendours of Notre Dame Cathedral. Getting rid of Estelle for a few hours did not solve the problem of how to deal with his mother's body.

The alternative was to take Estelle into his confidence, but he shrank from the idea of doing so. Her knowledge meant power, which could be used against him. Granted, the only other person Estelle knew in Canada was Vivien. Yet were Estelle to even hint at irregularity in Frank's financial dealings the implacably honest Vivien would be after him like a bloodhound. He would have to offer Estelle some kind of incentive, to buy her silence with a financial bribe she could not refuse and significant enough to keep her from confiding in her newfound ally, Vivien. But this would mean that he would be committed for life to paying her money. A wave of anger enveloped Frank and he began to shake. He grasped the newel post for support.

At that precise moment an idea blazed its way into Frank's mind with the intensity of a laser beam. His cousin Estelle Church would assume the identity of his mother Flavia Clarke. As such she would move into the Willowdale nursing home, while the body of the late Flavia Clarke, coffin shut, would be dispatched to the crematorium as that of Estelle Church. Estelle had been an actress; moreover she was roughly the same age as his mother. The animosity between Vivien and her mother would keep Vivien from going to Willowdale to visit. It was perfect. Estelle's impersonation meant his power of attorney continued to be valid. A monthly stipend to Estelle for the duration of her life was small payment for rescuing The Collection.

An outrageous idea, but it just might work. Frank stood leaning against the newel post breathing deeply and wondering how next to proceed when the doorbell gave its sharp jangle for the second time that morning.

Stealing into the front room, which afforded an oblique view of the front door, he could make out the silhouette of his Aunt Phyllis Coughlin, who was on the point of pushing the bell a second time. There was no question of his not answering; the veneer of normality must be preserved at all cost.

He opened the door. "Why, Aunt Phyllis. What a pleasant surprise!" Frank stood in a blocking stance, dead centre in the doorway.

"Good morning, Francis. I've come to see Flavia," announced Phyllis Coughlin, the younger sister of Frank's late father.

"Mother is resting at the moment," said Frank evenly. "She had rather an anxious night, so the nurse told me. And she dozed off just a few moments ago. I don't think she should be disturbed."

"I'll wait."

"I wouldn't advise that," replied Frank in his most pleasant tone. "We really want Mother well rested because we have to take her to the – the dentist, early this afternoon. Her lower bridge is giving her a lot of pain. And these days she finds leaving the house very exhausting."

His story about the dentist had been a flash of inspiration. Were Frank to have suggested his mother was moving out to Willowdale he would have been smothered in offers of help, with Aunt Phyllis insisting on ordering flowers for Flavia's room, on riding with her in the ambulance, on carrying her dressing case, on being in every way a tower of strength in time of trouble. Women of Phyllis Coughlin's generation nourished themselves on the misfortunes of others, and the spectacle of her sister-in-law being trundled off to a nursing home was an entertainment Phyllis Coughlin would not have missed for anything.

Frank had not budged from his position in the doorway.

"Well! May I at least come in and sit down for a minute? I walked up the hill from the bus stop." The last was delivered in a tone suggesting that greater virtue lay in taking public transportation, especially when one could well afford a taxi. Frank had no choice but to step aside and usher his aunt into the front room where she settled, not sat, on a plum velvet love-seat beneath a series of engravings depicting the heroines of Shakespeare in Pre-Raphaelite disarray.

Phyllis Coughlin had been a late child at a time when late children were discussed in the same hushed tones as divorce. Late children were a product of middle-aged concupiscence, when the parents were certainly old enough to have known better. As a result of her late entry into the world, Phyllis Coughlin was younger than her sister-in-law. A bare eighty-five, she went out daily except when the temperature fell below freezing. She carried a cane, more as a badge of authority than to help her walk. Like the British officer's swagger-stick or the pharaoh's flail, the cane bespoke prestige, social position, and the obligation she be given a seat on the bus.

It goes without saying she was a widow, as few men in North America make it past seventy-five. She had been left "very comfortable" by her husband, the late Rupert Coughlin. Not that her assets could begin to compare with those of her sister-in-law, nor was she dependent on Flavia's erratic charity to buy luxuries. This independence from her sister-in-law had over the years kept the two women on speaking terms.

Frank had never bothered to pay much court to his Aunt Phyllis. Childless, she made no secret of the fact that outside of small, token bequests to her late brother's children, Francis and Vivien, she planned to leave her money elsewhere. One half her estate was slated for a scholarship in her dear late husband's name; the other half had been left to her church.

Setting down her handbag and laying aside her cane Phyllis

Coughlin faced her nephew who sat, not at his ease, in a wooden armchair of no particular distinction. "I really came by to tell Flavia about the Medford wedding, although why one would wish to have a wedding in October is quite beyond me. One hasn't even had time to settle in before the snow is beginning to fly. But there's no accounting for the younger generation." Phyllis Coughlin spoke in the firm tone of the slightly deaf who stubbornly refuse to admit the need of a hearing aid. Only old people wore hearing aids.

"It was quite a charming wedding, all autumn tints. The bride wore bronze, her second marriage, you understand; but the dress was barely below the knee and fairly shrieked 'off-the-rack.' Her uncle gave her away – he's a stockbroker – and the groom wore a plain dark suit. I understand he has quite a promising future, something to do with computers – but all that is way beyond me. When I was a girl we learned to add and subtract. Long division was drilled into our heads, and I can't begin to tell you how many times I have written out my multiplication tables. Nowadays no one can add two and two to come up with four unless one has buttons to press. The church was bursting with bronze and yellow mums; I find them a coarse flower. The bride carried bronze carnations; I expect they had been dyed."

"Aunt Phyllis, I . . . " began Frank trying to stem the flow, but his deaf aunt ignored the interruption.

"I was late for the service; I waited forever for the bus, but the McSweens were kind enough to drive me to the reception. Grace McSween has been on a diet, but we all know she'll never be small. She cried at the reception; too much champagne punch, I expect."

"Aunt Phyllis," said Frank sharply, rising to his feet, "I really must get to the bank. Can I gave you a lift down the hill?"

Cut off in mid-story Phyllis Coughlin reached crossly for her cane. "Well, if I can't see Flavia I may just as well go down the street and visit Sybil Bradshaw. She's having a terrible bout of asthma. I expect it's all those cats."

"Can I drive you to Mrs. Bradshaw's?" asked Frank, moving toward the door.

"I'll walk," replied his aunt in a voice suggesting that to accept a drive was to stumble morally. "Tell Flavia I'll come by tomorrow, or the next day. Depends on the weather."

Frank watched with relief as his aunt made her slow progression down the walk leaning heavily on her cane. He closed the front door and went to stand at the living room window. Once Phyllis Coughlin suspected she was no longer being watched she appeared to forget about the cane and walked, not quickly but quite steadily, down the street and out of sight.

Frank locked and double-locked the door a second time, then crossed to what had been his father's study to make four phone calls. The first was to the manager of Care, Cooks & Chars to sever the connection. Frank explained he intended moving his mother to a nursing home and would no longer need the three daily nurses or Nurse Harrison to cover any absences. Nurse Gibson had shown up for her shift this morning; he had dismissed her but she was to be paid in full. No, Mrs. Clarke did not want any special nurses in the nursing home. He would no longer require a cook, nor did he really need the cleaning woman. Please send the final invoice to this address.

The next call was to the office of Maxwell, Perkins, Smith, and Latulippe where Frank spoke to the secretary. He had just about run out of copies of his power of attorney; he was going to need some more.

"Three or four?" inquired the secretary in a hoarse voice.

"How about two dozen?" suggested Frank, soothing her surprise by explaining that he was thinking of consolidating some of his mother's holdings. Too much diversification can be a nuisance, don't you know, and he hated to keep bothering the secretary for one or two copies at a time. He knew how busy she was. That the office must be in a turmoil over Mr. Maxwell's death. Poor Martin. Such a loss to the community. That he'd pick up his copies tomorrow.

"Very good, sir," she wheezed as if through hay fever.

The third phone call was to a firm of stockbrokers with whom he had not yet established an account. He gave the order to sell his mother's shares of Yukon Gas and Oil, Athabasca Tar Development Corporation, and Consolidated Fisheries. The stock certificates along with certified copies of his power of attorney would be delivered the following day.

Finally he telephoned his florist to arrange for a basket of flowers from the Clarke family to be delivered to the funeral home where Martin Maxwell lay in his best blue suit. Frank also sent two dozen roses in his own name to the widow.

These matters attended to, the time had come to talk to Estelle. Frank walked slowly up to the room where Estelle slept and knocked on the door. No answer. He knocked again.

"Who is it?" rumbled a voice made husky by sleep.

"Five minutes to curtain, Miss della Chiesa," said Frank with a heavy-handed attempt at lightheartedness. "It's Francis. We have to talk. I'll make coffee."

"Very well. Give me a few minutes to repair the ravages."

"I'll be in the kitchen."

Frank made his way downstairs where he put coffee into an aluminum percolator, and set it on the huge electric range. The kitchen had not been altered since the house had been built. Twin sinks, one of which was a washtub, sat beneath the window, and the round cooling apparatus rested on top of the refrigerator like a hat box. Such few appliances as the kitchen possessed were about ready to be enshrined in the Museum of Man.

The swinging door leading from the dining room opened to admit Estelle wearing her chocolate brown at-home with the matching scarf draped over her head. Dark glasses concealed her eyes. Frank thought she would have looked quite at home with a red earthenware pot balanced on her shoulder.

"Sit down, Cousin Estelle, we have to talk."

Estelle sat at the large marble-topped table, worn to satin by years of wiping, on which sat the coffee pot, two cups, cream, sugar.

Frank wasted no time. "Cousin Estelle, Mother died last night."

Slowly Estelle raised her hands and rested them on the top of her head, pressing the elbows together so that forearms framed her face. A cry starting around middle c came from her throat, gaining steadily in volume as it moved chromatically up the scale.

"Stop that! Stop it at once! We haven't time. You're not the least bit sorry, so please don't pretend you are."

Accustomed to taking direction on stage, Estelle lowered her arms and reached for the cream jug. "Very well. What now?"

"I have a proposition to make," began Frank, his voice urgent. "A proposition which would benefit both of us immensely."

"I'm listening."

"Vivien telephoned early this morning. She is very concerned about you. It seems you are, let us say, short of funds. Not to put too fine a point on it: you are flat broke. You came to Canada on the chance that Mother would take you in, solicitude and sacred claims of family and the last of your generation, and all that claptrap. Am I correct?"

"So far, yes," she replied uneasily.

"As you know, I had intended moving Mother to a nursing home, this very afternoon, in fact. But now she is dead. The government will take thousands of dollars in inheritance taxes and one half of whatever is left goes to building a memorial wing onto a senior citizens' residence in her name."

"I presume she has a notarized will?" The question came not from Stella della Chiesa, retired diva, but from Estelle Church, businesswoman.

"Yes, she does: Maxwell, Perkins, Smith, and Latulippe,

103

although she never dealt with anyone except Martin Maxwell, and he himself has just died – which could work to our advantage."

"*Our* advantage?"

"Our advantage. You see, Cousin Estelle, I have a plan, one which will make me rich, rich enough to support you comfortably for the rest of your life – if you catch my drift."

"Not completely."

"I will not bore you with details. Let us just say that so long as Mother is alive – that is to say as long as she is not officially dead – I can use my power of attorney to subvert funds which would go either to the government or to Maple Grove Manor. But once mother is dead, officially dead, that is, the document ceases to be valid."

Estelle took a thoughtful sip of coffee, then aimed her dark glasses at Frank. "And your plan is to have me impersonate your mother, move into the nursing home under a false identity, and enable you to defraud her estate while she herself is buried as Estelle Church."

Frank found himself at once taken aback and impressed. Behind the theatrical façade, Estelle was whetstone sharp. "Something like that. It would only be for a short time. After I have put myself in a position where I no longer need the power of attorney I will move you out of Willowdale. I will tell the director you are unhappy; you miss your own home; Willowdale is too far out of town for your friends to come and visit. Between us we'll come up with a story." Frank's immediate concern was convincing Estelle to move into Willowdale. How to get her out remained a problem to be solved some time in the future. "Then as Stella della Chiesa you can return to Europe, Southern France or Italy, some place where the winter is not harsh and bitter as it is in Montreal."

"I have two questions. First: where does your sister Vivien fit into all of this?"

"She is not in Mother's will, if that's what you mean; but she gets one half of Father's estate. She once took the bus –

the bus, if you please – all the way to Calgary to examine our property. She maintains it should be sold back to the city to be made into a park named after Father, instead of being flogged to a developer at a huge profit."

"It's a charming idea: The Desmond Clarke Memorial Park. I'll bet your father would have approved. But Vivien gets nothing whatsoever from Flavia?"

"Nothing."

"Will she be made aware of the – impersonation?"

"No, she won't. As far as she is concerned you will be dead."

Estelle sat silent for a moment. "That means in one blow, as it were, I have lost two of my three surviving relatives. I am reluctant to give up Vivien. I met her for the first time only last night, but she is one of the few women I have ever met who could become a friend. If she understood what was going on she could come to visit me."

"Absolutely not! Entirely out of the question. If Vivien ever suspected the truth she would blow the whistle on us at once. She is rigidly honest, an admirable trait, I suppose, but a tiresome one."

"I see, and I suppose you are right. But it is unfortunate nonetheless." If Estelle allowed her mind to dwell with regret on the ruby ring with which she had so generously parted it was only for a moment. "Now I have another question. What happens if I do not agree to the impersonation?"

Frank's blue eyes narrowed. "I will buy you a one-way ticket back to London."

"First class?"

"Economy."

"Supposing I were to tell Vivien what you have just told me?"

"I will deny it categorically and denounce you as an avaricious woman trying to insinuate your way into a share of the family fortune. After decades of neglect, I might add."

"Well, now. I have scant experience of the law, but I am

sure that what you are proposing is highly immoral, not to say illegal."

"It is."

"Just think of the field day the newspapers would have with the story, if we were found out. 'Diva Dies Twice.' 'Stella della Chiesa Caught in Scam.' An inglorious end to a glorious career."

"A calculated risk. And perhaps no more inglorious than being down and out in London, unemployed, on the dole. No longer a star but a statistic. Wouldn't you rather have an apartment in Rome, scene of past triumphs? Perhaps with Violetta's Villa, Maison Manon, Casa Constanza, or some such name over the door as memento of the good old days?" Frank leaned forward, skewering his cousin with his intense blue-eyed stare. "Listen, Cousin Estelle, you are an actress. Nobody at Willowdale knows you. Nobody at the notary's office knows you, only about you, now that Martin Maxwell is dead. Nearly all of Mother's friends, if such they may be called, are dead. Willowdale itself is so far outside the city limits it cannot be reached except by car. We will post a No Visitors sign on your door, and tell the switchboard to refuse calls. You are upset over the move and want time to settle in. You might even, on a whim as it were, resume your maiden name of McCutcheon. New home, new name. And it will make you harder to trace."

"Vivien has asked me to go and live with her."

"With her cats and her meditation and her causes and her home-baked bread which gets stuck under the bridgework? Vivien is seventy-two going on seventeen. I myself would prefer a cold-water flat in Ealing."

"And you wouldn't be willing to help us out – financially?"

"No, why should I? I have too much at stake to be charitable."

"And what assurance do I have that you would continue to support me after I had completed my impersonation?"

"The best assurance of all. You know the truth; where the

106

body is buried, to coin a phrase. You will be in a position to reveal the true story any time you like."

"I suppose you are right." Estelle took a thoughtful sip of coffee. "What about medical records? Your mother must have a file kept by her doctor with her complete medical history."

"Yes, she does. Fortunately it happens to be in my possession."

"I see. But it does seem odd. Do doctors in Canada simply hand over their files on request?"

"No. However, her doctor was on the point of retiring and moving to Victoria. There remained some question about who was to take over his practice. I persuaded the nurse to let me borrow Mother's file so I could have a photocopy made for the doctor who assumed her case. When I went to return the original the office was closed, and I never got around to going back, fortunately for us. For the record, the file will have been misplaced along with the daily diary the nurses kept on Mother. You will arrive at Willowdale with a clean slate, innocent of medical history."

"Ah, to be innocent – of anything. Could I have a little time to think it over?"

"There isn't any time. It's not as if we were deciding to sell a house."

"I suppose you are right." Estelle rose and crossed to the sink, where she stood looking out the window. If her attitude seemed theatrical, for once it was not self-consciously so. The full and frightening implications of Frank's proposal jolted her into spontaneity. She half turned towards Frank. "I can't do it; I just can't!"

"In that case you had better go and pack. As soon as Mother's body is taken from the house I will drive you to the airport, or anywhere else you may decide to go. Now I will have to call the police." He moved slowly towards the swinging door.

"Stop! Wait a moment." Frank turned towards his cousin, her body an arc of submission as she supported herself against the sink. "I'll do it."

107

"Good." Frank managed to conceal his surge of relief. "I think you have made the wiser choice."

Estelle stood straight, the demands of the scene taking over. "Before rigor mortis sets in we had better get dear Flavia down the passageway and into my bed. It will take both of us, but I saw a wheelchair in her room." Estelle moved majestically across the kitchen.

Frank followed, trying not to tread on her train for which the swinging door made an unsuccessful grab.

They climbed the staircase and paused outside the shut bedroom door. Old habits die hard, and Frank nearly knocked before turning the knob. He was almost surprised by the fact that his mother had not moved. She lay exactly as he had left her. He and Estelle crossed the large room, faintly acrid with the smell of age, to where the wheelchair sat beside the fireplace, holding two imitation logs which burned jets of gas. On more than one occasion Frank had helped his mother in and out of her wheelchair, but he dreaded touching her dead body. However, this was no time to be squeamish. While Estelle wheeled the chair over to the bed, Frank folded back the covers, then half dragged, half lifted his mother's body into a sitting position before swinging her into the chair, held steady by Estelle.

Holding onto the loose braid of white hair Estelle kept the body from slumping forward. "You had better fasten her into the chair lest she tip out. Use the belt from her robe."

The robe in question hung from a hook on the bathroom door. Frank tugged the belt free of the loops. Passing it under his mother's limp arms he fastened the ends behind the chair in a reef knot.

It took only seconds to wheel the limp figure of Flavia Clarke out of her bedroom and down the corridor to the room where her husband had slept alone. Frank found himself sweating from tension more than exertion. This same pervading tension caused Estelle's breath to come in gasps. In spite of the bizarre situation Frank could not help admiring the determination with

108

which she battled the emphysema, forcing her breathing to return to its natural rhythm.

"Let's get her into bed," wheezed Estelle, her sense of *mise-en-scène* taking over. "I presume I will have died in my sleep, so we had better pull the covers up.

The transfer of Flavia Clarke's body into Estelle's bed having been accomplished, Frank went to take the wheelchair back to his mother's room.

"Bring me one of your mother's housecoats," said Estelle, as if talking to a stage hand.

Frank parked the wheelchair in its customary place beside the fireplace. Reaching for the bathrobe on the back of the bathroom door he carried it down the hall.

Estelle was just on the point of closing a metal box which locked with a key. "Just a few trinkets and my passport," she explained. "For the rest I shall simply walk away. I presume there are provisions for safekeeping at the home?"

"Each room has its own safety deposit box." Frank appeared to study his cousin. "It seems to me that you are perhaps a shade, shall we say, flamboyant for a Westmount widow in declining health."

"Don't worry, I've already thought of that." With a slow, deliberate gesture Estelle pushed the scarf back from her lustrous black hair. Then she gave a sharp tug and the raven hair came off in her hand, revealing cropped, white stubble which stuck up in random points. "I feel like Amelia unveiling herself before Renato in *Un Ballo in Maschera*."

Frank tried not to register the shock he felt. Wordlessly crossing to the chest of drawers, Estelle replaced the wig on its styrofoam stand. Pulling several tissues from a box she rubbed vigorously at her mouth until all traces of scarlet lipstick had disappeared. Then, slowly, she reached for her dark glasses, removing them to reveal eyes innocent of makeup.

"Will this do?"

"Nicely," replied Frank, startled at the transformation. Shorn of her trappings Estelle looked ghastly. Even Flavia Clarke in death looked less cadaverous than the woman who now confronted him.

"And now if you will turn around I will put on your mother's dressing gown."

Frank turned while Estelle slid off her dark-chocolate jersey and pulled on electric-blue polyester.

"Very well, you may look – at nothing. By the way, the fingernails come off, as do the eyelashes. I will remove them at leisure in your mother's room while you call the police to come fetch poor dear Estelle. When the body has been removed, you can drive me to the nursing home. The sooner we begin this charade, the sooner it will end."

"As soon as the body has been removed I will make you some breakfast and bring it to your – Mother's – room."

"I don't think I could eat anything at the moment."

"You really should. It will be a fair drive, and there will be all the fuss about settling you in. We won't get there until after lunch. 'You must keep your strength up,' as my grandmother used to say." Frank's attempt at humour came out stillborn. Estelle did not even look at him as he left the bedroom.

Frank went downstairs to his father's study to telephone the police. He decided perhaps it would be prudent to call Vivien only after the body had been removed. He wanted no last-minute vigils at the bedside of the supposed new-found, dear-departed cousin. On an affective basis his mother's death had not touched him; nor did he intend to allow it to. Grief is a luxury only the virtuous can afford.

Police officers are often kinder than television would lead one to believe. The men in blue arrived almost at once and were fully prepared to accept at face value the story told by the distraught, dithering old man. He had been so worried lest his mother be upset. The very idea: her own cousin carted off without ceremony to the morgue. But naturally Estelle had no personal physician to sign the death certificate. How could she? She had just arrived from the United Kingdom. Could there please be as little fuss as possible. His mother had to go ahead with her move into a nursing home this very afternoon; otherwise she'd lose her room. She was already in a state over leaving her house. And now this. Yes, he had searched everywhere for Estelle's passport, had left no stone unturned. However he had unearthed a birth certificate. No, she had no next of kin; only himself, his sister, his mother. Such a dreadful shock. Poor Estelle.

The one obviously in charge had explained to Frank in a sympathetic tone that without a doctor to sign the death certificate the body had to be taken to the morgue. That was the law. But, he hastened to reassure Frank, the very picture of dismay and incompetence, there was nothing questionable about the circumstances of death; and the coroner or one of his assistants would certainly release the body to the undertaker in short order. With a comforting smile he left to supervise transporting the body downstairs on a stretcher and into the waiting van. Frank stood, rubbing the back of his left hand with the palm of his right. Estelle remained shut in the master bedroom removing her long red nails.

When the police van had pulled out of sight Frank went back into his father's study to telephone the undertaker and issue firm instructions that his cousin was to be cremated in a closed coffin. Then he telephoned his sister.

"Frank! I don't believe it! Estelle? Dead?"

"I'm not one for practical jokes, Vivien. Maybe she had a stroke. I'm not a doctor."

"You sound terribly matter-of-fact."

"Vivien, I hardly knew the woman. And I'm going to see she gets a decent burial, in the family plot. I'll get back to you about the service at the crematorium. I'll drive you up. There'll be just the two of us. Standing room only."

"Frank, that's not funny. I still can't believe it. I could tell she was tired from the trip, but—dear God! How has Mother taken it?"

"I haven't told her yet. I don't intend to until I get her

111

comfortably settled into Willowdale. A day or so won't matter. She didn't even much like Estelle."

"I just can't bring myself to believe it."

"You've already said that. And now I must go and get Mother organized for the move."

"When will you be going? Not that it affects me."

"Early afternoon. I'll drive her out in my car. There's something grim about an ambulance. I'll be in touch."

Frank rang off and went into the kitchen. So far so good. As he cracked several eggs into a bowl he came back to the idea that if his plan were to succeed Estelle's incentive had to be as well nourished as his own. Before cooking the eggs and preparing a tray, Frank ducked down the basement stairs and opened the safe. Removing the flat box holding the emeralds he carried it up to the kitchen and put it onto the breakfast tray. Green was such a restful colour: grass, shrubs, trees, banknotes, stock certificates, emeralds. Frank scrambled the eggs and carried the tray upstairs to his mother's room where he found Estelle pacing. He put the tray onto a low table and summoned her to a chair.

"What's that?" she asked, pointing at the green-calf box.

"Open it."

Estelle raised the lid and gasped. "Goodness me! Aren't they splendid!" She ran the tips of her fingers over the cold surface of the jewels.

"If our plan works out successfully they will be yours. I will hand them to you as you board your flight to Italy. Let us call them a bonus for a job well done."

"I suppose I should sing a few bars of Marguerite's 'Jewel Song' but I'm afraid I'm not up to it. When should I be ready to leave?"

"Around noon. The room will be ready at one. After you have eaten your breakfast I will pack you a bag. You won't need much besides nightgowns and housecoats. And now I must telephone the newspaper to place a notice in the obituary column. Even though you have no friends in Canada I will

112

still specify the service at the crematorium is to be private. No flowers."

"I suppose once you make that call we have passed the point of no return."

"We already have. Remember, I lied to the police. Now try to eat something. Leave the worrying to me."

"Whatever you say. And you had better put these away." Estelle handed Frank the box holding the emeralds. She reached listlessly for a fork. "I must confess motherhood has quite taken away my appetite."

# Chapter 10

Nurse Harrison sat on a vinyl-covered chair at the arborite and chrome kitchen table in her small apartment drinking sweet Australian port from a glass measuring cup with a handle, and brooding over her dismissal. Shifts had all been assigned at Care, Cooks, & Chars; if she wanted work she must return to the hospital, and hospital work meant hard work. From her present vantage point the Clarke case looked pretty good. That Clarke woman was a bitch on wheels but a good sleeper nonetheless. And the agency had told her only that she was off the case because the patient was moving.

Nurse Harrison reached for the telephone which sat on the table by her elbow. With an extra-long extension cord, the telephone followed her around the apartment like a pet dog. Nurse Harrison contributed much to the statistic that Canadians talk on the telephone more than citizens of any other nation.

She dialled the telephone number of Nurse Gibson; their being suddenly unemployed as a result of Mrs. Clarke's move created a common bond which temporarily erased their mutual dislike.

"Mabel, it's Flo Harrison."

"Where are you?"

"Home. There's no shift work. What's the story on Clarke?"

"The son's moving her out to Willowdale. Didn't even take

me along to help. Just gave me a tip and told me to beat it. Wouldn't even let me say goodbye to the old lady."

"How much did he give you?"

"Fifty."

"Fifty! Did he tell you he was moving the patient?"

"Yes, with the help of a cousin – from England."

"You mean that visiting relative who looks like an old whore?"

"I guess so."

There followed a brief pause as Nurse Harrison digested two facts. She had received no gratuity; Mr. Clarke had mentioned nothing about Willowdale. But for the moment she decided not to say anything.

"What are you going to do now, Mabel?"

"I'm going back to the hospital. I'm sick of private cases, babysitting with a bedpan. I start tomorrow. You?"

"Haven't decided. I may try for a nurse-companion. Live in. Get my meals."

"Well, see you, Flo."

"Sure thing, Mabel."

Nurse Gibson hung up the telephone. Nurse Harrison on the other end simply depressed the cradle until a dial tone began to sound. She dialled a number.

"Manoir Willowdale Manor," said a woman's voice.

"Brenda, it's Flo Harrison."

"Flo! How've you been?"

"Not bad. You?"

"Can't complain. Haven't seen you for a while."

"True. I haven't worked at Willowdale since old Mr. McMaster died. Say, Brenda, you have a new resident, a Mrs. Clarke, Flavia Clarke, moving in today. Is she going to need a special?"

"Hang on, Flo. I'll check."

Nurse Harrison waited. She liked working in nursing homes as well as she liked working anywhere. It was a lot easier than hospital work, and there was someone to talk to besides the patient. And even if the old bitch didn't need a private nurse Florence Harrison wanted her gratuity. A visit to the old lady, a few flowers might pay off.

The voice came back onto the line. "Flo? That Mrs. Clarke; sh    booked into room 336, but she hasn't checked in yet. I won't know if she needs a special until she gets here."

"Keep me in mind, will you?"

"Sure thing, Flo."

Nurse Harrison rang off. She hoped something might turn up at Willowdale. One of the other nurses would probably give her a lift for splitting the cost of gas. In any case, she intended to visit the old lady and maybe get a tip. And hadn't Ruby Turner gone onto a case at Willowdale? Yes, she had. And Ruby had her own car. Nurse Harrison reached for the telephone directory and flipped to the T's. Much as she disliked the idea she had to find work.

*     *     *

After telephoning her mother's house and waiting out twelve rings with one more for good measure, Vivien called a taxi and rode up the hill in style, high-hearted at the prospect of seeing Randolph's paintings after all these years. She toyed with the extravagant idea of asking the driver to wait. Habits of frugality die hard, however, and Vivien paid off the driver, tipping him only ten per cent of the fare as he had not held the door.

She had asked him to let her out half a block from the house, which stood on a corner lot. Walking up the street running alongside the house, Vivien pushed her way through a gap in the ragged hedge and crossed the lawn, more of a pasture really, and climbed the side steps onto the front porch. She did not want to be seen by the Petrie Sisters who lived across the street and monitored the scant activity on the quiet crescent. The sisters were indefatigable gossips, and Vivien did not want

116

it advertised that she had been seen sneaking into her mother's house. It was bad enough dodging the Petries in the supermarket or the library. Pushing the front doorbell Vivien made one more check to make sure no one had entered the house since she had phoned. The raucous sound of the bell was plainly audible through the front door, and she waited, anxiously hoping that the door would not swing open.

After a decent interval she rang again. The third and longest ring convinced her that the house stood empty. Remembering how resistant her mother had been to change, Vivien tried her own key in the lock, a key which had lain unused for some years now in a tiny drawer in her desk. Sure enough, the lock had not been replaced; the heavy door pushed open.

Little appeared to have changed in the house where she had passed her youth. It still had the look of stolid shabbiness, the clean but mended look that only great wealth or extreme poverty dares to cultivate. Up she climbed to the top floor, the stairs taking their toll less on her breathing than on her joints. At the top of the stairs she turned right into the room where she had slept as a girl, still furnished with rickety antiques. Above the spool bed, picked up for next to nothing at an auction, a rectangle of roughly two by three feet was clearly visible on the faded wallpaper.

Quickly Vivien crossed into the adjoining bedroom, once her brother's room, now stale from lack of use. Across the walls, once burgundy, now sepia, huntsmen stood poised, bows at the ready to release arrows at unwary stags. Above the bed, over the desk, two more rectangles hinted at what the paperhanger might once have seen. Only a pair of faded photographs, the Colosseum and the Roman Forum, still hung on nails driven into the wall decades ago.

Across the hall, in a third bedroom, now furnished with odds and ends no longer needed downstairs but too good to give away, the sole surviving picture was a watercolour of Edinburgh castle during a thunderstorm. Two brighter rectangles, where ladies carrying parasols walked forever in the shrubbery, indicated clearly two places where pictures had once hung.

Vivien went down to the second floor and crossed first to her father's bedroom where Estelle had unpacked, the casual chaos still untouched. For a moment Vivien allowed her thoughts to dwell on the cousin so newly acquired, so suddenly snatched away. Vivien was filled with regret, not only for the relative whom she had genuinely liked, but also for the realization that at her age one watches old friends die off. The garrison is slowly decimated with little hope of new reinforcements.

But Vivien had come for a purpose. Going from room to room she searched in vain for her husband's paintings. Overcoming her reluctance, Vivien opened her mother's door for a quick look. What cluttered the walls of the master bedroom did not come from the brush or the pen of Randolph Howard. Then, as if reaching for a life preserver in choppy waters, Vivien came up with a sudden thought. The revival of interest in the work of Randolph Howard had become known to her mother. She had brought all his paintings down to the ground floor. Even though Mrs. Clarke no longer used the public rooms she would still want her best things on display for the now infrequent visitors.

So anxious was Vivien to prove her hunch she hardly noticed the small elevator parked at the head of the stairs. Resting her hand on the banister she made her way carefully down the broad staircase. A fall at this point would be disastrous. Into the cheerless front room she hurried, only to find it unchanged: the Shakespeare heroines, the engraving of Salisbury Cathedral after Constable, even the parchment lampshade on which Mrs. Cooper's budgie had dropped all those Christmases ago. But not a single Randolph Howard painting or drawing was to be seen. Her father's study had not been touched. On the one wall not covered by bookcases hung the prints of racehorses she remembered as a girl. In the dining room a herd of ruminating cattle still hung over the sideboard facing the large mirror in its ornate gilt frame.

Suddenly exhausted, Vivien slumped onto one of the dining room chairs, the yawning realization taking hold. Not a single one of her husband's drawings or paintings remained in the house. Could they have been sold? Her mother certainly did not need money. More probably they had been casually given away. But Vivien knew her mother to have the instincts of a pack rat. Mrs. Clarke kept everything, as top-floor cupboards crammed with decades of discarded gowns could attest. Yet if her mother had not sold the paintings, nor given them away, then where had they gone? Only Frank had regular access to the house; and his power of attorney did give him control over his mother's possessions. But what possible reason would he have had to sell the paintings, especially when he well knew how badly Vivien wanted them back?

Vivien buried her face in her hands, uncertain of whether to laugh or cry. How foolish she had been to pin her hopes on those pictures. But she had. First to have lent them to the National Gallery for the Randolph Howard retrospective, then to have sold them judiciously, one at a time, would have made all the difference between budgeting and ease. She could have hung them in her house, enjoyed them while she remembered Randolph as he had worked in his painstaking, meticulous way. Now the paintings were gone. For a moment Vivien was swept with a regret so overwhelming as to deny the easy relief of tears.

She stared across the room, her eyes resting on Grandmother Van Patten's silver service which sat, just where it always had, in the centre of the heavy oak sideboard. But wait a minute, there was something odd. Vivien rose and went to pick up the teapot. This was not her grandmother's teapot with its rose-wood handle, squat yet graceful, the fluted sides tapering down into a pedestal base. This was not her grandmother's sugar bowl, its fluted top raised by the same oval ornamental knob that crowned the teapot. This was not her grandmother's cream jug whose handle described an elegant reverse s-curve. And furthermore – Vivien carried the cream jug over to the window where she removed her glasses and brought the bottom of the jug close to her eyes – this tea set was only plate. Someone had obviously taken her grandmother's valuable silver tea service and replaced it with cheap silverplate.

Slowly Vivien replaced the cream jug on the Sheffield tray. It did not take brilliance to figure out the truth. How else had Frank been supporting himself in style, denying himself nothing? Struck by a sudden thought Vivien crossed to her father's study where she remembered a James Wilson Morrice used to hang in a small space between two bookcases behind the desk. Predictably the space was empty.

Behind the endlessly charming façade, which Frank paraded before the world, lurked a venal man; a man who had been stealing from his own mother. Vivien was appalled. To steal was in itself reprehensible, but to pilfer from a parent? Like the proverbial taking of candy from a baby the theft of parental possessions seemed all the more reprehensible because so easy.

Vivien crossed the wide hallway to sit in the front room. She had looked forward to reliving those memories of Randolph she knew the paintings would trigger. Even her sadness at the death of Estelle could not totally quench the surge of anticipation with which she had entered the big house. Although there had been no children, Vivien's marriage to Randolph had been a successful one; she had come to accept her husband's body of work as his projection into the future.

By the standards of her community Vivien Clarke Howard had been well brought up, meaning she exemplified the virtues, more passive than militant, of good manners, clean hair, passing grades. Hers was not a spirit that lusted for confrontation; however she was adamant when given an issue she considered worth fighting for. Vivien shrank from accusing her brother, her one remaining close relative; but she knew for her own peace of mind that she would have to face him down. It was no longer a question of choice but of duty.

Vivien sat, nervously twisting the ruby ring her cousin had given her. She felt an odd, unpleasant sensation, as though there was a hole where her stomach should have been. Randolph was dead, his work casually dissipated. Estelle was dead, just after she had come unexpectedly into Vivien's life. And if what she suspected about Frank turned out to be true, Vivien knew she could no longer consider him a friend.

Suddenly she felt as if the four walls were closing in on her. Abruptly she left the house, locking the door behind her. She walked with determination down the front walk, defying the Petrie sisters to watch her departure. As she strode back down the hill Vivien looked into her future and saw more belt tightening, at least until her mother died. But until then, Vivien was not sure she any longer wanted Frank's help, certainly not if her suspicions were correct.

# Chapter 11

"Welcome to Willowdale, Mrs. Clarke – excuse me – Mrs. McCutcheon," boomed the director of Manoir Willowdale Manor. He was dressed in synthetics: dynel, polyester, nylon, corfam. He pumped the hand Estelle proferred to be kissed. On top of his avocado-shaped head sat a hairpiece, the look of which caused Frank to run a hand over his own hair, as if for reassurance. "We all hope you'll be very happy here. This way, please."

He led the procession towards the elevator. The director, Frank, Estelle in a wheelchair pushed by a nurse, a porter carrying the suitcase, all grouped themselves obediently in a wedge facing the door as the director pushed button number three.

"Lovely weather for this time of year," said the director in the self-conscious manner of one who talks in elevators.

Frank agreed, his whole demeanour almost aggressively casual, even though his armpits ran with sweat.

"Of course we need some rain," continued the director.

"Most certainly," replied Frank. Why was it that social discomfort caused people to discuss meteorology?

"But I guess winter will be here soon."

"Yes, it will," replied Frank, conscious that the palms of his hands were uncharacteristically moist.

"Well, here we are," announced the director as doors slid

open. Stepping briskly off the elevator he led the procession down a long hallway carpeted in yellow and orange chevrons and peopled with geriatrics in various stages of disrepair. An old man with iron grey hair, who was lashed into his wheelchair, waved vigorously at Frank. "They've got me prisoner. Please, help me to get away!"

The procession continued down the corridor. The wreck of a once-pretty woman in a tired satin peignoir leaned against the door-jamb of her room. She winked lewdly at Frank. "Wanna good time, sonny?"

"That will do, Mrs. O'Sullivan," said the director, embarrassed. "Some of our residents aren't quite themselves," he confided to Frank who thought, on the contrary, that the residents seemed to be very much themselves.

Estelle did not speak. A seasoned professional, she played the role of aged parent to the hilt. So frail did she seem that the nurse watched anxiously lest she tip out of the chair. The director opened the door to the very last room on the right and the cortège filed inside.

The room was furnished after the fashion of a decent motel except for the hospital bed. Two armchairs upholstered in nylon tweed flanked a low table on which sat a telephone. Above this was a hanging lamp whose bamboo shade turned out, upon inspection, to be plastic. A white chest of drawers, heightened with touches of gold paint and coated with varethane, sat beneath a matching mirror. The adjacent bathroom had assorted metal brackets clamped into the walls to help the resident to manoeuvre. On the wall over the bed hung a reproduction of a sad clown executed in heavy strokes of charcoal and gouache.

The porter put the suitcase onto the bed and withdrew, as the nurse helped Estelle out of the wheelchair and into one of the armchairs.

The director rubbed his hands together. "Naturally, Mrs. McCutcheon, you can bring anything you like to furnish your room: a desk, pictures, photographs, art objects. Make it as homey as you like. We advise you to keep small valuables in your safety deposit box. A great many of our cleaning staff come from the Islands and they, well, you know. The dietician will be in shortly to help plan your menus. If there is anything I can do, anything at all, please don't hesitate to ask."

"There is one small problem," began Frank. "Mother's medical records appear to have been misplaced. I know you are a busy man, I won't bore you with details, just another dreary tale of gross incompetence. But I am afraid the doctor will have to start from scratch."

"No problem, Mr. Clarke. Dr. Patrick, our resident doctor – absolutely tops, I might add – always likes to start from the ground up with each new patient. Is Mrs. McCutcheon on any medication?"

Estelle shook her head to indicate no.

"Good. Today is one of the days Dr. Patrick visits Willowdale. I'll make sure he comes to see you, ma'am." The director crossed to the door. "By the way, shall I put your first name or initial on the resident register?"

"F. McCutcheon will do," replied Frank. "I will wait with Mother until the dietician arrives."

The director bowed slightly and left the room.

The second he was out the door Estelle sprang to her feet. Pulling Flavia Clarke's scarf from her head and tugging herself free from Mrs. Clarke's spring and fall camel-hair coat, Estelle tossed them onto a chair. "God! What a place!"

"It's not the Savoy, but remember: it's only for a short time."

Estelle stood at the window, Marguerite awaiting the return of Faust. "Had I but known, or even suspected what I was letting myself in for. Even without the risk of discovery, to present myself like this, before strangers, before my public."

"Cousin Estelle – I mean Mother – you exaggerate. Old age is the name of the game out here. Think of a seesaw. On one end is a bedsitter in Battersea; on the other a suite of rooms in a Roman *palazzo*. Your weight can shift the balance."

Estelle sat, patience on a monument.

"Take comfort," continued Frank. "The worst is over. I have to congratulate you. The way you got yourself from the front door of the house into my car and then up here into your room would have fooled anyone."

"To be a great opera singer one must have more than a voice; one must be an actress as well. I imagined myself as the dying Violetta in the fourth act of *Traviata* as she awaits the final visit from Alfredo. Good heavens, Francis! How am I to deal with visitors? Anyone who comes to visit your mother will know I am not she." Agitation caused Estelle's breath to come in rapid pants.

"I have already explained that to you. A No Visitors sign will be posted on your door. The receptionist will be instructed to refuse to admit anyone. Nor will you take any phone calls. You will be totally incommunicado."

"Like Gilda hidden from the world by her father Rigoletto. But the garden wall was scaled and the maiden kidnapped. She concealed her true identity and died as a result."

"Gilda was a nitwit, sacrificing her life for a man, for anyone. You are not a nitwit."

Estelle went back to the window and stood looking out. "I wish I were as confident as you that nothing will go wrong."

"Trust me. Now as soon as the dietician comes I'll make myself scarce. But I'll drive out tomorrow. Anything I can bring you? Mother had a small colour TV."

"A telly would be nice. And perhaps a bottle of gin. I took the liberty of refilling my mayonnaise jar, but I'm going to need the moral support."

A knock at the door announced the dietician, a flashy middle-aged blonde with good legs shown off to advantage by perilously high heels. Frank decided the food wouldn't be too bad, and with a bow and a smile, he made good his departure.

\*     \*     \*

By the time Frank got back to his apartment dusk was begin-

125

ning to close in. For the first time in weeks he had skipped his daily nap, yet far from feeling tired he was bursting with nervous energy. He had just started to grasp the magnitude of the risk involved, although it had not yet begun to tarnish the thrill surrounding the deception. Furthermore, tonight he was to collect the Picasso drawing from Roch in exchange for the tea service.

Grandmother Van Patten's silver service, which Frank had obligingly stored for his mother, sat on a bow-front chest in Frank's small dining room. Buffing the teapot, sugar bowl, and cream jug with a rouge cloth for the last time, he wrapped each piece carefully in a tea towel and packed them into a heavy paper shopping bag with the Liquor Board logo printed on the side along with a French homily about moderation having the better taste. Carrying the bag out to his car, he drove along Dorchester Boulevard and down Beaver Hall Hill into Old Montreal.

"Precious Treasure!"

"Darling Angel!"

"Come inside." Roch pulled the door shut. "You are looking at a total wreck, a whited sepulchre. I have been working like a white. My escort service is beginning to take off like you would not believe. Even in one day! Word of mouth, don't you know."

"Where was the mouth when it gave the word?"

"Naughty Fanny." Roch shook a fat forefinger. "But one of my best clients—he just bought the A.Y. Jackson and the Henry Moore bronze—wants me to come up with nine tall, thin, black queens, money no object. It seems he has a fantasy about basketball; he went to a southern college."

"Send him three and he can do the rest with mirrors."

"If only I could."

"Perhaps you could put a notice on the bulletin board of the Pentecostal church."

"You're being very little help. And with all the West Indians in Montreal?"

"Why don't you try to find limbo dancers? They're tall and thin and athletic. That's how they get under the doors of toilet stalls. Going to the john in the Islands is marvellous fun."

"Fanny, you're not being serious. Let's have a look at the tea service."

By now they had manoeuvred their way through the apartment to the kitchen where Frank unwrapped the silver. After an appraising glance Roch nodded his head in approval. "Fine, very fine. I'd say late eighteenth century, maybe early nineteenth – and in mint condition. And I'm pretty certain I have a client. He got himself a pile of money making book and now he's trying to buy pedigree."

Frank reached for the drawing in its portfolio on top of the refrigerator.

"Sit down, Fanny, I want to talk to you for a minute." Frank sat. "I want to make you a proposition, a dishonest, honest offer. I am looking for someone to share the business with me, a partner as it were. I'm not getting any younger. More specifically I want someone to handle the escort service, Escorts Unlimited, as you have so gracefully named it. You would be perfect. We both know you're rotten to the core, but you present a marvellous façade."

"Roxanne, stop right there. I have never worked a day in my life and I don't intend to start now."

"Dancing attendance on that Gorgon Medusa mother is harder work than going down a condemned coal mine. Come off it, Fanny."

"I fear I must decline. Besides, I am at present involved in a – a small transaction which will keep me occupied for the next little while."

"Think it over." Roch leaned forward, hard and business-like. "Promise me at least you'll think it over. Most of the work is done on the telephone. And face it, Fanny; to risk indelicacy, there are big bucks in fucks, especially fantasy fucks. Catering cock, purveying pussy can be a tidy little hedge against inflation."

"I'll think it over; I promise," replied Frank, eager to get home and pore over his new Picasso.

"By the way, I may have a lead on a Tiepolo, saints with *putti*, pen and brown wash. If I manage to get my hands on it you'll be the third to know."

Frank edged his way carefully towards the front door of Roch's apartment, holding the drawing above his head so as not to dislodge a pyramid of etched champagne glasses stacked high on a gilt escritoire which intruded into the passageway. Casually he turned to Roch, who had followed him from the kitchen.

"Roch, supposing, just supposing you wanted to make someone disappear, just disappear, what would you do?"

"Roch! Fanny, darling, whenever you call me Roch I know it must be, as the young say, heavy. Don't tell me you're going to do in that ghastly mother of yours."

"No, not yet anyway." Frank manufactured a chuckle, trying to keep the conversation light. "But just supposing, as we used to play as kids. Just supposing you had a million dollars. Just supposing you were King of England. Just supposing you wanted to 'off' someone; what would you do?"

"First of all, being a true fairy, I'd wave my wand. Failing that I'd fit the undesirable with a pair of cement wedgies and tip her off the Jacques Cartier bridge."

"You've been watching too much television."

"Perhaps. However, I have not as yet had reason to 'off' someone, as you put it; but it would seem to me the first thing to do would be to isolate whoever it is. Separate him, or her, from other people, from their regular surroundings. Encapsulate him. Have the person by for a drink, preferably when the neighbours are on vacation."

"Not to worry. I was only speculating." Frank cast about for something to change the subject. "I say, Roxanne, I didn't know you had gone into the old clothing business." Hanging from a wall sconce, holding two small bulbs shaped like candle flames, was a topaz satin gown which, although elaborately

128

pleated and draped, still retained a timeless elegance which pushed it beyond fashion.

"Isn't it heaven!" Roch clapped his hands together. "It's by Worth. I had to have it, and it isn't even my size. It belonged to a singer. She was big time in her day: Stella della Chiesa. She once wore it for a recital in Paris. What's the matter, Fanny? You look as though you have just been goosed by King Kong."

"Where did you get it?" Frank's voice sounded tight, even to himself.

"It was part of an estate. The owner used to live in Europe. He died recently, and his lover was getting most of the movable items out of the house before the estate duty appraiser came around. Most of the stuff wasn't worth much. But I adore the dress."

Frank shrugged his shoulders, carefully feigning indifference. "I'm afraid I'm not much of an opera buff. Why sit through four hours of music when you can read the libretto in thirty minutes? And, speaking of clothes, Roxanne, where did you get that jogging suit?"

"Mail order, from the U.S. A store catering to the larger man."

"And the king-sized queen?"

"Dearest Fanny is deficient in charity. Just remember: it is easier for a full-figured girl to pass through the eye of a needle than for a mean bitch to enter the kingdom of heaven."

"No doubt you're right. But I have to dash. I'll be in touch."

As he made his way to his car Frank thought of the distance now separating that Worth dress from the crone at Willowdale, a distance which measured itself in memories, not miles. Those who still remembered Stella della Chiesa thought of her as a fading legend somewhere in Europe. The troublesome identity had become that of Flavia Clarke, alive to the world but accessible to no one but Frank. He slid behind the wheel of his car and drove back to his apartment.

He was hardly inside the door before he slid the drawing by

Sir David Wilkie into the portfolio and propped the Picasso in its place. Twenty-four hours ago he had closed his eyes and imagined this same drawing on his mantelpiece, its taut, elegant lines suggesting as much as delineating the two classic figures. Then he had been filled with peace and contentment. Tonight the mood eluded him. He studied the Picasso, but his mind darted back and forth between Estelle incarcerated at Willowdale and his mother boxed at the funeral home, funereal, but not homey.

By the time Estelle-Flavia felt up to receiving visitors Frank would tell the director his mother was unhappy at Willowdale and wanted to move out. But where was she to go? Frank had intended to put the big house up for sale as soon as his mother moved into Willowdale; now he had only to call the real estate agent who already knew of a developer interested in the large lot. Perhaps for the sake of appearance he ought to wait a few days. Since it was her most visible asset he did not want to appear in too much of a hurry. But once he had liquidated the major portion of his mother's estate, the question remained what to do with Estelle, now Flavia Clarke in the eyes of the world.

At the moment there seemed to be two choices. Either he could leave Estelle at Willowdale indefinitely in the dubious hope that she would finally succumb to old age and be content to remain, with the attendant risk of discovery. Or he could bring her back here to his own apartment. He had a spare room. The devoted son? Taking his old mother into his own home so she can spend her final days in peace. Here at least she could be kept under wraps until . . . until what? Until she died, of benign neglect. Estelle's leaving the country, even under her assumed identity, was out of the question.

There was no point in worrying about what to do with Estelle until she had fulfilled her function. Things would work out. He would make them work out. And the Picasso would be one of the highlights of The Frank Clarke Collection. Frank examined the drawing with admiration bordering on awe. How could a few lines of the pen be made to suggest a cascade of drapery?

The telephone interrupted Frank's thoughts.

"This is Jeanne-Marie O'Casey," said a whiny woman's voice. "I'm calling from the handicapped. We sell lightbulbs and pantyhose. Our bulbs are hospital bulbs, guaranteed to burn five thousand hours. We have sixty watts, one hundred watts – "

"I will take two dozen bulbs; twelve sixties and twelve one hundreds," replied Frank. "You already have my post office box number on file."

He rang off, uncertain of whether he really wanted to help the handicapped, as he had in the past; or whether to order items he neither wanted nor needed was a pact with fate, a trade-off with God to make certain his plan worked out. No sooner had Frank turned away from the phone than it rang again. He answered it.

"Frank, did you get Mother safely settled at Willowdale?"

Certain the caller was the lightbulb lady who had neglected something important to the order, Frank was startled to hear his sister's voice on the line.

"Yes, indeed. No problem at all. I wheeled her out to my car and the nurse helped me to lift her in. She seemed to enjoy the ride out, and there was a clutch of people waiting at the nursing home to help her up to her room."

"I'm very glad to hear it. Naturally I would have been ready to give you a hand, had the situation been otherwise."

"I was perfectly able to manage alone, really."

"Frank, now that the house is empty and shortly to be sold I can see no reason why I should not have Randolph's drawings and paintings returned."

"No reason at all, Vivien. The only problem is that I'm not sure what Mother has done with them."

"Are they still in the house?"

"Quite possibly. It's just that I haven't seen any of them

for some time." As he spoke Frank studied the six Howard drawings on the wall over the bed where they hung symmetrically in double rows of three awaiting assimilation into The Collection.

"Could you not ask Mother what she has done with them?"

"Certainly, when she settles in a bit. She has been quite disoriented by the move, and she probably wouldn't remember, even if I did ask her."

"I see. I would be glad to go through the house with you. Perhaps together we could find the pictures. They are difficult to conceal. It's not as if we were looking for coins or stamps."

"I won't need any help, thanks, Vivien. I have to go to the house tomorrow morning and I'll check upstairs. No need for you to bother."

"It wouldn't be a bother, I assure you." Frost coated Vivien's voice. "I certainly hope you are able to locate them. They ought to be in Randolph's retrospective exhibition at the National Gallery. I have already described them in a letter to the curator. I know she will be disappointed if they are not available. Should Mother have disposed of the works, I am sure the National Gallery would be willing to help us trace them, or suggest someone who could."

The mirror over Frank's walnut dresser caught the reflection of his eyes rolling in a fury of controlled impatience. But the voice going out over the wire remained as smooth as malt whisky. "Vivien, you're sounding terribly cloak and dagger about all this. The pictures are probably stacked in a closet somewhere. And you know those closets: Fibber McGee and Molly. Open any door at your own risk. All sorts of things will turn up when I empty the house."

"I daresay you are right. I would like to visit the house once, before you begin to dismantle it. At the risk of sounding sentimental, I want to see some of the things I associate with my childhood, like Grandmother Van Patten's tea service, and the lovely little Morrice which used to hang in Father's study."

"Sure, Vivien. I'll drive you up next week and give you the ten-shilling tour. I have to go; there's someone at the door."

That hoary old alibi was the best Frank could come up with, so much did he want to get his sister off the phone. As he put down the receiver Frank wondered if it might be a good idea to have the lock changed on the front door of his mother's house. It seemed unlikely that Vivien still had a key after all these years, but he couldn't be too careful. Sooner or later his sister would have to learn that he himself had sold the paintings, the tea service, and a number of other things besides. But he wanted to delay her discovery as long as possible, at least until he had liquidated the major portion of the assets. Also if Vivien learned the truth she would never agree to selling the Calgary real estate. Tomorrow morning he must call the locksmith.

# Chapter 12

At nine o'clock the following morning Frank pulled his car to a stop in front of his mother's house. Letting himself in, he went first to his mother's bedroom. He lifted the television set out of her room to set on the small elevator. A flick of the switch sent it down to the ground floor. He hefted it out to his car. It was still too early to go to the bank and pick up the stock certificates he had sold by telephone yesterday. Perhaps he would cash in the bonds today as well, taking out a term deposit in his own name with the funds. He might even convert the deposit into U.S. funds, depending on the rate of exchange.

Frank prowled through the house with an appraising eye. Little remained worth salvaging. He would keep the silver cigarette box from his father's study. Frank had no interest in the books, never having been much of a reader. He preferred his own experience to the second-hand observations of others. Nor did he want anything from the depressing dining room, not even the Waterford decanters; they were so macho chichi. He would flog the flat silver. When was he going to throw a knees-under-the-table dinner party for twelve?

Half-past nine found Frank at his father's desk reaching for the telephone. His first call was to the locksmith, who agreed to come by the following afternoon to replace the lock on the front door. The second call to the family minister confirmed the time of the cremation service, tomorrow morning at ten.

No, there remained nothing for Frank to do. He only had to be present at the funeral to sign the death certificate. Had he informed the cemetery office where the ashes were to be buried? No, he had not, and agreed to take care of the matter this very morning.

Frank replaced the receiver in the cradle, drew a deep breath, and dialled one more number. His Aunt Phyllis Coughlin must be told of the move; furthermore she must be discouraged, in fact forbidden, from visiting Willowdale. Frank always dreaded calling his aunt, who was never happier than when on the telephone. Although she stoutly refused to admit being deaf, she found the telephone amplified sound to a level where she no longer had to strain in order to hear. Consequently she enjoyed her Bell Canada chats to the point where it became nearly impossible to get her off the line.

"Aunt Phyllis, it's Francis."

"Francis, I do wish you would arrange for your mother's cleaning woman to set aside one day a week for Sibyl Bradshaw. The cats have quite taken over her house; the place defies description. I was barely able to put up with it yesterday for ten minutes. But I did have a stroke of luck. I was standing at the bus stop when Lorna Gallery stopped her car and offered to drive me home. So sweet of her. She had her daughter with her. I wish you could see the daughter's hair, dyed scarlet and sticking up in points all over her head. Someone really ought to go at her with the shears. And a safety pin through her ear. It's not as if she couldn't afford real jewellery. There's plenty of money there. I have always maintained that if you can't afford real jewellery you shouldn't wear any. The mother doesn't even seem to notice. But I must say she doesn't set much of an example herself. She wasn't even wearing a corset. How is Flavia today? I had thought of paying a visit."

"She is fine thank you, Aunt Phyllis. As a matter of fact it's concerning Mother that I telephoned you. She moved out to Willowdale yesterday, yesterday afternoon, to be precise."

Surprise and outrage reduced Phyllis Coughlin to uncharacteristic silence. Ultra-conservative even as a girl, Mrs. Coughlin had reached an age where she looked on change, any change, as the work of the Antichrist. "Why wasn't I told, at once?"

"It all came up rather suddenly," Frank began easily. "As you know, Mother has wanted to move out to Willowdale for some time now. The day before yesterday a room became vacant. When I told Mother, she insisted on making the move at once. I suggested she wait a day or so, but you know how stubborn she can be. She is very comfortably settled, but she insists she wants no visitors for at least a week to ten days. No visitors. None! And she has given the switchboard instructions to refuse all incoming calls. She wants a chance to collect herself and to adjust. When she feels up to seeing people, I'll be glad to drive you out."

"Well, I never!" came out as a tiny explosion. "She might at least have told me herself. Willowdale is so far away and inconvenient to get to."

Frank thought with satisfaction that Willowdale was virtually impossible to reach by bus. Phyllis Coughlin suffered from high blood pressure, or "nerves," as she preferred to call it; and nothing caused her pressure to soar as quickly as the inexorable tick of the taxi meter. Frank realized that unless driven, his aunt would never go out to Willowdale.

"As I said," continued Frank, "she made up her mind very suddenly. You know what she's like; you've known her far longer than I have." Frank laughed out loud at his little joke. "But she wants a period of total privacy." Frank raised his voice to a level that even his deaf aunt found excessive. "Mother wants no telephone calls and no visitors. Do you understand?"

Not wanting to push his luck Frank pulled a diversionary tactic. "But I almost forgot; I have something for you. The last thing Mother said as she left the house was 'See that Phyllis gets the painting of the Highland cattle, the one in the dining room, to hang in her apartment!' "

136

Phyllis Coughlin erupted into a cadenza of denials. She really couldn't. Wouldn't Flavia want it for her room at Willowdale? It would leave a mark on the wallpaper. It had come from the McCutcheon side of the family, not the Clarke. Wasn't Flavia kindness itself.

"I'll drop it by your building and leave it at the front desk this afternoon, or tomorrow some time. Goodbye for now, Aunt Phyllis." Frank rang off.

Even being cut off in mid-sentence failed to discomfit Mrs. Coughlin as the enormous problem of where to hang the Highland cattle in her tiny flat pushed the surprise at her sister-in-law's sudden move from stage centre into the wings of her consciousness.

Frank attached the safety chain on the front door of his mother's house and let himself out through the kitchen entrance, for which he had a key. If Vivien still had her own key to the house, unlikely after all these years, it would no doubt be for the front door. Frank wanted no one snooping about while the house stood empty.

After waving good morning to whichever of the Petrie sisters stood sentinel in her front window, Frank drove directly to the bank.

As he walked through the door, past a security guard who looked as though he collected chins, Frank's manner abruptly changed. No longer brisk, upright, efficient, he began to stoop. The spring left his step and he stopped for a moment, looking about as if confused.

Finally getting his bearings he shambled over to the vault and signed out his safety deposit box which an obliging young woman carried into a cubicle. It was such a heavy box; no, she didn't mind at all; he had only to buzz and she would be glad to put it back for him. Frank flashed his sweet, laser smile and shut the door. It did not take him long to riffle through the pile of securities and locate the certificates he wanted. Tucking them into his briefcase he pushed the buzzer. When he heard footsteps approaching he dropped his shoulders and pulled in his chin, allowing the flesh under his jaw to go slack, adding years to his appearance.

After thanking the young woman, who carried the box into the vault and locked the door, Frank made his way over to the counter to redeem the bonds, spreading them out on the counter as if they were indecipherable documents written in arcane script. A young man with a slight lisp came to the rescue. Frank did his best to explain: they were to be cashed in; his portfolio advisor had given him instructions; it was all so confusing. He wanted to buy – a term deposit? Yes, that was it; a term deposit, in U.S. funds.

"I'll see what I can do, sir," said the young man, apparently new on the job and looking for someone to help out.

"Move your ass, Dumbo," muttered Frank under his breath.

The amount being large, another clerk came over to help, one for whom redeeming bonds was not a total mystery. The bonds in question were registered to Flavia M. Clarke. Was the term deposit to be in her name? Frank appeared to hesitate. He wasn't sure; his financial advisor hadn't said exactly. Perhaps it would be better if the deposit were issued to him: Francis D. Clarke. He was his mother's attorney, after all. The bank had a notarized copy of the document on file. Oh, dear; he looked at his watch. It was getting late and he was due at the hospital for tests.

The ensuing flurry of activity left Frank with a thirty-day term deposit in U.S. funds purchased with his mother's Government of Canada bonds and issued under his own name. He left, but not until he had told the two clerks how wonderfully helpful they had been, all the time smiling his killer smile.

Frank walked out of the bank as though his feet hurt, then sprinted to his car. Three subsequent stops took him to the offices of three different firms of stockbrokers where he left certificates representing the stocks he had sold the previous day. He also left with each stockholder one of the three last notarized copies of his power of attorney. By tomorrow he would have his extra copies, to be picked up sometime later today. And even though he was spreading his business around several firms of stockbrokers, Frank wanted to proceed with caution. A sudden rush of sales for Flavia McCutcheon Clarke might look suspicious.

Frank then drove up and across the Montreal mountain to the cemetery office where an obliging but inept young woman wasted several minutes looking for the Clarke file under the letter K. The family plot held six graves in two rows of three, the whole dominated by a draped red granite urn on which had been carved the simple legend CLARKE. The urn represented Grandfather Clarke's attempts at permanence beyond the final fact. Naturally he occupied one of the upper graves beside that of his wife. The centre grave in the second row had been filled by Frank's own father. That meant that by burying the ashes of *soi-disant* Estelle Church in one of the graves flanking that of Desmond Bruce Clarke then Flavia Clarke would in effect be laid to rest beside her dear departed husband. Only the Grand Architect would know the difference.

Pleased with this turn of events – he was not after all a heartless man – Frank left the cemetery office, holding the door and standing aside to let a woman enter the building.

To his surprise, she spoke to him as she stood, dead centre, in the doorway. "Francis Clarke. Now what on earth are you doing here?"

"Millicent MacLean. I could ask you the same question." Although he continued to smile, Frank mentally took a stance of karate defence. Millicent MacLean: tireless gossip and absolute predator when it came to prying into other people's affairs. A surprising number of people mistook her insatiable curiosity for concern, and spilled information only too willingly into her lap.

"Oh, Francis. I hope it's not your mother." Her nasal voice went husky with sympathy.

"No, it's not. A cousin, whom we scarcely knew. And you, Millicent?" Frank deftly returned the ball. "Surely you're not up here for the outing."

139

"Unfortunately not. My sister, I'm sorry to say. Cancer: the female kind, you know." The words came out with such evident relish that even Frank was taken aback. "But tell me, Francis. When is *your* service? I would like to come, for Flavia's sake."

"The service at the crematorium is to be private, Millicent," replied Frank still holding the door, Mrs. MacLean having remained blocking the doorway. "Only family."

"Oh, but I'm sure an old friend of Flavia's, like myself, would not be unwelcome. Perhaps you could give me a lift up to the chapel. What was the cause of . . . passing on?"

Frank ignored the question. "Naturally I'll tell Mother you offered to come. But the service is to be private, really."

"I know it's an imposition to ask you to drive me up. My nephew will bring me, my late sister's son. A drive up to the crematorium will help take his mind off his loss."

A wave of irritation broke over Frank. "Millicent, if you so much as show your face at the crematorium I will personally eject you, with force, if necessary."

"Well, there's no need to be rude. I was only thinking of your mother," she retorted, her voice breathless with indignation. She had not shifted her position in the doorway.

"I know it's impolite to make personal remarks, Millicent," said Frank, "but your slip is showing."

With a gasp of outrage, Mrs. MacLean stepped backwards to check her hem, leaving the path clear for Frank, who ducked past her and out to his car.

\*　　\*　　\*

After making one more stop, at a liquor commission where he purchased two bottles of gin, Frank pulled onto the expressway for the drive out to Willowdale.

When he arrived, he found Estelle shut in her room and pacing the floor in extreme agitation.

"Francis, thank goodness you are here. How much longer

140

do I have to stay?" She paused as the porter came into the room carrying the television set Frank had brought. Frank tipped the porter and he left, closing the door.

"Now, now, Cousin Estelle – Mother, I mean – what seems to be the matter? Has something gone wrong?"

"No, nothing. But don't you see? I have given up everything. Everything!" A dramatic pause followed. "Not only do I have to present myself as a hag, but I have even relinquished my identity."

"I know you have. But you must have understood that when you moved in here. I'm afraid it's a bit late in the game to worry about any identity other than that of Flavia Clarke. But something has obviously upset you."

Estelle sat down abruptly. It is difficult to strike a tragic attitude in a lime-green tight-sleeved bathrobe which falls just to the ankle. "Yesterday evening I was half dead from sheer boredom, so I wheeled, yes wheeled, myself down to the lounge. I thought I would watch a bit of telly. The only other person there was a man, a very old man – although I suppose I'm in no position to throw stones. A talent show was in progress. A young soprano came on to sing the 'Bell Song' from *Lakmé*, in excruciating French, I might add. French diction must be so pointed, so forward. And she had two gestures: ten minutes to two and twenty minutes past eight. But I digress. The man began to speak. He told me about how he had been in Paris before the war. He had seen *Lakmé* at the Opéra with a marvellous soprano, his very words. Her name was Stella della Chiesa. He went on to explain how *Lakmé* is a slight work, really; it stands or falls on the beauty and charm of its star. Stella della Chiesa had both, so he assured me; beauty and the voice of an angel. He once had all her records, but they were sold when he moved out here.

"And there I sat in my wheelchair, no wig, no makeup, no nails, pretending to be that – that dreadful woman. Can you understand what it is to deny yourself? Can you imagine what it cost me not to admit who I really was, the Stella della Chiesa

141

who received an eight-minute ovation for her 'Bell Song'? It's bad enough that youth goes, beauty goes, the voice goes. The talent remains, but what good is it without youth? Talent and memory are all I have left. Now I must even deny my talent. And when you live only in memory you might as well be dead."

"I disagree," replied Frank. "That man, whoever he was, remembers Stella della Chiesa as young, vibrant, beautiful — a *prima donna assoluta*, not an old lady in a wheelchair. For him you will always be the stuff of legend. Wouldn't you prefer not to alter that memory?" Like many basically unfeeling people Frank understood the romantic machinery and was not above manipulating the gears for his own benefit.

Estelle stood and, placing a supplicating hand on Frank's arm, she looked straight into his eyes. "Take me out of here. I can't carry it off. If I were to go back to your mother's house, I could at least move around freely. With no one there I wouldn't have to pretend I'm what I'm not. I only agreed to all this because I was tired, and a little frightened. Please, take me away."

"No, Cousin Estelle, absolutely not. The house is way too vulnerable. Any number of people who know Mother might drop by unexpectedly. The risk of discovery is far too great. You must stay here. Furthermore, I think it would be a good idea if you remained in your room. I've brought you a television set; you have gin; your own bathroom. Continue having meals brought in."

"Can't I even go to the dining room?"

"I think it would be better if you stayed put. The lower the profile, the less the chance of detection. You are Flavia McCutcheon, widowed mother."

"You know something, Francis? I have always played by hunches, and I have never been wrong. Many years ago I was offered a new production of *Catarina Cornaro*. I had always been admired for the way I sang Donizetti. No expense was to be spared on the costumes and staging. The cast, the con-

142

ductor, could not be faulted. But I had a hunch, and refused. My agent was furious; the management pleaded with me, but I remained firm. The production was a complete fiasco. Everyone connected with it had much to live down. Well I have another strong hunch now, Francis. If you don't take me out of this place today, tomorrow, within the week, I will never leave. Don't ask me how I know; I just know. Call it instinct, but I know I am right. I will go anywhere you say, if you will only take me away from here." The urgency of her supplication robbed her of breath. She sat, gripping the arms of her chair and fighting for breath, which came in short, shallow gasps.

Frank gave a shrug of impatience. "Cousin Estelle, from what I have been able to gather you sang in the big league. And even though you may be retired you are still in the big league. This impersonation we are pulling off is not a small-time operation. There is a great deal of money at stake. And, like it or not, we are both in up to our necks. If your identity is so important, go ahead and prove who you are. Wave that passport around. Your name will be smeared across the papers; I will probably end up in jail. In other words, until I have been able to skim off the major portion of Mother's estate, you will stay right here. And that is my last word on the subject."

A nurse knocked and came into the room carrying a lunch tray, which she put onto the small table. With a smile she withdrew, closing the door.

"From *prima donna assoluta* to leek and potato soup with breast of chicken on white," said Estelle with resignation.

"It's only for a short while. For the next few days you are my mother, only that and nothing more. Remember that."

"I shall remember, Francis. I shall remember."

# Chapter 13

Frank was just putting the key into the door of his car when a woman's voice split the silence of the parking lot.

"Frank, for the love of Mike!"

He turned. "Claudia! What in God's name are you doing here?"

"I could ask you the same question. Don't tell me you live here!"

"No, I'm just visiting, an old family friend. I thought you were living in Toronto."

"I am, but my marriage broke up. I'm now the world's oldest swinger."

"Come now, Claudia. Tarzan is the world's oldest swinger. But I thought you had finally found love's young dream. At least that is what you told me over lunch the last time I saw you. How long ago was it?"

"Way too long. Anyhow, my Mr. Wonderful went off to Chicago on a convention last year. He was screwing a call girl when he had a heart attack. He recovered, but I was bored with him. I've got alimony coming out of my ears. And I've taken to wearing black as if I were a widow. Besides it has always suited me, and anyone in black can look like a lady."

Frank had to agree his ex-wife was looking well, considering she was exactly his age. Tall, thin, she had always worn a

144

slightly ravaged look, even as a debutante. Her age had now caught up with her face, gaunt yet handsome under the short page-boy of iron-grey hair. She had always dressed with style, meaning she dressed to suit herself, not to follow the dictates of trends. At first meeting, strangers often found her withdrawn, almost shy as she murmured that her name was to be pronounced as "cloud" followed by "ia." Frank remembered her as being about as shy as a used car salesman, and when she grew angry her vocabulary would have reddened the cheek of a longshoreman.

"What brings you to Montreal?" he asked.

"I'm finally moving Mother out of her apartment. She's ninety-two, can you believe. Eight more years and she'll be a bona fide antique. I've been meaning to call you, but so far I've been swamped. Anyhow I'm about to buy you some lunch. Name a place."

Frank led the way in his car, Claudia following in hers, to a fieldstone farmhouse which had been converted to a restaurant with waiters in sabots and a menu written in florid, illegible calligraphy.

Seated across the table from Frank, Claudia signalled the waiter. "Martini, gin, straight up, twist. Frank?"

"A martini, Claudia? Truth serum. Do you think it's wise?"

"Of course it's not wise, but I'm having one anyway."

"White wine for me, please. A carafe."

"Do you suppose these frogs know how to make a decent martini? Last time I ordered a martini they brought me some filthy red stuff that tasted like cough medicine."

"We call them francophones now, my sweet; unless you want to get yourself lynched."

Claudia lit a cigarette, holding it between nicotine-stained fingers. "You're looking good, Frank. Want to get married again?"

"Not at the moment, thanks."

"You were by far the most entertaining of my husbands.

And the easiest to get along with. Selfish people are always easy to live with, once you get the right wave length. I was a fool to have divorced you."

"The trouble with you, Claudia, was that you got hysterical if there was an erection within a radius of twenty-five miles that wasn't aimed directly at you."

She laughed and lifted her drink. "Mud in your eye. I suppose you're right. Women aren't really very bright. We set our caps for a man, move heaven and earth to land him, then spend our time making him pay for just what we want him to do. Why did you marry me?"

"That's easy. I liked you as well as any woman I ever met, and I loved your solvency. You married me because I was one of the few men you had met who was a decent lay and whom you could introduce to your friends."

"The clarity of hindsight. But there was more. Of all my husbands and lovers, and there have been a few, you were the one who taught me my skin. Maybe because you were so detached. I always suspected you were really making love to yourself, not to me. Unfortunately, passion and narcissism make poor bedfellows." Claudia blew smoke through her nose. "Why did you have to go and spoil things?"

"You kept me on a tight rein, and I got restless. You really didn't mind my having an affair with another man; you minded my having an affair, period. I needed to breathe. It was a pity, in a way. I didn't want to leave you. I just couldn't be on call twenty-four hours a day."

"But, shit, Frank, my best friend's *husband*?"

"Would it have made any difference if she had been your worst enemy?"

"No."

"Besides, you have to admit it was convenient."

Claudia laughed. "I suppose it was terribly middle class of me. And it is good to see you again. It's a pity we had to get divorced to become friends." She signalled for another drink by waving her glass at the waiter. "I realize now that I wasn't the easiest person in the world to live with. Now that I'm seventy, I think I'm about ready to be a really good wife. What's that Pennsylvania Dutch proverb? Something about 'Too soon old; too late smart.' And I'm beginning to feel like the North Pole. Everyone knows where it is but nobody ever goes there. I think it's called old age: when you finally admit to yourself you don't like getting laid on a water bed. And the last orgy I went to looked like the recovery room."

"Find yourself some good-looking hunk who can't afford his college fees and work out a deal. You've got the money. Put it to work productively."

"What a total bastard you are. But, God knows, you come by it honestly. By the way, how is Attila the Hen! I refer to that Presbyterian Sycorax who masquerades as your mother."

"Much the same, only older. I'm thinking of moving her to a home. Maybe even Willowdale, when I can persuade her to give up the house."

"God, how she hated me. Marrying her white-haired boy – and having my own money to boot. Did she put you back in her good graces after the divorce?"

"Yes, but she had a big row with Vivien, who was written out of the will. They haven't spoken in years."

"So now Vivien is out in the cold. How is she, by the way? I haven't seen her since just after Randolph died."

"Vivien is just the same. She was a flower child long before the sixties. She still believes in whole grains and fresh air and being kind to animals."

"Even though I married you, I always thought Vivien was the pick of the litter. I must give her a call and say hello, or would I be violating one of those invisible Clarke guidelines which no outsider can ever learn. Life with your family was like walking through a minefield in spike heels. Still, I'd marry you again, gladly."

Frank grinned. "Give me a frank account. How is your bank account? I'm an expensive hobby."

She finished her second drink. "Seriously, I'm thinking of

moving back to Montreal."

"No reason why you shouldn't. But remember how you always hated the winters."

"I know. But Montreal is a much more approachable city, for a single woman. Like me. Old. I guess you could call me retired, but from what? Toronto is full of single women dashing about between careers and lovers. But I have had the misfortune, or the lack of taste, to grow old. I am not ready to set sail for Little Old Ladyland, nor am I about to pull on a pair of leotards and a smile and do something serious about my hips. The road to good intentions is paved with hell." Catching the waiter's eye, Claudia pointed downward at her glass and at Frank's carafe. "And one of the big problems with sex is that it discriminates against the old, the shy, and the ugly."

"Everything in life discriminates, Claudia. Even the washing machine discriminates between white and coloured." Frank stole a glance at his watch. He wanted to get to the notary's office, and he knew from past experience lunch with Claudia could go on until midnight.

"In a way I have no business complaining," she continued, "but I'm just trying to get things into perspective. I have plenty of money and nothing wrong with me to speak of, none of the horrors that overtake women my age. I still have all my teeth and all my breasts. I don't wear rubber stockings. I belong to the generation who used the greasy kid stuff, so I am not suffering from side effects of the pill. My thighs do not look like cottage cheese, and my ass isn't hanging down to my knees. In short, I am a healthy woman of seventy."

Claudia dragged thoughtfully on her cigarette. "And I am still interested in men, their bodies, their minds, the way they move, the way they smell. I am not one of those bloody tiresome women who profess not to like the company of other women. I have always been very tolerant of other women; some of my best friends, etc. But I do not want my entire social life to be organized around members of my own sex. Last year I went on a Caribbean cruise. The promenade deck

148

looked like widows' walk. I sat at a table in the dining room
with two librarians from Nebraska, a social worker from Guelph,
and an unmarried daughter travelling with her mother, one of
those leeches who suck out every red corpuscle. There were
a few tame husbands, ship's officers, and fags. I didn't even
get to dance; I don't like dancing with other women. I wouldn't
make a very good dyke. Nor do I wish to be taken up by gays.
I don't really see myself as the only woman in a room full of
twenty-five-year-olds in jeans and construction boots who wear
both their earrings in one ear. I'd make an excellent fag hag
if I wanted to. I dress well; I like to drink; I enjoy parties; and
I can be a 'character' or a 'gas' or do schtick or whatever. All
those old routines we used to do. You remember: I learned to
ride a bicycle at six years old and I've been peddling my ass
ever since."

Frank chuckled. "I was up at the crack of dawn, and Dawn
loved it. Then I blew Bubbles."

"I love men in kilts. Once you get past the sporran you've
got it licked."

"You've been abroad; now try being a lady."

"A hard man is good to find."

"Nine out of ten doctors who tried Camels preferred women."

They laughed quietly. "Enough already," said Claudia aim-
ing her long ash at the ashtray, missing by inches. Frank
remembered her as a messy smoker, spewing more ash around
than an active volcano. She took one last drag on the cigarette,
then used the butt to light the next.

"I pay a fortune to live downtown," she said, "as downtown
as one can get in Toronto. And I am not afraid to go out at
night. But it's not much fun going to a restaurant alone, and
if you don't knee the *maitre d'* in the groin he puts you beside
a serving area or right across from the men's toilet. Half the
fun of a movie is talking about it afterward. I have tickets for
the symphony. Most of the time I use the other seat for my
fur coat. I make myself go out. It's so easy to fall back on a
book, television, a highball, or three for company. As I said,

I'm not complaining. I guess I'm just not wild about the idea of spending the next fifteen years alone."

Claudia paused to drag on her cigarette, drawing the smoke deep into her lungs. "But what about you, Frank? Are you still cutting the mustard? Or has The Great Zucchini turned into a mushroom cap?"

"Not really. I think my problem is that the flesh is willing but the spirit is weak. I still have fantasies; who doesn't? But at this point I realize there's no chance of bringing them to life, not even if I pay cash. The gap between imagination and reality is just too wide."

Claudia laughed quietly. "I guess that's the price you pay for over forty years of jumping anything that stood still long enough."

Frank glanced again at his watch. "Claudia, I'm about to expire from malnutrition."

"Poor Frank. I lured you here with a promise of lunch. Why don't you order for both of us. Anything but quiche. And another little martini wouldn't do me any harm. How's your wine?"

\* \* \*

The afternoon had already begun to wane by the time Claudia polished off the wine they had ordered with the meal, drank her third cup of espresso, and paid the lunch cheque. Frank had resigned himself to being held hostage for the afternoon. Claudia did not have much taste for solitude, in spite of protestations to the contrary. Frank remembered she didn't even want to go to the bathroom alone. Short of getting up and stalking from the table he had no alternative but to sit tight and hear her out.

Frank found himself surprised that, in spite of everything on his mind at the moment, he was truly glad to see Claudia again. He had always liked her, but she had been in love with him. Now as Frank sat studying his ex-wife across the table, he realized how few, if any, people in his life he really cared for. The price of an obsession is solitude. Claudia posed no threat, and she would make an excellent travelling companion when he went to Europe to search out drawings. She quite obviously still had her money and for that reason alone was well worth cultivating. Frank decided that, having re-established contact with her, it might be a very good idea to keep in touch.

After a long and maudlin goodbye scene in the parking lot, during which they reiterated that they must get together soon, very soon, Frank poured Claudia behind the wheel of her car and she tore out of the parking lot on three wheels.

At a more sedate pace he drove back to his apartment. By now it was too late to swing by the notary's office. It was also too late to call stockbrokers with orders to sell. Lunch with Claudia had set him back one full day. Frank struck the steering wheel in a gesture of impatience. Still, it had been his own choice. If Claudia had made him captive, he had been a willing victim. To calm himself he thought of his mother's Government of Canada bonds tidily turned into a U.S. dollar term deposit issued in his own name. Tomorrow morning after the funeral service he would have to get busy.

No sooner had he closed the front door behind him than the doorbell rang. It was almost as if the person outside had been awaiting his return.

Frank opened the door to find Nurse Harrison standing in the hall. For a fraction of a second he did not recognize her out of uniform and wearing what looked like her second-best dress. Eyeshadow coated her lids. His first impulse was to shut the door in her face, but caution dictated at least token courtesy.

"Oh, excuse me, Mr. Clarke; but I was wondering if I might have a word with you." Her voice managed at once to be obsequious and bullying. "I found your address in the phonebook by matching it up with the phone number you gave me in case of emergency."

"Come inside, Nurse Harrison." Frank led the way into his living room. He did not offer to take her coat, he did not offer her a drink. "Sit down, please."

After looking uncertainly around the room, she seated herself on one of a pair of art deco armchairs upholstered in black velvet, self-consciously not resting her elbows on the lucite arms. Knees pressed together, she sat straight, her hands folded over her purse.

"What can I do for you?" Frank's tone was brusque.

"Well, sir, I learned from the agency that you moved Mrs. Clarke out to Willowdale. Very suddenly too. I was sorry not to have a chance to say goodbye to the patient, such a lovely lady. I have a friend, Ruby Turner, who is working on a case at Willowdale; and I asked Ruby if she would drive me out with a nice begonia I had for your mother."

If Frank felt apprehension bordering on panic he did not let it show. "Yes, go on," he said flatly.

"Well, I inquired at the desk for your mother's room. 'Mrs. Flavia Clarke,' I says. 'We have no one of that name,' the girl says. 'Did a new patient come in yesterday?' I says. 'Yes, a Flavia McCutcheon,' she says. I remembered that was your mother's maiden name, wasn't it? 'But she's to have no visitors,' the girl says. 'What a shame,' I says. 'I brought her this plant.' 'Leave it with me,' she says, 'I'll see she gets it.' I thanked her and made as if to leave, checking the register to find the room number, 336. I once worked at Willowdale so I know the building. I went out the front door and around to the parking lot and in the side entrance. I went up the fire escape to the third floor and knocked at the door of your mother's room."

"But there is a No Visitors sign on the door. And it means just that: no visitors!" Frank fought the urge to strike the woman. Her pancake makeup would come off on his hand.

"Someone who's been on the case as long as me can't hardly be called a visitor. There wasn't any sign on the door. If you gave orders to have one put there they haven't been followed.

I wanted to offer my condolences on her cousin's, Mrs. Church's, death. Such a lovely lady she was too, and so elegant. I read about her death in the paper this morning. I always read the obituary column; I like to keep track of my ex-patients. You never know when they might leave a little something to a nurse, out of gratitude." Nurse Harrison's voice rang smugly, hinting at revelations to follow. "So I knocked at your mother's door. 'Come in,' says a man's voice. I opened the door. There was an old woman in the chair with a man and two nurses standing beside her."

"Probably the doctor," said Frank.

"No, sir. The doctor at Willowdale is Dr. Patrick. He's an older man, bald with glasses. This man was young. But the woman in that chair was not Mrs. Clarke. 'Excuse me,' I says from the hall. 'I must have the wrong room.' I shut the door, but 336 was the number, sure enough. As I walked away I realized I had seen that woman somewheres before. It took me a bit to realize she was that relative, in the black wig, the one as was supposed to have died. 'Goodness me,' I says to myself, 'why is that woman in Mrs. Clarke's room at Willowdale and not Mrs. Clarke?' I know it's none of my business, but I venture to say there's others would be curious too, and maybe as to who, if anyone, is going to be cremated tomorrow morning." Nurse Harrison toyed with the strap of her calfskin handbag, a gift from a former patient and hardly used at all.

"What, precisely, are you getting at?"

"Well, sir, I don't want to make no trouble for nobody. I'm just a poor woman trying to put something aside for her old age." For the first time Nurse Harrison looked directly at Frank. "I was thinking you might be willing to help me out."

Frank thought quickly. To pay money for her silence, allowing himself to be blackmailed, would be to admit he had something to hide. Moreover blackmail never stopped with one payment. Neither admitting to nor denying her suspicions, but mounting a counter offensive seemed the better course.

"Why should I want to help you out for poking your nose

into matters that don't concern you? And since you have taken the trouble to drop by, perhaps you could tell me what has happened to my mother's silver tea service."

"Her tea service?"

"You heard me. I noticed yesterday morning it was gone. Now if you will just return it to me quietly I will not take any further action. Remember, the agency employees are supposed to be bonded. You would never work again in this city were you to be accused of theft."

Nurse Harrison's fleshy cheeks trembled with outrage. "I never did anything of the sort. If there's things taken it's Gibson what did it."

"Nurse Gibson may drink a little, but she is not a thief."

"Then it's the cleaning woman, or that foreign cook."

"No, Nurse Harrison. It was on the dining room sideboard the afternoon I had tea with Mrs. Church. The following morning it was gone. You took that night shift, if you remember."

"But you yourself told me to go home early. How could I have taken it with you there?"

Frank smiled patiently. "You had all night to hide the service, in a shopping bag, in the bushes beside the front porch. Once the front door had closed you had only to carry it away."

Her face flushed, Nurse Harrison rose to her feet. The quilted coat she wore looked like a tea cosy. "Mr. Clarke, I did not take your mother's silver. I swear it!"

"Think it over, Nurse Harrison. Simply return the tea service in the next day or so and we will say no more about it. Goodnight." Frank moved to open the front door through which Nurse Harrison flounced in medium-heel pumps she could not quite control.

Frank shut the door firmly behind her. In a way he felt lucky that the discovery had been made by someone who did not understand the true value of the information. But it nettled him to have Nurse Harrison in the know; Frank had a keen dislike of loose ends. Maybe, just maybe, Nurse Harrison would have to be dealt with. It would mean hiring a hit man, an added expense, not to mention the sheer nuisance of finding one. Finding a reliable hit man was even more difficult than finding a good cleaning woman, although their functions were similar. They both tidied up mess made by others, for a fee. Only a hit man did not expect bus fare and lunch.

Frank put the intrusion of Nurse Harrison temporarily on hold as he tried to figure out the identity of the man in the room with Estelle when Nurse Harrison opened the door. By her own admission it had not been the doctor; nor did the description fit the director. And to the best of Frank's knowledge the rest of the Willowdale staff, dietician, physiotherapist, recreation director, was female. Nor did Estelle know anyone in the city, outside of Frank himself and Vivien. He thought of calling the nursing home and asking Estelle about the man in her room, but he did not want to break his own rule of no incoming calls. He would have to speak to Estelle tomorrow about making a no-visitors request herself; it would have more impact coming from her.

Less than forty-eight hours had passed since Frank had discovered his mother dead. In the brief seconds during which he made his decision, the whole scheme had seemed impossibly easy. All he had to overcome was Estelle's initial reluctance before everything else fell neatly into place. But problems had begun to crop up. How long would it be before Nurse Harrison called his bluff? Who was that strange man in the room with Estelle? How soon would someone with more credibility than Nurse Harrison make the discovery of Estelle in his mother's room? Frank took three deep breaths, forcing himself to remain calm. He would find solutions. He had to. There was no turning back now.

*   *   *

While Frank sat pondering the dual problem of Nurse Harrison and the unidentified man in Estelle's room, Nurse Harrison walked towards her bus stop, her outrage at being falsely

155

accused of theft slowly turning to anger at how she had been deflected from the purpose of her visit. She had arrived at Mr. Clarke's door prepared to blackmail him, only to be called a thief and turned out the door. Or had he been bluffing? Although not intelligent, Nurse Harrison had native cunning. She knew she was innocent of theft, but it remained Mr. Clarke's word against hers. Innocent or guilty made no difference; the accusation would stain her reputation with the agency. Still, Nurse Harrison knew something fishy was going on at the nursing home. Whatever it was needed investigating. She knew from watching television that a private investigator could find out the real story; but she also knew he would charge enormous fees, drink heavily, and chase women. Would she be able to recover her costs? How to uncover the truth and then how best to exploit the knowledge occupied her as she walked, her handbag tucked safely under her arm as it held her last cheque from the agency.

The night blew soft with that mellow October air which belies the imminent onslaught of winter. Nurse Harrison decided to save steps and cut through the park to Sherbrooke Street and her bus stop. It was a well-lighted park, with broad walks, a football field: safe, visible. So deeply immersed was she in thought that she did not hear footsteps approaching until the two young men, footpads in jogging shoes, were beside her.

"Excuse me," said one as he jostled her off balance while the other made a grab for her purse. She stumbled, losing one of her shoes, but holding on grimly to the straps of her handbag. Making a fist of her free hand she punched the young man grabbing for her purse in the nose, not hard, but hard enough to make him back off in surprise. In a flash she picked up her discarded shoe which she held by the toe as a club. Striking out with the heel she landed a sharp blow on each of her assailants, as attested by "Jesus Christ!" and "Goddamn!"

Nurse Harrison began to run towards Sherbrooke Street, only a couple of hundred yards away. Clumsily, one shoe on, the other in her hand, she cantered away from her attackers, who faded into shadow. Totally unaccustomed to running, moreover on grass, Florence Harrison appeared to gain momentum through the same principle of physics that sends an avalanche down the side of a mountain. Stumbling, panting, close to hysteria, she approached Sherbrooke Street and attempted to slow down as she reached the edge of the sidewalk. Miscalculating her momentum she was propelled across the sidewalk where the foot still wearing the shoe caught the edge of the concrete walk, tipping her forward into the street and directly into the path of an oncoming automobile travelling well beyond the speed limit. Stiff with lacquer, Nurse Harrison's hair survived the accident unmussed; and the eyeshadow gave an almost piquant expression to her wide-open, terrified eyes.

# Chapter 14

In the morning, after checking the obits, Frank turned back to page one and scanned the headlines. Although there had been no names for the biscuit box in today's Births and Deaths, Frank was far too preoccupied to care. He had passed a fitful night, floating uneasily in that limbo between sleep and waking when perceived reality finds itself invaded by phantoms and fantasies, disjointed and unreal. Nurse Harrison, a rope around her short neck, swung gently from the branch of a dead elm tree; she lay quietly, as if asleep, riddled with submachine-gun bullets in a north-end back alley; she rested comfortably in a block of cement at the bottom of the St. Lawrence River beneath the Jacques Cartier Bridge.

Still groggy, he almost failed to notice the story on page five, a short item about an accident, on Sherbrooke Street. The phrase, "near Westmount Park" happened to catch his eye and he read the brief account once, then a second time, and again a third, before snipping it neatly out of the paper. He sat stunned, the extent of his good fortune just beginning to be realized. Not once during the night, not even when his feverish fantasies turned her towards martyrdom – with Nurse Harrison in a shift being devoured by lions or turned on a wheel of spikes – had he even remotely conceived of the possibility of a simple, straightforward accident.

Frank slipped the item about Nurse Harrison into the biscuit box. As he showered and shaved, he ran through his list of chores for the day: driving Vivien to and from the funeral service, collecting his powers of·attorney, speaking to the director of Willowdale about Estelle's isolation, finding out about the man in her room. Oh, yes, he must remember to deliver the Highland cattle to Aunt Phyllis and let the locksmith into the big house.

Frank drove to Vivien's condominium to pick her up. So immersed was he in his colossal good fortune, almost an omen, had he allowed himself to believe in such nonsense, he took no notice of Vivien's stony silence as she climbed stiffly into the front seat of his car for the drive up to the crematorium.

Through the narrow, twisting roads of Mount Royal Cemetery they drove, past kneeling marble angels, draped basalt urns, and slender granite obelisks, to the crematorium situated on the crest of the mountain affording a sweep of autumn landscape. At the entrance skulked a solitary official. The arrival of the minister brought the population to four.

Frank and Vivien stepped inside at the minister's request to sign the death certificate, attesting that Estelle Church, aged eighty-seven years, residing in the City of Westmount, Province of Quebec, widow of Neville Church, died on the fourth day of October in the year one thousand nine hundred and eighty-three, and after divine service conducted by him was cremated at the Mount Royal Cemetery in the aforesaid Province of Quebec on the sixth day of October in the same year.

The minister signed, Vivien signed, Frank signed, before the three of them went into the small chapel, bathed in shafts of coloured light from stained glass windows Frank privately classified as tart nouveau.

"Let's not sit together," he whispered to his sister. "If we sit in separate pews we will look like more people."

"That's not funny," replied Vivien, for whom death was no laughing matter. They compromised by sitting in the second row.

During the brief service, Frank fixed his gaze on a point

somewhere behind the minister's right shoulder. As he listened to the familiar words of the funeral rites, Frank found himself assailed by feelings he had heretofore ignored, or denied. Up to this point his mother's death had been viewed as a problem to be solved, not as an emotional milestone to be surmounted. Anything even remotely approaching grief had been vigorously suppressed. But now, seated beside his sister in the empty chapel, Frank found his defences crumbling.

Flashes of memory flickered into his consciousness, eroding the image he had fastened onto of an overbearing, self-centred old woman. There was that other woman who had helped him to wash and dress and eat after he broke his arm in a fall from a tree. There was the woman who had allowed Vivien and Frank to dress up in her discarded evening clothes while Vivien played out her fantasies of being an actress. There was the woman who had stood between Frank and the beatings Mr. Clarke felt were his son's due, on the premise that adversity builds character. Memories of the woman who had laughed with Frank over the eccentricities of guests in hotel dining rooms, whose knowledge of old china verged on expertise, whose unshakable assurance that simply because she was who she was doors would open, surged in on Frank and temporarily blotted out the termagant she had become. For a few moments Frank had to face the idea that the body in the coffin belonged to his mother, the person who for seventy years had been the dominant figure in his life.

Lost in reverie, Frank barely noticed that Vivien had stood and was moving towards the door. The minister held out a hand, like an usher in a concert hall, as he waited for Frank to follow. It was not until he had walked out of the chapel after Vivien and shaken hands with the minister that Frank realized, with the sudden tightness in the stomach one feels as a car skids, that he had reached the point of no return. Up to this moment he could still have confessed the deception, produced his mother's body, and taken the consequences, most probably a stiff fine. No longer. And the road not taken led directly to jail.

Vivien stood outside the car, pointedly not getting in although Frank had not bothered to lock the door. Still almost dazed by the bombardment of unfamiliar emotions, Frank remembered that he had a long list of things to do, none of which he felt much like doing. A machine had been set in motion which did not permit time for regret or remorse.

He opened the door on the driver's side. "Coming?"

Vivien Howard faced her brother across the roof of his car. "Frank, what happened to Randolph's paintings, the ones at Mother's house?"

Totally unprepared for the question, Frank almost shook himself to clear his head before answering. "I don't know. I think they got moved upstairs."

"Yes, they did. But they are no longer there, or anywhere else in the house."

"Are you sure? And how, may I ask, do you know this?"

"Quite sure. I let myself in two days ago, while you drove Mother out to Willowdale. I went through the entire house, top to bottom, and not a single painting or drawing could I find, unless they are stacked in the basement, and I think that unlikely. Did you sell them?"

"Me?"

"Yes, you! Look at me, Frank. Look straight into my eyes. Did you sell those paintings?"

"No."

"You're lying. I can tell by the way your pupils dilate. Your pupils always dilate when you tell a lie. I have been able to tell since you were a small boy. And even though I could not see your eyes I know you lied to me on the telephone yesterday. I know Mother wouldn't have sold them. She certainly didn't need the money and she never gets rid of anything. "What did you do with the money?"

"I spent it."

"Frank, I have never blamed you for being the favourite child, or for being the sole heir outside of Maple Grove. But I had counted on those paintings; they were my – pension plan. You had no right to sell them. They weren't even yours."

Taken aback by Vivien's accusations, Frank tried for what he thought a reasonable tone of voice.

"If you want to pick legal nits, Vivien, they weren't yours either. Randolph gave the paintings to Mother and Father. They accepted them. The paintings therefore became their property. When Father died his possessions went to Mother. The paintings were hers."

"What right had you to sell her things?"

"My power of attorney gives me control of all her property."

"You disposed of those paintings long before you had power of attorney, along with Grandmother's tea service, and Father's Morrice. You have been stealing from your own mother."

"Haven't I helped you out financially over the years?"

"Yes, you have. But I had no idea your handouts were underwritten by the sale of Randolph's paintings. I would have refused, had I known. You can be as legalistic as you like, Frank, but morally those paintings were mine. I can still hear Randolph saying to Mother, 'If you ever get bored with this, ma'am, just give it back and I'll paint you another.' He wanted those paintings to come back to me when Mother dies; he told me so many times. They were all I wanted from Mother's estate. I don't want to live on humiliating handouts from you, whenever you happen to remember. I have always shied away from taking legal action. There is something dreadfully ugly about members of the same family in court. But you have behaved dishonestly. You have abused a position of authority and trust."

The prospect of being taken to court by his sister did not please Frank one bit. Even if her case were weak she could cause delays, tie up the final settlement, call his transactions into question.

"All right. Suppose I were to reimburse the money. Suppose I were to pay you whatever I received for the paintings."

"You sold too soon. There will be a retrospective of Randolph's works at the National Gallery. After that exhibition, prices for his paintings will soar. And even if you were to offer me what Mother's paintings are currently worth, the fact remains that you have behaved dishonestly. How much else you have sold is open to speculation. However, it is not for me to judge, but for the law."

Frank walked around to stand on the same side of the car as his sister. "Be reasonable, Vivien. I did not sell those paintings to do you out of anything. I sold them because I needed cash—and so did you. You make me out to be little better than a common thief."

Vivien looked straight at her brother with an expression far more eloquent than words. Then she started to walk away, her rubber-soled black Wallabies just visible beneath her ankle-length black cotton skirt.

"Don't you want a lift back home?" Frank offered.

"No, thank you; I'll walk."

"It's a long way."

But Vivien had moved out of earshot. Frank started his car and turned it towards the south gate of the cemetery. "Sure you won't change your mind?" he asked, slowing down beside his striding sister. By way of reply she shook her head, and Frank drove away.

It really did not seem terribly likely that Vivien would take him to court. For one thing she had no money. And justice, like other highly-priced commodities, is more readily accessible to the rich.

As he pulled through the gates of the cemetery Frank could not help feeling satisfaction at how he had resisted the urge to sell Randolph Howard's drawings. A couple of times when funds were low he had been sorely tempted. Maybe he should return them to Vivien, partial restoration for the paintings he had sold. But with the sudden blossoming of Randolph Howard's reputation, Frank realized the drawings would be a valuable asset to The Frank Clarke Collection. The words alone had a comforting ring. And regardless of right or wrong, Frank understood he would not return the drawings to Vivien. He would have liked to, but the claims of The Collection pulled far more strongly than family ties. Even the shame he could not prevent himself from feeling at the idea of defrauding his sister did not really change anything.

Frank eased his car into the flow of traffic. By the time he pulled to a stop in front of his building, he had fallen into such a heaviness of spirit, he could barely pull himself from behind the wheel. He had alienated his sister, browbeaten and humiliated Estelle, and turned his mother's body into an accessory by falsely signing a document. He had behaved abominably. But even more compelling than his keen awareness of wrongdoing was the certainty that given another chance he would behave in exactly the same way. Like someone caught in the grip of drink or drugs or gambling, Frank had become obsessed with The Collection. His memorial after death had taken over his life. He was, he thought to himself, circumscribed by his obsession just as his three goldfish were trapped inside their transparent but impenetrable wall of glass.

Frank plodded up the stairs to his apartment and let himself in. He picked up his briefcase, and was sorting over in his mind the errands he had to do, when it occurred to him that he had better feed the fish before going out. As he was about to shake the dry flakes of food into the water, Frank glanced into the bowl to see the fantail, his favourite of the three, floating motionless on the surface, its gills totally without movement. Almost to his surprise Frank heard a sound, as of someone weeping.

Some moments passed before he realized the tears were his own.

* * *

Vivien Howard had continued to stride along the cemetery road until she was certain Frank had lost sight of her in his rear-view mirror. Once his car was safely out of sight she had slowed to a more moderate pace. Pride has its price. Not only was she some miles from home, she was a fair distance from a main thoroughfare where she could catch a bus. The day enveloped her like a quilt. Filled with echoes of summer, the air had not yet begun to reverberate with the metallic overtones of winter. She continued to walk, past grassy islands dotted with gravestones and isolated by bands of asphalt, an archipelago of the dead. Many of the gravestones resembled altars where the living propitiated their bad consciences with visits and flowers, which faded and died within hours. It occurred to Vivien that no one ever offered anything of value to their dead. No headstone ever found itself draped with a mink coat; no jewel casket was ever laid lovingly on the grass. Only flowers; sometimes plastic.

It was such beautiful weather, Vivien thought she would visit the Howard family plot, and Randolph's grave. Then she remembered that it was located on the other side of the cemetery. A few years ago she would have relished a walk through the grounds on a beautiful autumn day. Now she realized it would take all her energy just to reach the cemetery gates. Reluctantly she abandoned the idea of making a detour and began to walk in the direction of the exit.

By the time she found her way out of the cemetery, having taken two wrong turns, she was heartily tired of walking. Her knees ached; her feet hurt; her back had begun to grumble. The temptation to flag down a taxi was almost overwhelming, but a cab ride to her house would have cost several dollars. Vivien reconsidered and, fishing a brilliant orange senior citizens' ticket from her handbag, she walked to the nearest bus stop.

One hour and two transfers later she opened her front door and went wearily inside. After hanging up her folded black shawl she lowered herself gratefully into a chair and, bending over with no little discomfort, she unlaced her shoes. A sigh of pure satisfaction announced that she had at last freed her feet from their painful confinement.

At that precise moment the doorbell rang. "Damn!" thought Vivien, still mindful after all these years of her mother's injunction that to answer the door without shoes was what they did in the slums. The bell rang a second time. Vivien slowly pushed herself upright and crossed in stocking feet to open the door, slipping on the safety chain before turning back the lock.

"Mrs. Vivien Howard?" inquired a young man standing on the doormat of fake grass whose ornamental plastic daisy resembled a notarial seal. He wore the livery of a courier service.

"Yes, I am she."

"Package for you, ma'am."

Vivien released the chain and opened the door. The young man handed her a heavy package wrapped in brown paper.

"Sign here, please."

Putting the package onto the roll-top desk, Vivien wrote her name in the indicated space, and the man left.

Vivien cut the string and tore off the brown paper. Inside was a metal box, roughly twelve inches long, eight inches wide, six inches deep. An ordinary size-eight white business envelope scotch-taped to the top carried her name. Inside the envelope, on a piece of Manoir Willowdale Manor letterhead was the message: "For my daughter Vivien Howard, to be held until further notification." The box had been locked, but neither the package nor the envelope contained a key.

A frankly astonished Vivien studied the box, the first communication from her mother since the battle of the figurines. However, astonishment soon gave way to a host of new feelings, foremost of which was raw curiosity. What lay under the locked lid? She burned to know. And the lock, made for a small key with a hollow bore, would be easy to pry open. But Vivien was a woman of character; no Christmas present had ever been opened before Christmas morning. Until such time as her mother was called to Abraham's bosom, the mystery box must remain shut.

And yet; and yet. Did the very presence of the box hint at the possibility of reconciliation? Vivien reread the note: "until further notification." Was there to be further communication? And if so, when? But, resolved, Vivien carried the box into the kitchen. Standing on a chair, she put the metal strongbox onto the topmost shelf of a kitchen cupboard. Out of sight, out of mind, as her mother was fond of saying.

Suddenly exhausted by the morning's events, Vivien went into her bedroom and lay down. While trying to imagine what might be in the box, out of sight perhaps but definitely not out of mind, she faded into sleep.

# Chapter 15

Phyllis Coughlin resided at Trillium Towers, a complex of flats for still mobile geriatrics which boasted a restaurant, a resident nurse, and weekly bingo. Earlier that morning she had sat in the robin's-egg blue and canary-yellow dining room watching a square of butter melt into her soft-boiled egg as her mind addressed itself to the problem of how to get out to Willowdale Manor without being obliged to pay for a cab. In spite of Frank's repeated injunction about no visitors, she could not postpone the pleasure of smothering her sister-in-law with condolences on having to leave her home. Furthermore Phyllis Coughlin refused to think of herself as a visitor; she was family. And who was Francis, whom she had known since his conception, to tell her she was not to visit her own late brother's widow.

Mrs. Coughlin had a mind which filed away stray bits of information with an almost mathematical precision. She remembered that Grace McSween had an aunt living at Willowdale, very happily it would seem, what with French lessons and bi-weekly crafts. Grace McSween had let this information drop some time during the Medford wedding. Every two weeks or so Mrs. McSween said she armed herself with a potted plant and drove out to Willowdale for an hour's visit.

As was her custom each morning after breakfast, Mrs. Coughlin returned to her room for an hour or so on the telephone before she went out. This morning her first call was to Grace McSween to request a lift the next time she drove out to the nursing home. But of course, replied the good-natured Mrs. McSween. How about this very afternoon? She was just on her way to the florist to buy a nice mum plant; they did last so well. Or perhaps a gloxinia. Did Mrs. Coughlin think her Aunt Thelma might prefer a gloxinia?

Mrs. Coughlin opted for the gloxinia and asked what time she should be ready to leave.

Early afternoon found Grace McSween pulling onto the freeway with carefree abandon while she rattled on to Phyllis Coughlin about the Medford wedding and how lovely it had been; the hum of traffic almost but not quite obliterating the sound of her voice in Mrs. Coughlin's deaf ears. As good manners dictated she look at the person to whom she was speaking, Mrs. McSween was the sort of driver who kept a passenger's eyes nervously glued to the road.

By the time Mrs. McSween pulled into the parking lot at Willowdale and stopped the car with a bone-rattling jolt, Phyllis Coughlin's nerves were in a state. The two women threaded their way through wheelchairs pushed by bored nurses and pushed through swinging doors into the foyer, carpeted in orange and yellow chevrons chosen for their cheering effect on the patients. They agreed to meet at the front desk in an hour's time, and Grace McSween with her potted plant disappeared into the elevator.

Phyllis Coughlin approached the receptionist who was presently engaged on the telephone.

Finally replacing the receiver the young woman smiled at Mrs. Coughlin. "May I help you?"

"Mrs. Flavia Clarke. Which is her room?"

The receptionist consulted a ledger. "We have no Mrs. Clarke registered here."

"But of course you do. My sister-in-law, Flavia Clarke. You can't have mislaid her in two days!"

The receptionist consulted her register a second time. "A Mrs. Flavia McCutcheon moved in two days ago. Could it be the same party?"

"Naturally it's the same party. Although why she has reverted to her maiden name, I'll never know. What is her room number?"

"Room 336. But Mrs. McCutcheon is not receiving visitors, at least not until further notice."

"But I'm her sister-in-law."

"Sorry, madame, but her son was very firm on the subject. No visitors, no telephone calls."

"I see. Very well, then, since I'm here I may as well visit Celia Thornton. We went to school together. She used to be very musical; played the piano beautifully. But she gave it all up when the children arrived."

"Mrs. Thornton is in Room 217."

Inclining her head just a shade by way of *noblesse oblige*, Phyllis Coughlin walked across and into the elevator where she pressed button number three. Stepping out onto the third floor, she paused for a moment, uncertain which way to turn.

"They've got me prisoner. Help me to get away," wheezed an old man apparently tied into his wheelchair, who made a grab for the hem of Phyllis Coughlin's camel-hair coat.

"You are mistaken, my good man. This is a nursing home, not a jail," she replied, impatient with any form of senile decay which, in her opinion, revealed lack of character.

In the lounge, two of the more mobile residents were arguing over whether to watch an English or a French television channel.

"French bitch!" cried one.

"*Maudite vache anglaise!*" shouted the other.

Pulling, shoving, they hit at one another with feeble fists until a nurse, her professional smile pasted on, stepped in to referee.

"Girls, girls," she scolded, separating them none too gently as she pried gnarled fingers from yellow-streaked white hair.

Standing resolutely between them, she proceeded to administer the kind of lecture on sharing one might give to four-year-olds with a bag of jelly beans.

To the right were the even-numbered rooms. Steadfastly refusing the help of her cane, Phyllis Coughlin made her way down the passageway past tonally inaccurate reproductions of the French Impressionists.

An old woman in a sleazy peignoir lounged in her doorway. "If it's action you're looking for, honey, try the second floor," she offered.

Phyllis Coughlin swept by and onwards to the end of the corridor where she stopped in front of room 336 and rapped sharply on the door with the head of her cane.

"Come in," growled a voice, almost masculine in its gruffness.

Phyllis Coughlin opened the door, and walked into the room.

In an armchair sat a woman engaged in the act of blowing her nose with great vigour. Only after the person had taken the tissue from her face did Phyllis Coughlin realize that this woman was not her sister-in-law.

"Excuse me," said the woman to Phyllis Coughlin in a voice which could never be mistaken for Flavia's, "but I seem to have caught a cold. Were you looking for someone?"

"Yes, I was; but you are obviously not she. I must have the wrong room. Excuse me." Phyllis Coughlin withdrew, closing the door behind her. Standing once more in the hallway, she double-checked the room number: 336, beyond any doubt. Tilting her head back so as to look through the very bottom of her bifocals, she managed to make out the typed letters beneath the room number: Mrs. Flavia McCutcheon. Mystified, and not a little cross, Phyllis Coughlin walked towards the elevator.

"I told you to go down to two, dearie," said the hussy in the tatty dressing gown.

"Please get me out of here," whispered the old fool in the wheelchair.

171

Peace had descended on the lounge, which was presently deserted.

Totally forgetting her erstwhile musical friend on the second floor, Phyllis Coughlin returned to the lobby and crossed to the master list of residents on a wall in a large glass case. "F. McCutcheon: Room 336" was clearly spelled out in white letters slotted into the black board.

Mrs. Coughlin marched up to the desk. "Where is my sister-in-law?" she demanded, interrupting the receptionist who was talking to one of the nurses.

"I beg your pardon?"

"My sister-in-law, Flavia Clarke, McCutcheon – or whatever she chooses to call herself. The woman in her room is not my sister-in-law." Mrs. Coughlin banged her cane on the floor for emphasis.

"I told you Mrs. McCutcheon is not to have visitors," replied the receptionist in a voice tinged with institutional reproach.

"I am not a visitor; I am her late husband's sister. She must be in some other room. Now I want to know which one."

Accustomed to dealing with the dotty, the receptionist clamped her teeth together and parted her lips. The result passed for a smile.

"The woman in Room 336 is Mrs. Flavia McCutcheon. She arrived two days ago. She was to receive no calls or visitors. That is all the information I have at present. If you have any further questions you will have to speak to the director."

"Where is he?"

"He had to go out. I expect him back in an hour or so."

"I'll wait." Phyllis Coughlin went to sit in a chair facing the elevator, where she sat for the rest of the hour watching the depressing spectacle of her contemporaries shuffling, limping, wheeling themselves by.

The most logical explanation that presented itself to Mrs. Coughlin was that somehow rooms had been mixed up, and somewhere in this building her sister-in-law sat behind a door with someone else's name on it, probably that of the woman

172

who presently occupied Flavia's room. It was outrageous, when one thought of the monthly rates charged by Willowdale. Good heavens! A king's ransom for a room and they can't even keep track of who is where. Mrs. Coughlin had every intention of giving the director a piece of her mind.

The elevator door opened to reveal Grace McSween, somewhat depleted after an hour with her aunt.

"Are you ready to leave, Mrs. Coughlin?"

"I have to speak to the director."

Grace McSween glanced at her watch. "I'm afraid I am due at the dentist in an hour or so, so I will have to leave now. The girl at the desk will call you a taxi."

"It can wait," replied Phyllis Coughlin rising to her feet. It really was Francis's responsibility to sort things out; he was Flavia's attorney, after all. And she was going to call him the second she got home.

"How is Mrs. Clarke?" asked Grace McSween as they walked to the car.

"She was asleep," snapped Phyllis Coughlin.

"A move can be so tiring."

The two women seated themselves in the car. Disinclined to chat further, Grace McSween found some nice Mozart on the radio. Phyllis Coughlin felt relief at not having to converse, preoccupied as she was with the condition of her nerves, the whereabouts of her sister-in-law, and disappointment at not having been able to give the director what for.

# Chapter 16

After pulling himself together, Frank flushed the dead fantail down the toilet. Then he telephoned three stockbrokers whom he had not called in over a week and gave the orders to sell that he ought to have given yesterday. To expedite matters he offered to deliver the stock certificates along with a certified copy of his power of attorney later that day. He then called the locksmith and cancelled the order for a new lock on his mother's front door. Vivien knew the truth about the paintings so what was the point?

Frank drove up the hill to his mother's house where he let himself in through the rear door. Going at once into the dining room he lifted the painting of the Highland cattle in its ornate gold frame off the wall. A shaggy bull standing on a knoll surveyed his ruminating cows against a blurred backdrop of lakes, mountains, and mist. Frank blew dust from the top of the frame. Along with windows and telephones, cleaning women never touched picture frames.

Lifting the painting into the back seat of his car, Frank drove down the hill and across the Lachine Canal, a romantically named ditch filled with water the colour of putty. He pulled to a stop in front of Trillium Towers, where he left the painting with the receptionist for delivery to his aunt.

"Scotch cows! How different!"

Frank charmed her with a smile and returned to his car. His

next stop was the bank, where once again the obliging young woman, only too anxious to help this sweet old man, carried the heavy strongbox into a cubicle to place on the desk. Frank took out several stock certificates. How beautiful they were, crisp and angular, like new money. Each certificate was surmounted by an engraving in pastel tints of a chastely sensual male or female nude, a bit of casual drapery concealing that which would have been most interesting to observe. Suitable for framing, every one.

But damn Vivien! No sooner had he crawled out from under the Nurse Harrison situation than Vivien was threatening to take him to court, even though she couldn't afford to. Fortunately she did not realize how vulnerable he was at this moment, nor must she ever find out. He really had to try for reconciliation, or at least détente. At all costs, Vivien must be dissuaded from following through with her threat, and Frank had just the ticket.

He lifted out a small chamois bag from the safety deposit box and slid it into his jacket pocket.

After leaving the bank he went to the notary's. The suite of offices occupied by the firm of Maxwell, Perkins, Smith, and Latulippe had been furnished with beige discretion. Everywhere muted browns and rounded contours suggested tact, prudence, secrecy. Behind a desk sat a secretary, red-eyed and looking as though she were in the last throes of a tragic love affair.

"Good borning, bay I help you?" she inquired in a voice clotted with cold.

"Good morning. I am Frank Clarke. I believe you have some copies of my power of attorney."

"I'b sorry, Bister Clarke, but they aren't ready yet. They have been run through the photocopying bachine, but Bister Perkins hasn't had a chance to sign them. He was sick yesterday and he's dot id the office just dow. It's this cold . . . ." A sudden sneeze engulfed her as she gave herself up in total sensuous abandon to its delicious, wracking spasm.

"I see," he said crossly. "And when do you suppose I may collect them?"

Still euphoric from her sneeze, the girl pulled him into focus through bleary, blissful eyes. "Toborrow, toborrow borning. Without fail. We are so terribly behind we . . . ."

Frank could see another sneeze on its way. "Tomorrow morning then," he said, ducking out the door before it struck.

A disgruntled Frank rode down in the elevator. Without notarized copies of his power of attorney there was little point in delivering stock certificates to brokers. An unnecessary day's delay. Damn! However, there seemed to be little he could do but wait. He must continue to maintain as low a profile as possible.

Consumed with restless energy he drove out to Willowdale. Before going up to Estelle's room he asked to speak to the director and was shown into an office that reflected the man himself: a synthesis of synthetics. Formica coated the desk, nylon covered the floor, varethaned veneer clad the walls. On a plastic table beside a vinyl chair sat a melmac ashtray for visitors.

Frank sat waiting impatiently; the office did not lend itself to quiet reflection. He crossed the lobby to stand at the open door of a large bright room which resembled a kindergarten classroom; but the students, seated either on vinyl stacking chairs or in wheelchairs, were all comfortably into their eighties. A middle-aged woman, whose fixed smile hinted at desperation, and whose French roll was beginning to unravel, was trying to teach a French class. A green blackboard on wheels faced the room whose occupants erupted into a hiss of whispers each time the teacher turned her back to write.

"Now, then, everyone, repeat after me," she began, pushing her voice way up into its head register so she managed to sound at once cheerful and hysterical: "*La machine à écrire de mon oncle est dans le bureau.* All right, everyone together. One, two, three; *un, deux, trois.*"

She gave a downbeat and the class, which sounded as though

176

its collective jaws had been shot full of novocaine, broke into a garbled mumble even the keenest linguist could not have interpreted.

"Very good, class. That was very good. Now, why don't we try it one at a time. Mr. Graham, please don't do that. Mrs. Bates, why don't you go first. Remember: English is a lazy language; French is not. Go on now: *La machine à écrire de mon oncle est dans le bureau.*"

Mrs. Bates rose unsteadily to her feet, grasped her aluminum walker shaped like a lectern, looked around as if to savour her moment of celebrity, and spoke: "*La plume de ma tante est dans le jardin.*"

A wheeze of merriment broke up the class as the teacher, with a shrill, staccato laugh, tried unsuccessfully to tuck stray wisps of hair back into place.

"Very good, Mrs. Bates; very good indeed. Doesn't that take us back a while, class? Mr. Graham, please don't do that. All right now, Mrs. Markland, you try the sentence. Don't forget to make the lips work – and your tongue. Think of pushing the words out of your mouth with your tongue the way – the way you push the kitty out of doors on a cold night. What's that, Mrs. Markland? You left your hearing aid in your room? Please remember to bring it to your lesson next time. We can't very well learn a foreign language if we can't hear the words, now can we? Mr. Graham, I really must ask you to please stop doing that. Yes? Is something wrong back there?"

The sound of whispers and giggles eddied through the back rows. Flushed, and giddy with her success as stand-up comic, Mrs. Bates had suddenly let go; a small puddle on the linoleum under her chair mute testimony to her overexcited condition.

Obviously accustomed to this sort of mishap, the teacher headed for the door in search of a nurse to deal with the situation. Frank ducked back into the director's office where a further ten-minute wait did not sweeten his disposition. Finally the director bustled in, erupting with apologies and inquiring what he could do.

"It has come to my attention, Mr. Macafee," said Frank, clipping his syllables, "that Mrs. McCutcheon has been receiving visitors. I had thought to have made it quite clear she was not to be disturbed."

"We have posted a No Visitors sign on her door. But you must understand, Mr. Clarke, Willowdale is like a big home. We welcome visitors with open arms. It would be impossible to monitor every room."

"But the No Visitors sign has been removed from Mother's door."

The director shook his head in feigned annoyance. "Probably one of the residents took it. There are a few who will take anything that isn't nailed down." He smiled indulgently.

"It could be bolted to the door, could it not?" Frank struggled to remain calm. "You see, Mr. Macafee, like many women who are . . . . comfortably well off, shall we say, Mother is plagued by hangers-on who take shameless advantage of her generosity. You can well understand that until she has settled into life at Willowdale, I do not want her bothered." Frank flashed a smile at the director, their smiles clashing like rapier blades across the desk. "It has come to my attention," Frank continued, "that a man came to visit Mrs. McCutcheon yesterday. He was in her room, along with two nurses."

"Oh, you must mean Mr. Perkins, her notary. She sent for him to come out. We can't very well refuse to admit someone who has been invited by the resident, now can we? We are not a prison, Mr. Clarke, but a home."

The urge to reach across the desk and punch the platinum-plated prick right in the mouth found itself checked by a sudden chill. Why had Estelle sent for the notary? How did she even remember the name of the firm?

"Can you not lock the door?"

"The fire department would be down on us in minutes. But again I must urge you to understand that we are not running a penal institution. If a visitor chooses to ignore the No Visitors sign, there is little we can do."

"Then do that little," snapped Frank, striding from the office and over to the elevator. He waited and waited, unaware that on the second floor a patient in a wheelchair was trapped in the automatic door and shrieking feebly for help.

Eventually he opted for the stairs. Wheezing and cross, he made his way down the hall to Estelle's room.

"Hey, mister, do me a favour," shouted a behemoth in pink terrycloth. "Find out if there's bingo this afternoon."

Frank ignored her. Walking past the old man tied into his wheelchair, who appeared to have dozed off, Frank passed the senile siren in her satin peignoir. At the sight of Frank she cupped her antique breasts in her two hands. "Wanna ticket to paradise, Big Boy?"

"Not at the moment, thank you."

Frank knocked on the door of Estelle's room and went in without waiting for an answer.

"Good morning, Francis," said Estelle from her chair, her voice a strangulated croak. "You must excuse my voice. I seem to have a touch of laryngitis."

"Good morning – Mother." Frank pushed the door shut. "Estelle, why was Todd Perkins here yesterday?"

The question caught Estelle off guard, but only for a moment.

"I wanted to find out about the will, my will, as it were. It occurred to me that I would be better equipped to deal with this fraud we are perpetrating if I knew more about what I really owned."

"Why did you not ask me?"

Estelle looked directly at Frank. "I was not certain you would tell me the truth."

"I see," replied Frank, still suspicious but afraid of alienating his cousin. "But in future there is no need for you to concern yourself about the will, or any other business matters. I will take care of that end of things."

"I had no idea there was so much money at stake. It really won't be a burden for you to support me, after all this is over."

Estelle began to cough. What began as a tickle in the throat grew and swelled into wracking spasms which caused her slight body to double over. When the attack had passed she rose unsteadily from her chair and crossed to the dresser for a handful of Kleenex. Looking up, she caught sight of herself in the mirror.

"Good God! I look like the old countess in *Queen of Spades*, and I'm not even a contralto." She returned to the chair. "But I console myself by saying that when this masquerade is over I can once more wear my wig, my eyelashes, nails, clothes. And there must be a great deal of pressure on you. Poor Francis. How is your end of the business going?"

"Pretty well. I have had a couple of small setbacks, but I can handle them."

"I'm sure you can. Still, I have little to do but sit here and think of everything that could possibly go wrong. We are in it together, after all. But it's silly of me to worry. I know you are perfectly capable of looking after things. By the way," Estelle's voice came and went from resonance to a whisper, like the sound on short-wave radio, "early this afternoon a woman knocked at my door. 'Come in,' I said. Although I have difficulty seeings things up close I can see quite well across the room. I could tell she was startled to see me. 'Excuse me; I seem to have the wrong room,' she said, and left."

"Could you describe her?" asked Frank, apprehensive.

"She was an old lady. I suppose you could have called her well-dressed – if you happen to like that tweedy, birdwatcher look. She carried a cane . . . ."

"Phyllis Coughlin!" said Frank, smacking his fist into his palm. "How the hell did she get out here?"

"Is something wrong?"

"I don't know. It could have been your sister-in-law."

"I didn't even know I had one."

"I'll have to find out. Maybe I will move you out of here, after all."

"Not for a day or two I hope. I really do have this dreadful cold. I'm not well enough to go anywhere at the moment, I'm afraid."

Frank had an idea. "Perhaps you should go to the infirmary for a couple of days. That way you would be out of circulation."

"You could well be right. We have come this far; it would be a shame not to see it through to the end."

"I'll go and speak to the head nurse."

Before she could reply, Estelle was seized by another fit of coughing, even more violent than the last. Frank found himself embarrassed by the spectacle of Estelle doubled over, choking, hanging onto the arms of her chair to keep from tipping forward. The embarrassment began to translate itself into alarm. What if Estelle were really ill? At her age, and with her emphysema, any infection became potentially dangerous.

"Are you all right?" he asked anxiously.

"Yes, I think so."

"I'll go right now and find the head nurse and tell her to speak to the doctor. He should really come and give you a thorough checkup. Our plan aside, you don't sound too well."

"It's only a cold. How I used to live in terror of colds, the singer's nemesis. Now it is simply a passing inconvenience."

"I'll come by again tomorrow. So long for now."

"If I may quote from Mimi's Farewell: '*Addio*, Francis, *senza rancor*.' Goodbye – without bitterness."

# Chapter 17

Before leaving Willowdale Frank talked to the head nurse who assured him, through dentures which looked like piano keys, that the doctor was due for his bi-weekly visit that very afternoon and would certainly examine Mrs. McCutcheon. Frank suggested his mother be moved to the infirmary. Oh, yes, the woman continued, if Doctor Patrick thought it a good idea, his mother would be taken to the infirmary. No, she couldn't move Mrs. McCutcheon without the doctor's authorization; he was to see her very shortly, after all. But Mr. Clarke was not to be concerned. His mother would get the best of care.

Frank walked out to his car. At least Todd Perkins had never met Flavia Clarke, so it was possible that he didn't suspect the woman in Room 336 was not Frank's mother. But Aunt Phyllis remained another matter. How dare she not obey his explicit injunction, the importunate old hag! Never mind; he would come up with a story. A mixup had occurred in assigning rooms; his mother was on the second floor; the office had forgotten to make the correction in the records. And by the time he finished raking Aunt Phyllis over the coals for going out to Willowdale in the first place, she wouldn't dare return.

If Estelle managed to get herself moved into the infirmary for a few days he would be covered. By tomorrow he would have his powers of attorney and could get cracking on sales. Another three or four days should do it. He did not intend to liquidate the entire estate, only the lion's share; enough to secure The Frank Clarke Collection being safely housed in the Frank Clarke Gallery.

There remained the problem of Vivien. Frank felt reasonably certain her threat of court action would remain just that, an outraged threat not to be followed up by a writ and a summons. And Frank had a plan for mollifying Vivien. He would not call it a bribe exactly, more of a bonus for doing nothing, an incentive for inertia.

Frank slid behind the wheel of his car. Reaching into his jacket pocket he took out the chamois bag he had removed from the safety deposit box. Tugging it open, he slid out a bracelet, sapphires and diamonds forming a supple chain. The rich blue of the large square sapphires excited the diamonds, which threw off pinpoints of blue. Frank held the bracelet up to watch the multi-faceted gems shatter light into prisms. He then replaced the bracelet in the bag and put it back into his pocket.

Pulling his car out of the parking lot, Frank decided against returning home for his customary nap; he felt too overwrought to sleep. He would drive straight to Vivien's.

As he turned into the slow lane of the expressway, his thoughts returned to the time when his mother had bought the bracelet. At that point he was back in her good graces as his wife had kicked him out. The egg that laid the golden goose (as Claudia herself had called Frank), had been caught with another gander. Having lived off his wife for over three years, Frank had faced the choice of working for a living or reconciling himself with his mother.

Shortly after the reconciliation he and his mother had taken off for an extended European tour. Travel for Mrs. Clarke consisted mainly of spending large sums of money to maintain the illusion she had never left home. She demanded bacon and eggs in Palermo, orange marmalade in Crete, English muffins in Istanbul, Yorkshire pudding in Grenada, and hot baths everywhere. Frank worked very hard, ever equipped with a phrase book, a tip, a smile. She had no use for foreign languages; all one need do is speak slowly and loudly and they were bound to understand. He ran interference, cajoling tea from waiters in cafés, coaxing room service to add a three-minute egg to the tray of café and croissants, tucking a jar of black currant jam into his overnight bag on a cruise through the Greek Islands, and listening to her complain at every meal about the unsalted butter. He had agreed to undertake his mother and he kept his side of the bargain.

They had hired a car to drive from Rome up to Florence; Flavia Clarke disliked trains. And although the official reason for stopping in Florence was to savour the treasures of the Renaissance, she had been primarily interested in the shops. Had she worn roller skates she could not have travelled more rapidly through the palaces, cathedrals, galleries, pronouncing them all "magnificent" before heading into the market place.

No sooner had they unpacked than he and his mother were put ceremoniously into a taxi by a liveried doorman for the drive to the Ponte Vecchio, that venerable bridge lined with small, elegant goldsmith shops perched precariously over the Arno.

Mrs. Clarke held three iron-clad beliefs about shopping abroad. One: all foreign shopkeepers are out to cheat you. Two: if you display even momentary weakness, such as politeness, you will be taken advantage of. Three: the person with the traveller's cheques and the letter of credit is in total command. As a result, she was unflaggingly suspicious and rude.

Seated stiffly on an upholstered stool in a small, impeccable goldsmith shop, his mother poked diffidently at gold objects spread before her on black velvet. The beautifully tailored Florentine salesman, white teeth flashing in a handsome, tanned face, remained unflappably courteous. She announced she was tired of looking at gold. Didn't he have something else to show her? Opening a safe the salesman drew out a diamond and sapphire bracelet, but only after he had cleared away the gold and the black-velvet tray to substitute another of white silk.

With just the right amount of flourish he laid the sapphire and diamond bracelet in front of Mrs. Clarke. Frank could see her grow tense, her attraction for the jewels almost carnal.

She lifted the bracelet from its bed of white silk, as though it were a piece of undercooked bacon, and started to bargain. She knew perfectly well one never paid the asking price; what was the salesman prepared to accept?

Politely but firmly she was informed that in this shop the price on the ticket was the price one paid. By then Frank's patience had worn thin and he suggested to his mother that they were not in the straw market. At this overt demonstration of insubordination, she threw back her head, almost as if she might whinny, and walked from the shop, leaving him to follow with her handbag and the cardigan she was never without, even during a heat wave.

He smiled at the salesman. "*Mille grazie. Buon giorno,*" and he followed his mother into the street.

"Mother!" His voice was low, but it carried. She stopped short. "I will do a lot of things for you, but I will not carry your handbag. And take your sweater." He thrust the objects into her hands. "And furthermore you were insufferably rude to that salesman. You want that bracelet, and you know perfectly well you'll kick yourself back home when you realize how close you came to buying it."

Bullies are easily cowed. "Do you really think I was rude, dear? My head was pounding." Mrs. Clarke suffered from "headaches," an ailment which struck her down whenever things were not going her way.

"Why don't you take a taxi back to the hotel and lie down. I'll pick up the bracelet and spend an hour in the Uffizi. Then we'll have tea."

Mollified by his suggestion, Mrs. Clarke complied. But he wouldn't stay away too long, now would he? And she did hate to take taxis when she had to pay in strange money; she never knew how much to tip. Frank told her to ask the hall porter, and pushed her into a cab. Then he went back into the shop, bought the bracelet, and made a date with the salesman, for eleven P.M. in the Piazza della Signoria, when Frank had his mother safely tucked into bed after dinner and several games of double solitaire in the hotel lounge.

Sliding the jeweller's box into his pocket with satisfaction, a tiny piece of his future, after all, he had walked the short distance to the Uffizi Gallery for a visit to the Botticelli room. As he studied the familiar but always strange *Allegory of Spring*, Frank had a feeling of time arrested. Yet even a roomful of paintings by the Florentine master could not touch in his imagination the memory he carried of the Botticelli drawing he had once seen in the British Museum, the allegorical figure of Abundance in pen and brown wash heightened with white. The graphic rather than painterly treatment only enhanced the floating, etherial quality of the young woman whose diaphanous, clinging gown made her seem airborn. Less was indeed more.

Standing in rapt admiration of Abundance with her attendant putti, he had dreamed for the first time of amassing his own collection of drawings. The seed of acquisition fell upon fertile ground. Reassuringly he patted the jeweller's box in his breast pocket. One day this bracelet would buy a drawing for the collection he intended to assemble for his own private enjoyment.

Now Frank pulled off the Decarie Expressway at the Sherbrooke Street exit, thinking it was fortunate that Vivien was old enough to look upon gem stones as glamorous rather than quaint. He drove to her building and rang the buzzer.

Vivien was in the kitchen making tea, still groggy from sleeping heavily during the day. At the sound of the buzzer she walked to the door and, without removing the safety chain, she opened it enough to see her brother standing there.

"Just your friendly neighbourhood mugger," said Frank with forced good humour. "Would you mind sliding your handbag through the crack? I'm putting my mother through college and I could sure use the cash."

An unwilling Vivien unlatched the chain. "I have just made tea. Would you care for a cup?" She did not feel in the least like talking to her brother, but the heavy hand of good manners rested on her shoulder.

"Love one."

Vivien went into the kitchen to prepare a tray, giving Frank time to check out her desk in the small front hallway. A brief note lay unfolded on top of some unopened mail. Under the Willowdale Manor letterhead was a brief message: "For my daughter Vivien Howard, to be held until further notification." Frank stared in disbelief. He picked up the sheet of paper to read the message a second time. "For my daughter?" Now why in God's name had Estelle been in contact with Vivien? And what had been enclosed with the cryptic message? What the hell was Vivien going to think, hearing from her mother after all these years of silence? Surely she wouldn't consider going out to Willowdale for a visit. Just what Frank needed. The letter did not necessarily imply reconciliation, but it could signal the beginning of the end.

The sound of cups rattling on a tray caused Frank to drop the note onto the desk and move to the window as if absorbed in the nonexistent view.

"Milk, no sugar, if I remember correctly," said Vivien as she poured.

"Right."

"Now what is it you have come to see me about? You are not given to making unannounced social calls." Vivien sat stiffly. She had no intention of making the visit easier for Frank.

"You're right," replied Frank. His manner of easy affability was by now so thoroughly practised he slid into the role without effort, a seasoned actor revisiting a familiar part. "I have a little something for you." With a swagger and a flourish, which in the very performance mocked themselves, he handed his sister the chamois bag.

Today Vivien found her hands more than usually stiff. She

tugged unsuccessfully at the drawstring which refused to give way. In the process she gave Frank a chance to observe a large ruby ring on her left hand. Frank hesitated only a second before recognizing the ring as the one Estelle had been wearing when he picked her up at the airport. (Vivien had been decorous at the crematorium, black gloves emerging from beneath her black rebozo.) Now Vivien sat, wearing Estelle's ring, the letter from Estelle open on her desk.

Something was going on that Frank could not understand. Things had begun to spin out of control. The original plan had seemed so foolproof, so easy. But his cast of characters had begun to ignore their lines and directions; they were ad libbing and freewheeling all over the set. Frank had an uncomfortable feeling of losing control, and he did not know just how to go about lashing his actors back into line.

Vivien put down the bag with a gasp of impatience. "I can't get it open. My fingers . . . ." She broke off, ashamed and humiliated by this show of weakness.

Frank came to the rescue, teasing the bag open and sliding out the bracelet.

"A little something to dress up your wardrobe."

Vivien had never seen the sapphire and diamond bracelet, its having been purchased after the rupture with her mother; but she had heard about the jewels at length from her aunt, Phyllis Coughlin, who didn't much care for sapphires herself.

"This must be Mother's sapphire bracelet, the one you bought in Florence. Why are you giving it to me?"

"I thought you might enjoy having it."

"Did Mother tell you I was to have it?"

"No, but does that matter?"

"It most certainly does. What right have you to give away her jewels? No more right than you had to sell Randolph's paintings, or Grandmother's tea service, or Father's Morrice. Your power of attorney was granted so you could administer, not pillage. I will not be bribed with a bracelet. Jewels such as these are for the young and the rich. I disqualify on both counts. And even were I tempted, which I am not, I could not even manipulate the catch, let alone the safety chain."

"Excuse me for breathing, but I thought you might enjoy wearing the bracelet. Mother has no further use for it. If I take it to the nursing home it will be stolen in a flash, unless she keeps it locked up."

"As long as you are trying to bribe me with jewels, why not Grandmother's emeralds? Or have you sold them too, or taken the real stones from their settings to replace with paste?"

"Do you want the emeralds?" asked Frank, all the time thinking his sister's idea of replacing real stones with fake was a good one and why hadn't he thought of it first. The fact that he had promised the emeralds to Estelle seemed subordinate to the problem at hand.

"They are not yours to give. Nor could I begin to afford the insurance. I would not sell them because they belonged to Grandmother. They would have to sit in the bank. Listen to me, Frank, you have come to butter me up, to offer me bribes, so I will overlook your selling Randolph's paintings. Well, I won't. And tomorrow I intend to speak to whoever takes care of Mother's affairs about the way you have been selling off things that were not yours. I will not be deflected by a bracelet."

Vivien stood. "And furthermore, before we get to the bottom of all this, let me assure you I intend to do nothing about the Calgary properties you have been urging me to sell."

Frank dropped the bracelet back into its chamois bag and pulled the drawstring tight. "You know something, Vivien? You are – and always have been – a colossal pain in the ass. Now listen to me, and listen carefully. I sold Randolph's paintings – and the Morrice – and disposed of the tea service. Why not? They were coming to me anyway. And you got some of that money, don't forget. From me, not from Mother. I shall continue to assist you financially, just so long as you do not interfere. You say one word to the notary and I won't give you one more dime."

"If you have finished your tea, Frank, I have things to do."

"Then do them. I came here carrying an olive branch. Well, dear sister, you can take that olive branch and shove it."

He stalked out of Vivien's apartment, furious. Damn her! If she really meant to hire a lawyer then he would hire a better one. Anyhow what could he expect? Vivien never did have enough sense to come in out of the rain. And even if she walked with God she could still fall flat on her face.

*       *       *

The telephone in Frank's apartment was ringing as he let himself in.

"Mr. Clarke," said a man's voice. "This is Doctor Patrick, from Willowdale."

"Yes, Doctor Patrick."

"I examined your mother this afternoon. She is a sick woman, Mr. Clarke. She has caught a very bad cold and I am afraid it could easily develop into pneumonia. I have moved her into the infirmary. I am reluctant to put her into hospital. The move itself could be traumatic, and she is getting excellent care here at Willowdale."

"Naturally, Doctor Patrick, I will be guided by whatever you think best. Just how serious is her condition?"

"At the moment it is difficult to say. She may recover. It is only a cold, after all. But she does have emphysema. Her lungs have lost their elasticity. We have been using suction to clear fluid from her lungs, another reason I want her in the infirmary. She is an old lady, Mr. Clarke. Her ability to fight infection is no longer what it once was."

"I see. It goes without saying I want whatever is best for her, doctor, and I'll rely on your judgment."

"Very good, Mr. Clarke. I will call you tomorrow."

Frank replaced the receiver mechanically in its cradle as the idea, staggering in its implications, took shape in his mind that Estelle might die. Frank understood Estelle to be an old lady.

But once one has reached seventy, "old" is registered less in years than in the ability to survive. The possibility of Estelle's dying had not seriously presented itself to Frank. He knew some day she must die, but up to now he had thought of her death as coming at some indeterminate time in the future, only after he had succeeded in his plan. In spite of her advanced age, Estelle's behaviour belied her years, due in part to her total absence of spontaneity. Everything she did or said was first monitored by an intense self-awareness which saw itself bathed in an endless limelight. That she might actually die, that the light in which she moved might be switched off now, struck Frank with full force. His power of attorney would cease to be valid – for the second time. The corpse, coffin shut, would be dispatched to the crematorium where the incriminating contents would be reduced to ash. But incinerated along with the body would be his dream of immortality, The Frank Clarke Collection.

At the moment there was nothing whatsoever he could do but wait. At ten o'clock tomorrow he would be standing outside the bank, powers of attorney tucked safely into his briefcase, prepared to race against time. Though the fragile health of an eighty-seven-year-old woman did not impress Frank as something on which he should depend, he felt that, just possibly, Estelle would pull through.

# Chapter 18

Phyllis Coughlin entered the dining room on the second floor of Trillium Towers where each night she took her dinner, sharp at six. The hostess informed Mrs. Coughlin that her regular dinner companion, Zoe Braithwaite, would not be in this evening. Mrs. Braithwaite was having one of her attacks and wanted no dinner. Did Mrs. Coughlin wish to join another table? Mrs. Coughlin did not. In spite of an hour's stretchout with a cool damp facecloth across her forehead, she found her nerves stubbornly refusing to calm down. The events of the afternoon had left her in a state: the terrifying drive out to Willowdale, Grace McSween's chatty drivel, and then that total stranger in Flavia's room. And she had not been able to reach Frank by telephone, although she had called repeatedly. And if that weren't enough, she had to decide on which wall she would hang the Highland cattle. Small wonder her nerves were in absolute tatters.

She toyed with the shepherd's pie and pushed the parsnips around her plate. She ate a piece of Melba toast and drank a cup of tea. Then, without waiting for the crème de menthe parfait, she rose suddenly and returned to her room. Collecting her cane, her handbag, her coat, all in a neat pile at the foot of the bed, she picked up the telephone and ordered the switchboard to call her a taxi. The request was so unusual that the receptionist felt she had to verify.

"Did you say a taxi, Mrs. Coughlin?"

"That is precisely what I said: a taxi – and at once!" She put down the receiver. One of the more boring features of old age was having to repeat things, like small children trying to get attention.

Seated in the back seat of a taxicab, driven by a black driver, rainbow decals on every window, reggae music exploding from the radio, Phyllis Coughlin found her resolve beginning to falter. But in a firm voice she spoke the address of her niece, Vivien Howard. And although Phyllis Coughlin set little store by amulets and talismans she was secretly relieved to have a St. Christopher medal on the keychain in her handbag.

The trip passed without incident. Mrs. Coughlin climbed with difficulty from the cab, paid her fare, tipping the smiling driver a quarter, and walked to her niece's front door.

The doorbell startled Vivien for the third time that day; her staircase was turning into a public thoroughfare. Who could it be at this hour? "Aunt Phyllis!" she exclaimed with surprise, knowing her aunt never went out after supper.

"Good evening, Vivien. May I come in?"

"Please. Would you like a cup of tea? There's still some in the pot, but I could make fresh."

Vivien went to fetch a clean cup.

Her aunt noticed the two used teacups. "I see you had someone in," she remarked as Vivien re-entered the room.

"Yes," replied Vivien without further explanation; she had always disliked her aunt's prying ways. Vivien poured tea and handed the cup to her aunt. "Is it still warm?"

"Warm, but a bit stewed." Mrs. Coughlin put down her cup and turned her full attention to her niece. "Vivien, I am perplexed." She then proceeded to relate in chronological sequence the events of the past two days, her visit to the big house, her nephew's refusal to let her see her sister-in-law, his telephone call to tell her Flavia was moving, her trip out to Willowdale, the total stranger in Flavia's room, and her unsuccessful attempts to reach her nephew by telephone. Mrs.

Coughlin was uncharacteristically succinct. "Well, what do you think?" she said in conclusion.

As the full implication of her aunt's story was only beginning to take shape in her mind, Vivien parried. "To be honest, Aunt Phyllis, I don't know what to think. You know that I no longer speak to Mother, and I seldom see Frank. However I am certain there is a perfectly logical explanation."

"Good heavens, Vivien, if your mother is not in her own house, nor in the room that is supposed to be hers at Willowdale, then where is she? I wanted to see her safely settled in. It is a terrible wrench to leave one's own home. And there is always something one needs, or that has been forgotten. I also wanted to thank her for the painting of Highland cattle she told Francis to bring me. But then Flavia was always the soul of consideration."

Vivien knew that particular painting had been her mother's favourite, far surpassing in Mrs. Clarke's estimation anything done by Randolph Howard. She realized how odd it would be for her mother to give it away rather than take it with her to Willowdale. "I cannot tell you where she is, Aunt Phyllis. But I'll tell you what I'll do. Tomorrow morning I intend to visit the family notary; I will ask him to make inquiries. I promise you the second I have some news I will be in touch. There is nothing more we can do at the moment except try to get a good night's rest."

"Do you think I should go and see Francis?"

Vivien shook her head. "I wouldn't ask Frank, if I were you. I suspect he has told you all he intends to tell you. A third party will be more reliable. More tea?"

"No, thank you." Phyllis Coughlin fairly crackled with impatience. "Then, if there's nothing more to be done at the moment, I'll run along. Call me a taxi."

Only too anxious to be rid of her aunt, Vivien went straight to the telephone.

"You ought to turn on more lights," said Mrs. Coughlin, as they waited at the window for the taxi to arrive.

"I'm trying to cut down on my electricity bill."

"You could have a fall. And at your age, my dear – ah, here we are." And Phyllis Coughlin walked out slowly, but without leaning on her cane, to the waiting cab.

Vivien stood in her front window, just above street level, watching her aunt's taxi drive away and trying to fit together the fragments of the puzzle. The woman in her mother's room at Willowdale was not Mrs. Clarke. And for the first time in years she had received a note from her mother. It suddenly dawned on Vivien that the handwriting was really not at all what she remembered her mother's to be, though it was possible she might have asked one of the nurses to write down the brief message as dictated. Unless the message had been written by the woman in her mother's room.

Could the body cremated in the coffin have possibly been . . . ? No, it was impossible. Frank might be larcenous but he was not a hardened criminal. Vivien stacked the teacups on the tray which she carried out to the kitchen, the shrill voice of suspicion steadily increasing in volume. She had a hunch that the most important piece of the puzzle might well be found in the locked box.

With extreme reluctance, and the uncomfortable feeling she was betraying a confidence, Vivien pushed a straight-backed wooden chair firmly against the counter. She levered herself up, and carefully reached down the strongbox. She placed the box on her small kitchen table and sat down. If she wanted to know the answer she must force the lid open. Vivien shrank from the violation of trust, but she had to discover the truth.

From the drawer where she kept tools for household repairs Vivien chose a screwdriver. The flimsy lock proved stubborn, and Vivien no longer had much strength in her hands. With a gasp of impatience she twisted the screwdriver one more time, and with a grinding sound the lock yielded. Then, almost as if wilfully committing a sacrilegious act, Vivien raised the lid slowly with both hands. What she found inside caused her to cry out.

Resting on the quilted lining of the box were jewels like none Vivien had ever seen. A rope of perfectly matched pearls the size of peas, which fastened with an emerald clasp as large as a postage stamp, lay twisted in a necklace of diamonds and beryls, their transparent blue-green the colour of the ocean as it exists in imagination. Visible beneath the opulent tangle was the corner of a navy-blue booklet. Vivien teased it out of the box. On the cover the lion and the unicorn faced each other above the legend: *A Mari Usque Ad Mare*.

For a moment Vivien sat holding the passport, reluctant to open it for fear of what she would see. But then when she did, there was Estelle Church looking directly at her, fully made-up, bewigged, ravaged by the uncompromising camera.

Mechanically, Vivien placed the passport back in the box and lowered the lid. What she had begun to suspect as she listened to Phyllis Coughlin was now glaringly confirmed. Vivien thought of her recent visit to the big house, of the elevator parked at the top of the stairs when she knew her mother used it to travel down as well as up. Why had Frank driven their mother out to Willowdale in his car instead of calling an ambulance? Had there really been a nurse to help him, or had he made up that part of the story as well? He had already proved himself an adept liar.

The strange woman in Flavia Clark's room at Willowdale must be Estelle herself. She and Frank were up to something which sounded frankly criminal. And, Vivien's mind fought against what she had to conclude was true: the body which had been cremated must have been that of her mother. Vivien was shocked by the realization, more profoundly shocked than she had ever been in her life.

But there was one last check she must make. Lifting the telephone directory onto the table, she looked up the number of Willowdale Manor and dialled it on the wall phone beside the refrigerator.

"Manoir Willowdale Manor. *Bonsoir*. Good evening."

"Good evening. Do you have a Mrs. Flavia Clarke registered? She would have moved in the day before yesterday."

"We have no Mrs. Flavia Clarke. But a Mrs. Flavia McCutcheon moved in two days ago. However she is not taking any calls."

"I see," said Vivien. "Thank you."

She rang off and returned to sit at the kitchen table. There was nothing more she could do at the moment except find a way to pass the long night until she could go to the notary's office and learn, albeit reluctantly, the truth.

*　　*　　*

It was after getting safely out of the taxi in front of Trillium Towers that Phyllis Coughlin took a fall. She knew it would be sheer madness to let the leather-jacketed driver help her out of the cab. He would seize her handbag and tear off in a squeal of tires. She paid her fare, tipped the driver fifty cents as he had not been playing the radio, and climbed unaided from the back seat. The taxi drove away. Then, miscalculating the curb, she tripped, landing with a loud retort on the concrete. Immobilized, she lay on the sidewalk until a passerby alerted the night receptionist at the Trillium Towers desk. An ambulance arrived in due course which bore Mrs. Coughlin off to Emergency where she was found to have broken her leg. To break anything at eighty-five is almost invariably fatal. Not so, however, for Phyllis Coughlin, who was made of the same stuff that won India for the British and then lost it.

In spite of shock and acute discomfort she insisted on a private room and a special nurse. And in a perverse kind of way Mrs. Coughlin was almost glad of the fall. Now Blue Cross, to whom she had been paying premiums for years, had the opportunity to do something nice for her.

# Chapter 19

That night, exhausted by the day's events to the point of over-stimulation, Frank took a sleeping pill; something he rarely did. Sleep came eventually, heavy and sodden. When, the following morning, consciousness had fully invaded his mind, dispelling those phantoms which hover between sleep and waking, Frank did not climb immediately out of bed. He lay, his body still, his mind racing with the first burst of energy which follows sleep. A strategy was taking shape.

As any trust officer well knows, one of the most common eccentricities shared by wealthy widows is the conviction that they are really paupers. They anxiously telephone their trust officer to inquire whether they should keep the thermostat at sixty-four to save money, whether they should shop at supermarkets instead of the friendly little corner store with its twenty-per cent markup, whether they should take in a lodger to lighten the financial load. Even as dividends roll in and coupons pile up, these anxious ladies remain convinced that any day they will be foreclosed and forced into the street.

It was Frank's idea to present his mother as just one of these anxious women. Believing she would not be able to make ends meet, what with the nurses and all, she had requested that Frank sell off anything of value in the house. As Frank himself intended to tell the story, he would insist on how he had tried to allay her fears, to persuade her the bills could all be paid without flogging the silver. But – and he would not have to emphasize this point – his mother was well known for being a very headstrong woman. Whatever she wanted done got itself done. And with extreme reluctance Frank had sold off many of her possessions. He had no choice. Whether Vivien believed him or not was not the issue; his word had only to stand against hers. As long as Frank managed to convince the notary or lawyer or judge that he had acted solely on his mother's behalf, then he was in the clear.

Thus resolved, Frank swung himself out of bed. After pouring hot water onto tea leaves, he made his customary check through Births and Deaths, finding only one familiar name: Blakelock, Nigel, a private collector with whom Frank had dealt in the past. The idea came to Frank that perhaps he should contact the executors of the Blakelock estate to learn if any drawings had been left; and if so, to whom.

Hardly had he clipped the obituary for the biscuit box when the telephone rang. A voice claiming to be from his mother's bank wanted to speak to Mr. Clarke. Frank identified himself.

"About the term deposit, Mr. Clarke. You wanted the certificate issued under your name, even though the bonds had been registered to your mother. I spoke with the manager, and he told me to issue the term deposit certificate in Mrs. Clarke's name. You see, it is a large amount of money, well in excess of the annual gift allowance; and there could be a presumption of gift. That means the revenue department might charge your mother gift tax on the deposit. On that amount the tax could be considerable. I tried to reach you yesterday. I knew you would not want to lose two days' interest. I can change the registration next month, if you wish."

"I see," said Frank, uncertain of whether to be pleased or angry at the woman's efficiency. "Just leave it for now. I'll let you know."

Frank dressed quickly and was halfway out the door when the telephone rang again. He wanted to ignore it, but remembered it might be Dr. Patrick. Frank's suspicion turned out to be correct. In the brief conversation that followed Frank learned that his mother's cold had developed into pneumonia; she had a fever and was barely conscious. The doctor assured Frank that Mrs. McCutcheon might still pull through, but in a tone of voice that quenched hope.

A grim and agitated Frank left his apartment and drove to the notary's office to collect his powers of attorney. The secretary, still drenched with cold, was talking on the telephone. Having attempted to disguise her red eyes with heavy black eyeliner, she looked not unlike a racoon. Time was running out, and he silently cursed the delay.

After putting down the receiver the secretary told Frank that Bister Perkins wished to speak with him. Frank fidgeted while she rang Todd Perkins' phone.

Todd Perkins marched briskly into the reception area and shook Frank's hand. As the new senior partner of the firm, he was having problems with his image. Heretofore the pin-striped, three-piece look had been upheld by Martin Maxwell, now defunct. The muted mantle had passed to the athletic shoulders of trendy, disco-hopping Todd Perkins, terror of the singles' bars. No one could have found fault with the three-piece suit, except perhaps that it was brown. But the cowboy boots clashed, as did the tired Afro hairdo, sorely in need of refurbishing. To have removed the heavy gold ring from his left ear would have exposed a large, unsightly, *National Geographic* hole in the lobe. Like the secretary he was in the throes of a bad head cold, which made him appear slightly out of focus, as if he stood behind a rain-washed window.

"Mister Clarke, glad you dropped by." His ability to pronounce "m" announced he was on the road to recovery. "Would you care to step into my office? There are a couple of things I think we should discuss."

"I am in a bit of a hurry this morning. Do you suppose I could just collect my copies of the power of attorney and drop by again, later in the afternoon perhaps."

"Actually it's the power of attorney that I would like to

discuss with you, among other things. It won't take long. This way, please."

Frank followed Todd Perkins down soundless beige carpet into an office commanding a spectacular view of the St. Lawrence River. In one of two Barcelona chairs facing the teak desk sat Vivien, dressed in black. Frank felt like someone confronted by a vampire who realizes he is without a crucifix.

"Good morning, Francis," said his sister, pointedly studying the view from the window.

"Good morning, Vivien." It did not escape Frank that his sister had reverted to his formal name. He could also see she was having one of her bad days. A black chiffon scarf covered but did not conceal the orthopaedic collar which supported her aching neck.

"Mrs. Howard just arrived, only a couple of minutes ago," said Todd Perkins cheerfully if thickly through cold. "Your unexpected arrival is a bit of luck. It will save us all some time, as I have matters to discuss which concern you both."

"Mr. Perkins," began Vivien, leaning forward in her chair, her regal manner a by-product of the collar. "I have several questions to ask you, matters which I think should be discussed privately."

"If your questions have anything to do with your mother's will or the power of attorney granted to your brother, I think they will be covered by what I am about to say. Cigarette?"

Todd Perkins reached into his vest pocket for a silver cigarette case and pressed the latch. The lid opened to reveal five small, squashed cigarettes which bore the unmistakable appearance of having been hand-rolled. "Oh – sorry," he said, quickly whipping the case out of sight. "I know I have some American cigarettes here somewhere," he continued, nervously patting his pockets.

"Don't bother, I don't smoke," said Vivien.

"Neither do I," said Frank thinking that the idea of a swinging notary carried its own interior contradiction.

Todd Perkins sat down. "In that case, let me tell you about

the recent visit, visits, I should say, that I had with your mother. I went out to the nursing home two days ago to confer with Mrs. Clarke, then again yesterday for her signature. I meant to call you when I got back to the office, but I felt so rotten because of this cold I went home instead. She's a remarkable woman, your mother. Truly remarkable."

On the point of breaking in to ask what exactly it was that Mrs. Clarke needed to sign, Frank was beaten to the draw by Vivien.

"The point is," she interjected sharply, "that woman is not my mother."

"Now, now, Mrs. Howard, I understand you have had differences with your mother in the past." Todd Perkins' voice was thick with professional patience. "But she has obviously had a change of heart. I venture to say you will be quite surprised by her new will."

"New will!" Frank positively barked.

"Yes, Mr. Clarke. We always encourage our clients to make a completely new will rather than adding codicils, especially if there are to be major changes. That way it is less open to question in the courts."

"Changes or not, the woman at Willowdale is not my mother. And I also have questions about the power of attorney." Vivien placed her hand on the desk to emphasize her point.

"Mrs. Howard, Mr. Clarke," Todd Perkins raised his hands, palms outward. "Regardless of your personal feelings, which believe me I respect, I honestly feel that if you allow me to explain the reasons for my visit to Willowdale you will find a great many of your questions will be answered." For perhaps the first time since Martin Maxwell's death, Todd Perkins began to realize the full implication of taking on the older clients, formerly handled by Maxwell himself.

"Your mother telephoned me to come out to Willowdale. She asked me to bring copies of the power of attorney and of her will. To begin with, she has revoked the power of attorney."

"Revoked!" Frank almost leaped from his chair.

"Yes, Mr. Clarke, she has revoked your power of attorney and she asked me to draw up a new power of attorney naming your sister, Mrs. Howard, to act in your place."

Vivien sat upright in her chair, rigid with attention; but she did not speak.

"I would like to see the signature," demanded Frank.

"She didn't sign. She couldn't, poor woman. Her right hand was so seized up with arthritis she couldn't hold the pen."

"Arthritis? But what about the signature?"

"As I said, she didn't sign. She made an x with her left hand and the two nurses who were in the room signed as witnesses. It's perfectly legal, I assure you. Just as long as you have two notaries, or one notary and two witnesses. Now about the will." Todd Perkins reached for a sizable document, and began to read.

" 'On this sixth day of October – nineteen hundred and eighty-three, before MTRE. TODD G. PERKINS – the undersigned Notary for the Province of Quebec, both residing and practising in the City of Montreal, Appeared: DAME FLAVIA McCUTCHEON, of the City of Westmount, therein residing at Manoir Willow-dale Manor, unremarried widow of the late Desmond Bruce Clarke, in his lifetime, Executive of the same place. WHO being of sound and disposing mind, memory, judgment,' et cetera, et cetera."

Todd Perkins looked up. "The provisions about burial charges, debts against the estate, death duties, and so forth, are just the same as they were in the previous will, now revoked. I suggest we skip all that and get on to the substantive changes." He began to read, " 'I furthermore direct – ' "

"Skip the legalese for God's sake and tell us precisely what the changes are." Frank could barely contain himself.

Todd Perkins put the will down on top of the desk and leaned back comfortably in his oatmeal-coloured swivel chair.

"Very well, then. As you probably know, your mother had originally divided her estate into two equal parts. This division still stands. One half goes to Maple Grove Manor to build a memorial wing. However she has made a change in the disposition of the remaining half."

"What in hell . . . ." began Frank, the words escaping from an excess of pressure, like steam from a radiator valve.

"The remaining half of her estate she has left outright to her daughter, Mrs. Vivien Howard, along with all her personal belongings."

"But the signature . . . ." Frank could scarcely speak.

"Again she made a mark and the two nurses signed as witnesses."

"Are there any further changes?" asked Vivien as the truth began to sink in.

"Yes. She directs that the inscription in the lobby of the memorial wing read as follows: 'The Flavia Clarke Memorial Wing Erected in Loving Memory of My Beloved Cousin Stella della Chiesa.' The letters of the name Stella della Chiesa are to be in capitals and twice the height of the other letters."

Vivien raised a hand to hide the smile that was beginning to reshape her mouth. Then, with a quick, tearing sound, she undid the Velcro fastener on her orthopaedic collar which she removed to tuck into her canvas tote bag.

"She also directed," continued Todd Perkins, "that her son Francis have available to him a room in The Flavia Clarke Memorial Wing, rent free, for the duration of his natural life."

A searing cramp knifed through Frank's lower intestine, jerking him to his feet with a barely suppressed grunt. "Where is the washroom?"

"I believe every room at Maple Grove has its own washroom, Mr. Clarke."

"I mean here, goddammit."

"Oh, sorry, just down the hall to your right."

Directing every last ounce of self-control towards his sphincter, Frank hurried down the passageway and into the washroom, where he lunged at the toilet. The agony and the ecstasy were both so overpowering that he could barely find the strength to pull himself back together.

Although he had never been a good sport or a team player, Frank had still been deeply influenced as a boy by the concept of grace under defeat. All those hearty boys' annuals filled with stories about the Foreign Legion, that last shuddering gasp of chivalry, had imprinted themselves, almost subliminally, into his consciousness. He had felt grudging admiration for those fair-minded lads of the sixth form who, after being soundly trounced at cricket, shared tea and scones with the victorious team. Frank had spent his entire life behind a veneer of good-natured indifference; his drives and compulsions rigorously suppressed and redirected so as to never impinge upon the way he wanted to be perceived. If, on occasion, hairline cracks had appeared in the enamelled surface they were never permitted to widen into fissures. Frank had created himself in his own image; ikon and individual had fused into one. It was way too late to change. He had gambled and lost; now he must cut his losses and walk away with style.

Frank washed his hands and splashed cold water on his face. He straightened his tie, ran a comb through his hair. If there was a taste of ashes in his mouth as he re-entered Todd Perkins' office, Frank knew he had been responsible for the incineration.

"Mrs. Howard has told me about some very valuable emeralds, and a sapphire and diamond bracelet," said the notary. "Perhaps it would be a good idea to put them into the bank for safekeeping."

"Do you have a piece of scrap paper?" asked Frank. Taking a gold pencil from his pocket he wrote down the combination of the safe in the basement. "The emeralds are in a safe, in a storage closet, near the furnace. I'll send the bracelet around by messenger. And here is my house key. I will have no further use for it." He stood shakily. "Now if that's everything, I'll just run along."

"One more thing, Mr. Clarke, before you go. I have two envelopes from Mrs. Clarke, one for each of you, which she instructed me to give to you after we had discussed the changes in the will." From a desk drawer Todd Perkins took two envelopes.

Frank tore his envelope open. Written in a hand he did not recognize were the words: "*Et c'est là l'histoire de Manon Lescaut.*" Crumpling the page into a tight ball he dropped it into the wastepaper basket.

Vivien opened her envelope. The message was short. "Dante: *Inferno*, Canto xxx." Vivien knew even without checking the poem that she would find a reference to Gianni Schicchi. Folding the paper she slipped it into her purse.

Todd Perkins walked Vivien and Frank to the elevator. Frank and Vivien stepped inside.

As the elevator door shut, squeezing Todd Perkins out of sight, Vivien could no longer sustain the steely composure she had rigidly maintained in the notary's office. Her conflicting feelings found outlet in tears. Frank silently handed her a clean handkerchief. They did not speak until the elevator had reached the lobby where, by unspoken consent, they found a private spot behind a massive cast-concrete pillar. By now Vivien had regained her self-control. From her bag she produced a pair of dark glasses which she put on to hide her reddened eyes.

"I suppose Mother's body was cremated yesterday," she began.

"Yes. Her ashes are to be buried in the grave beside Father."

"And Estelle is impersonating Mother at Willowdale."

"Yes. But she is desperately ill. The doctor called me this morning. She has pneumonia and her lungs are full of fluid. The doctor did not sound very encouraging. He said there was no need to visit as she was barely conscious. She is a dying woman."

"I see."

"When did you learn about Estelle and Mother?"

"Last night. Aunt Phyllis came to see me. She had been out

to Willowdale and her story made me suspicious. That afternoon I had received a box by messenger, supposedly from Mother. I opened it and found Estelle's passport and jewels. She must have had a premonition of death. I don't know what you two had planned, but it appears to have backfired."

"So you got Estelle's jewels as well."

Vivien ignored Frank's comment. "I don't think I should know any more than I do. Regardless of what you have done I would not want to see my own brother go to prison. Even though you were unscrupulous enough to use Mother's dead body as accessory to your scheme, I will not, out of respect to Father, press charges."

"That is very magnanimous of you, dear sister, now that you have everything."

"Would you prefer us to return to Mr. Perkins' office and confess the truth? Regardless of where Mother's fortune ends up, you will go to prison. Shall we return to the elevator?"

Frank stood silent, staring at the travertine floor.

"Now listen to me, Francis. I will not take action over your selling Randolph's paintings. It would be sordid to drag our family name through the courts. Moreover, I will soon be in a position to buy back those paintings I wish to recover. When Estelle dies I will be very well-to-do, possibly even rich, although we were both brought up to believe that word vulgar. I shall endow a scholarship in Father's name, as a memorial. I will therefore be prepared to sell the Calgary property. Your share of the proceeds should enable you to live. Even though you were trying to defraud Mother, and possibly even me, I will not see you destitute, if only because you carry the family name. You may arrange the sale with Mr. Perkins when the time comes.

"One last point," Vivien went on, "and on this I absolutely insist. We will bury Estelle as if she were Mother, from Mother's church, with Mother's own minister officiating. There will be a reception afterward in the church hall. You will attend both the service and the reception and behave in a suitable manner. You will be courteous and charming to those few friends of Mother's who are in fit condition to attend. You will accompany me to the crematorium. This much I demand of you. And in return I will guard the secret until I die. And now, Francis, I will say goodbye. By the way, thank you for your handkerchief. I shall launder it and post it back to you."

"Don't bother, Vivien. I have others."

"Goodbye, then."

"Can I give you a lift?" asked Frank, still outwardly the gentleman.

"No, thank you. I'll take a taxi."

Vivien walked from the lobby into the street, and out of his life. Enveloped in the immense apathy that follows crisis he could not bring himself to care.

Uncertain of what to do, he returned home. The stairs up to his front door seemed endless as he pulled himself up by the handrail, one step at a time, the way an old man climbs stairs. He walked heavily into his bedroom and, without even bothering to remove his jacket, he fell onto the fur spread, a relic from his fauve period he had not bothered to replace. Sleep would have come as a relief, but his eyes stubbornly refused to close as his mind churned with the events of the past few days.

A simple telegram from a cousin he had never met had set up a chain of cause and effect which had left Frank destitute. To a disinterested third party Frank would have seemed very comfortably off. The revenue from the Calgary property would enable him to live much as he had up until now. He owned the building in which he lived. If his furnishings were eclectic they were also valuable. Furthermore he had already squirrelled away not a few bits of money from his mother's estate, even though the large U.S. dollar term deposit that the overly zealous bank clerk had registered in his mother's name would now go to Vivien.

When it came down to food, clothing, taxes, Frank had far more than he needed. But he did not see survival as a day-today activity. For him it meant a projection beyond death, a strategy to beat the oblivion that he had come to fear far more than the bare act of ceasing to live. And in terms of The Frank Clarke Collection, not to be very rich meant having to abandon the dream.

The idea, dismal and infuriating, that he was far worse off than he had been before his mother's death, now tormented Frank. Vivien was to inherit one half of their mother's estate, Maple Grove Manor the other half. Vivien now stood to inherit one half of their father's estate. Frank had nothing from the will; moreover, with his power of attorney legally revoked, he could no longer touch his mother's assets. Granted, he was still at liberty to expose the falsified will, but that revelation would sink him up to the neck in a morass of criminal proceedings. He was trapped by his own strategem and outfoxed by the person he had coerced into becoming his partner in crime.

A sudden hot flush of pure rage swept Frank; his skin prickled at the notion of her daring, just daring, to dictate a new will. God! How she must have hated him. And Vivien had won the prize, for having offered to take Estelle in and give her a home. The whole goddamned episode sounded like a nineteenth-century cautionary tale for children or a bad operatic plot.

Damn Estelle! Damn her to hell! Frank lay on the bed, hoping she would die soon. He thought of calling Willowdale to inquire how she was doing, but he really didn't care to know. At the best of times Frank did not overflow with compassion. Having just been tricked out of a fortune, he had none.

Then the anger passed, leaving Frank numb with disappointment at the realization there would never be a Frank Clarke Collection housed in The Frank Clarke Gallery. He was not to stand, a little older, a little frailer, in his own temperature-and-humidity-controlled room surrounded by master drawings whose presence attested to his taste, cultivation, and philanthropy: his gift to the world. Not only did he have to face the dream denied, he also had to come to grips with the idea that his very *raison d'être* had been yanked from under him, like a rug in a low-comedy routine. He had taken the pratfall, but there was no laughter.

Frank lay staring at the ceiling, wondering what to do with the rest of his life. To travel around Europe and the Americas ferreting out such fine drawings as had not already been absorbed into major collections was to have filled the next ten years. He had gained his freedom, but without money he now had to face the prospect of an empty old age in which activities take the place of action. He certainly was not the type to go weekly to the Senior Citizens' Centre in order to take recorder lessons or brush up his French. He did not wish to play bridge with his peers nor be lectured by a rookie cop on the hazards of carrying a handbag in public places.

The telephone on his night table rang. Frank let it go five times before picking up the receiver. "Yes?"

"Fanny, dearest, it's Roxanne. Fanny, I just had the most provoking news."

Frank understood he had only to listen. "How so?" he asked without interest.

"Remember I told you I had a buyer all lined up for the opal? What I didn't know is that he was out on bail, which he has skipped. At the moment he's floating around somewhere in the continental U.S. We never did complete the transaction, and now I'm stuck with a brooch I don't know how I am going to unload."

Frank sat up. "Don't worry about it, Roxanne. I'll buy the opal back from you."

"Oh, Fanny, do you mean that?"

"Yes." Frank wanted to reclaim the opal. Vivien did not know about the jewel and Frank realized the brooch would be the only thing he would have that had belonged to his mother. Certainly not out of sentiment, Frank wanted the brooch as a relic more than a keepsake. "What are you asking for it?"

Roch named a price. In earlier times Frank would have started to bargain, but he couldn't seem to find the energy.

"Okay, Roch. I'll come by with a cheque in about twenty minutes." Frank hung up.

Half an hour later, the opal in his jacket pocket, Frank faced Roch across a glass of Pineau des Charentes at Roch's kitchen table.

"My dear," began Roch. "Let me tell you about the bizarre experience I had yesterday. A young man came by with a diamond watch he claimed to have found. We got to talking. Ass like an apricot. But, can you imagine, he asked me if I had any hard-boiled eggs."

"Shoplifting is hungry work," said Frank staring absent-mindedly into his glass.

"Now, now, Fanny, we mustn't jump to conclusions. But the point is, he didn't want them to eat. Not at all. They were to go up the yellow brick road."

"I see. Did you shell them first?" Frank stifled a yawn.

"What a question! I may be kinky but I'm not sadistic. What followed was quite delightful, but I did feel a little as though I were making mayonnaise."

"Cuisinart sex?" asked Frank, unable to come up with anything better.

"I suppose you could call it that. And now, my dear Fanny, have you thought over my proposal, about running the introductions agency?"

"Yes and no. I might be interested."

"Splendid! I can't tell you what a relief it is. The whole business takes far more time than I have to give. I can't entrust the job to just anyone, as you can well understand. And these days a dollar is a dollar is a dollar. Did you get your other business wound up?"

"Yes." Frank did not think it necessary to elaborate.

"Good. Now this is how I work, but don't let me cramp your style. Each client who registers with the agency is given a code number. I reverse the initials of the name. Say John

Doe is the thirty-eighth person to register; he becomes DJ-38. We urge our clients to use phone booths. You will keep a file on what we have to offer. Part of the job, the time-consuming part, is recruiting new talent. Some clients are easy to please; they want the same thing over and over again. It is astonishing how pedestrian most fantasies are. I can't tell you how many requests I get for beatings administered by someone got up as a nanny or a governess. I file that one under Mary Poppins. Rape and violent seduction fantasies are also popular. I have a two-hundred-and-forty-pound weight lifter who is simply dying to be assaulted anally. If only King Kong were still around. You will need a stable of black males; a great many fantasies revolve around black men. Fewer around black women, although I keep a couple on call. Men married to yentas often fantasize about something exotic and submissive. Stay away from children, unless they are impersonated by adults. No one under twenty-one as client or help. And I am convinced there is a vast geriatric market out there waiting to be exploited."

Roch tapped his fingernail against his front teeth. "Do you suppose if we come up with some nimble numbers to provide sex for those on life support systems that we would be reimbursed by Medicare?"

Frank could not jolly himself into the frame of mind for arch banter. "Roch, get on with it. This is a business like any other."

"You're right. For the rest, you are depraved enough to come up with angles I probably haven't even thought of. You will take twenty-five per cent from clients who come through me, seventy-five from those you recruit yourself. The client pays you; you pay the employee. That way there is no gouging or blackmail. Also it enables clients to get on with their fantasies without having to talk business. We give credit up to a week, but the clients always pay. They can do without new cars, fur coats, winter cruises; but they can't live without their fantasy fucks. Fanny, are you listening?"

Frank nodded.

"And remember," Roch continued, "discretion is the key-word. We are a lonelyhearts club, nothing more, and, on the books, strictly non-profit. And never forget that a satisfied customer is the best advertisement. Now, what do you say?"

"Thanks, but no thanks. It's the part about recruiting new talent that I can't, or won't, handle. I am too old to deal with tawdry tarts and piss-elegant queens. And for commissions that will barely keep me in goldfish food. It's a sleazy, small-time operation, and I don't want any part of it."

"Aren't we being just a tiny bit grand, my Fanny?"

"Roch, my name is Frank!"

"Well shut my mouth and call me madam!"

"I'll call you . . . some time." Frank rose abruptly and strode from the kitchen, leaving Roch with his mouth partly open and his chin folded down over his Adam's apple.

In the entrance foyer the Worth gown still hung from the sconce. Frank made a slight bow. "So long, Stella," he said quietly before leaving the apartment and closing the door.

# Chapter 20

Frank returned home. Regardless of the major setback he had just undergone, he could not see himself operating an escort service, a prostitution ring by any other name. A shoddy occupation, and in Frank's opinion there was nothing in the world more boring than other people's sexual fantasies, except perhaps a federal budget.

Frank still had a card up his sleeve and he saw no reason to delay producing it. Realizing that Claudia was probably staying at her mother's apartment, Frank looked up the number of his ex-mother-in-law. No specific plan had formulated itself as he dialled the old Wellington-7 number, now 937. However, asking Claudia to have dinner with him some time soon might lead to, who could tell? Aware that older people need more time to stop whatever they are doing and get themselves organized to answer, he let the phone ring ten times. He was just about to hang up when Claudia's voice came onto the line.

"Hello!" The word came out more as a challenge than a greeting.

"This is mild-mannered Clark Kent. I'd like to speak to Mary Worthless. I have the adult cassette she ordered."

"This is Nelvana of the Northern Lights. Mary Worthless is out, I'm afraid. Every afternoon she sits in the subway, wrapped in a shawl, peddling hash brownies."

"What took you so long? Were you in the bath?"

"No, I was otherwise engaged. Frank, I'm glad you called. I wanted you to be the third to know. I'm getting married."

"Not again!"

"Yes."

"Are you going to stand there and say, 'This is the sixth happiest day of my life'?"

"Of course. They say love makes the world go square. And you are the one who put me up to it, after a fashion. Remember that spiel you gave me over lunch about making your own good time?"

"Sort of."

"Well, I'm doing it. He owns a moving company. He came to give me an estimate on packing up Mother's things and putting them into storage. It was love at second sight; the first time I wasn't wearing my contact lenses. He's sixty-four, but after a lifetime of lifting furniture around? Totally awesome, as they say in California."

"I suppose congratulations are in order."

"Not really. I suppose I am behaving like a damn fool. But the way I see it, if we have three good months together I will be just that much ahead. Listen, do you have any plans for dinner tonight? I'd love you to meet him. Let's go out and celebrate, on me!"

"Thanks anyway, Claudia; but I'm tied up, I'm afraid. Some other time." To be in the company of contented people was more than Frank could face.

"Will you come to my wedding? Next week some time? October is a busy month for movers, so we have to plan the wedding around his schedule."

"Sure, Claudia, I'll come to your wedding. Just let me know when. My schedule is pretty loose at the moment."

Frank rang off. He realized that Claudia's marriage would push her to the outer fringes of his life. Her attention and energies would naturally focus on her new husband, and Frank himself must be relegated to the role of casual friend. He felt a sudden pang of jealousy. Not sexual, he had moved beyond that; the envy he felt was that of one sitting on the sidelines watching the party spin past. Regardless of any residual affection, he and Claudia would meet occasionally for lunch. Frank knew he would find little common ground with a man who had spent his life moving furniture, and there would be the tension which exists between husbands past and present. Frank understood that Claudia had moved out of his life, and he felt sorrier than he would admit.

It was turning out to be, in anglo understatement, quite a day. Newly disinherited, he had seen his sister walk out of his life, and had learned his seventy-year-old ex-wife had found if not love at least companionship with someone else. Three shells, but no bean. Moving them around made no difference; they all came up empty.

Temporarily out of ideas, uncertain of what to do, and unwilling to absorb any more surprises, Frank went to the movies.

"Do you have a golden-age pass?" inquired the cashier, inclining her lacquered coils of hair toward Frank.

"Golden-age pass, my ass!" snapped Frank, slapping down a five-dollar bill.

"There's no need to be rude," she huffed, pushing his ticket through the opening.

Frank gave her a look that would have shredded paper. Then he went into the theatre to follow the misadventures of an odd little creature who seemed to exist solely on beer, watermelon, and Smarties. At the end of the film Frank could not understand why everyone on screen did not board the spaceship for the flight into nowhere. Frank himself would gladly have climbed the gangplank and zoomed off over the rainbow. He knew nothing whatsoever about outer space, but at the moment it seemed like a very good place to be.

\*     \*     \*

Early the next morning, around the time dark is first threatened by light, Estelle's laboured breathing stopped for good. Dr. Patrick telephoned Frank with the news. Awakened from fitful sleep, Frank felt neither glad nor sorry. He did, however, request a favour of the doctor. Not wanting to be the one to break the sad news to his sister, Frank asked the doctor if he would be good enough to telephone Mrs. Howard. The fact would come as less of a shock from a doctor than from a brother. In truth, Frank did not want to speak to Vivien.

By now wide awake, Frank got up, made tea, and sat waiting for the paper to be delivered. The phone rang again. This time it was the manager of Trillium Towers to inform Frank that Mrs. Coughlin had taken a fall and was now in hospital. Frank promised he would visit his aunt this very morning.

When the paper did finally arrive Frank turned as usual to Births and Deaths. But the zest was gone. Why bother to clip obits now? he thought to himself. They would only serve to remind him of The Collection and the immortality he had almost managed to grasp. On his way to the bathroom Frank dropped the biscuit box filled with yellowing clippings into the kitchen trash bin.

Remembering his aunt's fondness for chocolate-covered cherries, Frank bought a box and took it with him to the hospital. Although in obvious discomfort, his aunt was fully alert. Without even pausing to thank him for the candy she pelted him with questions about his mother. Where was she? How was she? Why wasn't she receiving visitors?

"It's about Mother that I've come to see you, Aunt Phyllis," replied Frank, who went on to say, quite simply, that his mother had died during the night.

Mrs. Coughlin burst into tears, less Frank understood from grief over his mother's death than from this further mute reminder of her own mortality. Frank withdrew, leaving his aunt to mourn in private. He promised to return the next day. At the door of the hospital room he turned. "Is there anything I can bring you, Aunt Phyllis?"

By way of reply his still weeping aunt shook her head.

Frank paused for a moment at the door, watching his aunt grieve for the death of a woman she had never met. Small matter. The sorrow remained genuine, even if its true object had died some days ago. Frank would have been the last person to disabuse his aunt. At her age, what pleasures remained but food, disapproval, and grief? Like Frank's mother, Phyllis Coughlin belonged to that now nearly extinct species, the dinosaur widows: women who inhabited a Ptolemaic universe in which the centre was self. They were a totally different generation from Frank, one whose distance measured itself in attitudes more than years. Compared with his aunt, old and shrivelled in her hospital bed, Frank felt young and vigorous. He had his health; after an almost sleepless night, he felt marvellous. And in spite of the immense disappointment of being done out of his mother's inheritance, he could not deny the feeling of relief at no longer, like a juggler, having to keep the balls revolving in perfect synchronization.

As he turned away from his aunt, too absorbed in mourning to notice him leave, Frank felt a surge of his old buoyancy. It took him completely by surprise, like a sneeze or a cramp, and was just as difficult to ignore. With the burdens of the past two days lifted from his shoulders, he could not suppress the spring in his step as he walked down the antiseptic corridor towards the elevator. Even filtered through the dreary hospital atmosphere, the crisp October day held promise. As Frank pushed the button, and stood waiting, he could not ignore the almost subversive feeling that something was going to turn up. And why not? It always had.

\*     \*     \*

Vivien Howard let Frank know through the notary that she herself intended to take care of funeral arrangements. Even though Frank and Vivien sat together in the same pew during the funeral service for Flavia McCutcheon Clarke, whose shut coffin was almost hidden under an enormous spray of white carnations and huge white chrysanthemums, they only nodded at one another. They didn't even find anything to say while at the crematorium. At the small reception which followed, when they stood side by side shaking hands with those few survivors whose principle concern was that with Flavia now dead no cheque would be forthcoming at Christmas, Frank and Vivien spoke nothing to one another. There are times when silence becomes easier to bear than tense, polite conversation.

After the mourners had dispersed, Vivien took a large basket of long-stemmed white roses she had set aside from the funeral flowers and brought them in a taxi to the hospital where Phyllis Coughlin now held court in plaster. Having just submitted herself to the luxurious indignity of a bed bath, Mrs. Coughlin was anxious for the distraction of visitors bearing news. Such regret as Phyllis Coughlin had initially felt at poor dear Flavia's passing was by now more than counterbalanced by satisfaction at having outlived her. Also, the mere fact that Flavia had died meant she had been found, and the funeral established her whereabouts once and for all.

"I have brought you some of Mother's flowers, Aunt Phyllis," said Vivien from the door of the hospital room.

"Please take them away, Vivien, they use up the air."

Before crossing to sit beside her aunt's bed, Vivien stopped a passing nurse and asked her to take the roses to one of the wards.

"How are you feeling, Aunt Phyllis?"

"Immobile, uncomfortable, idle, not that anyone cares. Flavia would have. Poor dear. Who would have thought I was to outlive her?" Phyllis Coughlin reached for a tissue to wipe her dry eyes. "Now I know it does not really concern you, Vivien dear, but have you seen the will?"

"The will?"

"Flavia's will. I asked Francis about it yesterday, but he said he hadn't spoken to the notary. By the way, did you know that your mother was in the very next room all along? Francis explained about the mixup. To think I could have had one last visit with Flavia . . . ." This time a few genuine tears did materialize.

Vivien waited for her aunt to compose herself. "I have not read the will, Aunt Phyllis, if that's what you mean. Here, let me fix your pillow. Is that better?" Vivien sat. "However the notary did run through the bequests."

"I see." Phyllis Coughlin crossed her hands demurely on the sheet, but her eyes glinted with curiosity. "And what did she leave me?"

"She didn't leave you anything, Aunt Phyllis."

"I beg your pardon?"

"It's true, I'm afraid." Vivien felt profoundly uncomfortable, but she had given her word to Frank. And Aunt Phyllis must never be allowed to suspect a thing. Vivien played it straight. Briefly but succinctly she went on to explain how at the eleventh hour her mother underwent a change of heart and altered her will so that only Maple Grove Manor and Vivien herself were the beneficiaries. Phyllis Coughlin's eyes grew wide with indignation and disbelief.

"I don't believe it. Nothing to me? And she knows I have left bequests to both you and Francis." She spoke as if Mrs. Clarke were still alive.

"If you say so, Aunt Phyllis. Mother and I have not spoken in many years, as you know. I honestly have no idea why she changed her mind."

"Are you absolutely certain I am to have nothing at all? Her own sister-in-law! Not even a token bequest? Nothing but those wretched cattle?"

"Quite certain, Aunt Phyllis. Naturally if there is anything you need, you have only to ask."

"I will not need your charity, Vivien, thank you very much. I don't mind telling you I am highly displeased. You will have to go now. I am due for my bath."

"Is there anything you want, Aunt Phyllis? Anything I can bring you?"

"Nothing, thank you. Good afternoon."

Vivien withdrew, relieved to think that in spite of acid rain and the threat of nuclear war, messengers bearing bad tidings were no longer struck down where they stood.

No sooner had her niece left the room than Phyllis Coughlin reached for the telephone and dialled a number. "Francis? It's your Aunt Phyllis. As well as can be expected, thank you. Francis, will you pass by my apartment and fetch my mail? I shall ask the receptionist to open my letter box. I will also ask her to let you into my flat. In the bottom bureau drawer you will find two shawls, folded, on the right. The lavender one is from Flavia; give it to the woman who does up my room. Bring the green and yellow one to the hospital along with my mail. I want to put it around my shoulders when I sit up. Tomorrow morning will be fine."

She rang off, then dialled a second number. The call, to her own notary, was brief. No, she didn't want to change her will, only to add a codicil. The bequest she had made to her niece, Vivien Howard, was to be taken out. She certainly did not need the money now. The very idea. Naturally he could bring the document to the hospital for her to sign. She wasn't going anywhere for a while.

Phyllis Coughlin settled back against her pillows. Now that Francis was out of Flavia's will he wouldn't be quite so cocksure. He knew he stood to inherit something from her. And that knowledge ought to keep him on his toes whenever she needed errands run. Yes indeed, her nephew could be very useful to her.

# Epilogue

Winter came and went twice. The board of directors of Maple Grove Manor had for some time been aware of the conditions relating to the memorial wing as set forth in the will of the late Flavia Clarke. An architect had been engaged to draw up plans, even before the funeral. Influential men sat on the board, one of whom managed to have funds released so that construction could begin the minute frost was out of the ground that spring.

After a long convalescence while she waited for her broken leg to mend, Phyllis Coughlin had been moved out to Willowdale. As she needed a walker for short distances, a wheelchair for longer trips, it had been deemed inadvisable for her to return to Trillium Towers. Her doctor had urged Willowdale, and Frank had made the necessary arrangements. He also assured his aunt that he would personally supervise her being settled into the right room, the one with her name on the door.

As soon as the memorial wing was completed, approximately one year after construction had started, Frank moved into his room. And why not? He sold his duplex for a tidy profit and purchased a Matisse reclining nude, executed in bold strokes of charcoal. He furnished his room with his choicest possessions and sold the rest. Such meals as he took in the dining room turned out to be more than adequate. Moreover, whenever the roof leaked or the furnace grew temperamental someone else dealt with the problem.

In due course the steamer trunks filled with Estelle's costumes arrived in the port of Montreal. Vivien donated the lot to the Royal Ontario Museum to become a permanent part of the costume collection. She sold Estelle's jewels, along with her mother's sapphire bracelet, and used the funds to endow a scholarship, The Stella della Chiesa Memorial Scholarship, designed to help further the careers of young singers. The ruby ring Estelle had given her Vivien kept as a memento.

On the day of the official opening of The Flavia Clarke Memorial Wing Erected in Loving Memory of My Beloved Cousin STELLA DELLA CHIESA, Vivien Howard was on hand to unveil the inscription chiselled onto the marble facing of the main wall in the lobby. Floral arrangements stood everywhere, the largest and most aggressively opulent being that from Francis Desmond Clarke, as Frank, standing on the sidelines, duly noted. Phyllis Coughlin, confined as she was to a wheelchair, had decided against making the long trip from Willowdale for the opening. It was hot; everybody would be standing so she wouldn't see a thing; it would exhaust her. In truth she still rankled over being left out of Flavia's will.

The occasion was said by everyone present to have been a lovely affair. The mayor made a speech. Mrs. Howard pulled a silken cord to unveil the wall, after which delicious refreshments were served on the sun porch.

Frank did not linger for the punch, however. Being the dutiful nephew he was, he had promised his Aunt Phyllis he would drive out to Willowdale and report in detail on the occasion. As he leaned over to unlock his car, he could feel, stiff in his inside jacket pocket, the envelope he had picked up from the notary's office immediately before the opening ceremony. It was the first certified copy of a document which he had finally persuaded Aunt Phyllis to grant him. Frank had no need to review the preamble; he knew it by heart.

"On this thirteenth day of June, nineteen hundred and eighty-five, Before: Mtre. Todd G. Perkins, the undersigned Notary for the Province of Quebec, practising in the City of Montreal, Appeared: DAME PHYLLIS CLARKE, retired, of the City of Montreal, Province of Quebec therein residing at Manoir Willowdale Manor, unremarried widow of the late Robert Alfred Coughlin (hereinafter called the 'Constituent'), who does by these presents, nominate, constitute and appoint her nephew, FRANCIS DESMOND CLARKE (herein the 'Attorney'), of the City of Westmount, Province of Quebec, therein residing at Manoir Maple Grove Manor, to be her true and lawful Attorney and for her and in her name, place and stead, to do any and all of the following things, namely: